On a Night Like This

On a Night Like This

Ellen Sussman

An AOL Time Warner Company

This book is a work of fiction. Names, characters, places, and incidents are the product of the author's imagination or are used fictitiously. Any resemblance to actual events, locales, or persons, living or dead, except for Sweetpea, is coincidental.

Warner Books, Inc., 1271 Avenue of the Americas,
New York, NY 10020

An AOL Time Warner Company

Printed in the United States of America

ISBN 0-446-53141-3

This novel is dedicated to Neal
and to my daughters, Gillian and Sophie,
with love.

Acknowledgments

I would like to thank Jonathan Strong and John Barth, my gifted teachers.

Some brave friends read early drafts of the novel, and for their patience and encouragement I thank Susan Goodman, Ken Sonenclar (a writer's dream of a friend), Kimberly and Les Standiford, and Jeanne Duprau.

Thanks to Dr. Bruce Wintroub for sharing his knowledge of melanoma.

Over the years my many writing students have inspired and challenged me. Thank you all.

I am extraordinarily lucky to have found a terrific agent and a brilliant editor. Thanks to Elyse Cheney and Jamie Raab.

And thank you, Neal, for everything you have taught me about love.

On a Night Like This

Chapter One

Blair lifted the man's arm and slid out from under him. She tucked a pillow back in her place, and he embraced it easily. She smiled at that. Men. She gathered her clothes from the floor and tucked them under her arm, picked up her shoes, stopped in the doorway. She looked back at the man, his long, lean body curled away from her, his hair a tousled mess, his face half buried in the pillow. *I could climb back into bed and stay there awhile,* she thought. She closed the door quietly behind her.

The hallway of his apartment was dark and she slid her hand along the wall until she found a light switch, flicked it on, squinted in the sudden brightness. She hadn't looked at the clock. Had she slept all night or only an hour or two?

She headed down the hall, drowsily dropped a shoe, which thudded on the hardwood floor. Another door opened and a woman appeared, pajamaed and sleep-rumpled. Blair recovered her shoe, stood and shrugged, naked, too slow to cover herself up.

"Are you a roommate or a wife?" Blair asked.

The woman peered at Blair. Someone without her glasses. "Roommate," she mumbled.

"Good," Blair said. "Go back to sleep. I'm leaving."

"Where's Perry?"

Perry. That was his name.

"Sleeping. Sorry I woke you."

The woman plunged back into the darkness of her room. Blair continued on down the hall.

She found the kitchen, dropped her clothes and shoes on the old pine table, grabbed a glass and poured herself water from the tap. She drank, then opened the fridge. Filled the glass with white wine, sipped at it, took it with her back to the table. Microwave clock read 11:45. She had barely slept. Amanda would still be awake, maybe waiting for her. She found a phone, curled into a chair at the table, dialed and drank.

"Hey," Amanda said into the phone.

"I'm sorry," Blair told her. "I'm late."

"Or early," Amanda told her. "I thought maybe you'd crawl in sometime tomorrow."

"I don't crawl, Amanda."

"Then you'd tango home. Who's the guy?"

"Maybe I'm at the library. Studying for a master's degree in quantum mechanics."

"You coming home?"

"Did you get worried? Damn, I should have called."

"I didn't get worried. I'm not a baby."

"What did you eat for dinner?"

"I finished the lasagna."

"Damn you. I've been dreaming about that lasagna."

"I'll make you some eggs."

"You go to sleep."

"I'm not tired."

Blair smiled. "OK, then I'd love a mushroom omelette. With cheese. Tons of cheese."

She hung up the phone, took one last swig of wine, pulled herself up and out of the chair. When she half-turned, pulling her sweater over her head, she saw someone standing in the doorway.

"You scared me," she said. Perry. Naked and watching her. She reached for her jeans, pulled them on. Stuffed her bra and underpants into her backpack.

"Who was that? Your boyfriend?"

Blair smiled, shook her head. "My daughter," she said. "Sixteen years old. Waiting for her mom to come home and tuck her in."

"You're some teenager's mom?"

"That I am." She slipped her feet into her shoes and turned toward him.

"You can't stay?" he asked.

"I don't stay," she said. "Something you should know about me."

"Too bad," he said, covering her hand with his own.

Blair put her hand on his chest, pressed her palm into him. "But I had fun. Tell me where we are. How I get home. That sort of thing."

They had met at a bar. He had driven them back to his place. She hadn't paid attention to anything except his slow voice, his hand on her thigh, the soft blur of streetlights from her tequila high.

"I'll drive you," he said.

"No," she told him. "I'll find a cab. Go on back to sleep."

"That's it?" he asked.

"You mean, are we now formally engaged? I don't think so."

He smiled. "I mean, can we try this one more time?"

"Maybe. Give me your phone number."

"You don't give out yours?"

"Smart man."

He walked to the kitchen counter, pulled out a drawer, rifled through, found a business card, which he passed to her. He was comfortable being naked—she liked watching him.

"I'll call you," she said.

"Maybe," he told her, smiling.

She pulled her backpack onto her back, headed toward the door. She looked back at him, blew him a kiss. He was watching her.

"Do you always do this?" he asked.

She stopped, leaned back against the door, suddenly tired. She waited.

"Is this what men do? And you do it better?"

"No," she said.

"Been burned too many times?" he asked.

"No," she said.

"I give up."

"I'm dying," she told him. "It's easier this way."

Neither spoke for a moment. It was the first time she said it. Something in her chest tightened. Blair leaned over, placed his business card on the side table by the front door.

"AIDS?" he asked, and she could imagine his mind flashing: *Condom, we used a condom, hallelujah for condoms.*

She shook her head. "I wouldn't do that to you," she said. "Just cancer. Nothing to be scared of."

"Except relationships," he told her.

"Right," she said. "Everyone's a therapist these days. Gotta run. It's been grand."

She opened the door, walked out, pulled it closed behind her.

• • •

Blair caught the last bus to the Haight, walked a couple of blocks, turned down her street. On the edge of the Haight, on the edge of a park, on the edge of elegance. She lived in a rented cottage behind a mansion. A dilapidated mansion in the middle of finely refurbished

Victorians, most graced with pastel colors, hers boasting a loud, honking purple. The neighbors hated it. Of course. Which was Casey's plan.

Casey sat on his front steps, smoking a joint at midnight. She wasn't surprised. Her landlord had inherited money and the mansion; he coasted through life, women and drugs. She put up with him because she loved the cottage.

"Come join me," he called out before she turned down the driveway toward her haven.

"Gotta go. Amanda's waiting."

"One hit," he urged. "You'll sleep better."

Couldn't argue with that. Blair walked down the path to the front patio, joined him, midstep.

"Where were you?" he asked, passing the joint.

"None of your business," she said, taking in a good, long hit of the pot.

"Sex," he said. "I can smell it."

"You're disgusting," she told him. She took another hit.

Blair looked through the darkness toward her cottage, her daughter inside, making omelettes. She stood. "I gotta go. Amanda's making me an omelette."

"Can I join you? I'll bring wine."

"No." She started off, across the ruined grass of the front yard.

"Are you sick?" Casey called out.

Blair stopped, turned around.

"How'd you know?"

"I don't know. A hunch. Maybe that's the smell."

"You're smart for a rich kid."

"What's wrong, Blair?"

"I'm going to die?" she said. But somehow it came out as a

question this time. How do you answer a question like that? She shook her head—it still sounded as if the words had been formed in someone else's mouth. "Thanks for the smoke."

She turned and headed back behind the house, following a string of white Christmas lights that she used to line the path from the driveway to her cottage, tucked in the far corner of the backyard. The cottage was really a tiny apartment over a garage, but it was built in 1910, all in pine—walls, floors, ceiling—and was graced by a tree that hung over and around the house, making it feel more tree house than garage.

"I'm sick," she muttered to herself, trying a different take. *No. That's beside the point. I'm dying is the point.* "I'm dying" is what she needed to tell her daughter.

She climbed the wooden stairs to the cottage and caught the pungent smell of sautéed onion and garlic, saw Amanda's willowy shadow against the white curtain in the tiny kitchen, heard the African-drumming CD that Amanda listened to late at night with the lights dimmed low; she paused for a moment before turning the doorknob. *Not yet,* she thought. *Not tonight.*

She pushed the door open, breathed in, smiled. The small pine-walled living room was tented with lilac-dyed muslin billowing from the ceiling—Blair always felt like she was entering her own exotic harem.

"Amanda, my sweet girl!" she called.

Amanda appeared in the doorway, boxer shorts, cotton camisole, untamed red curls, beaming. "You better be hungry."

"Ravenous."

Blair dropped her bag on the floor, beelined for her daughter. She ruffled her hair, planted a kiss on her ear.

"You got taller," she said, looking her kid straight in the eye.

"Since this morning?"

"Yeah. I think you beat me. Finally."

"Turn around."

They turned back-to-back, butt-to-butt, head-to-head. Exactly the same height. But Amanda was fair-skinned and her mother dark, and Amanda's body was narrower, her bones sharper. She looked like she was about a minute away from becoming a woman, having shed her child's body only seconds before.

"You didn't sneak past me," Blair said, patting their heads together. "Yet."

They moved toward the table, a battered wood schoolteacher's desk, which sat in the middle of the tiny room that served as their dining room. Blair dropped, exhausted, into one of the wooden chairs.

"I'll get dinner," Amanda said. There was barely room in the kitchen for both of them.

Blair watched her daughter. She somehow felt she could see Amanda in all her incarnations—she was the joyous five-year-old, the headstrong eight-year-old, the surly twelve-year-old, and now this, the lovely young woman—in a flash of an eye. Even now, with a tattoo peeking above her tank top, she was Blair's baby. A few months ago, Amanda had come home with ROVE tattooed on her chest, just below her collarbone. Blair used to think she knew her daughter completely, knew every expression, every gesture. Rove? What did it mean? Was this Amanda's first hint of mystery?

"My boss said I can work an extra night at the café if I want to," Amanda said.

"You want more work?" Blair asked. "Why?"

"I want the money."

"You don't need the money. When was the last time you bought new clothes?"

Amanda owned two pairs of jeans—one red and the other lime green—and an odd assortment of bowling shirts, Hawaiian shirts, tuxedo shirts—whatever she found at the vintage clothing store down the street. She looked like a kid playing dress-up, the clothes always too big for her, bound around her waist by bejeweled belts. She looked like no other kid at her high school, and Blair was proud of her for it.

"I buy CDs," Amanda said. *And help pay the rent,* Blair thought. She grabbed her daughter's hand as she passed by and pulled her close.

"You're too grown up, my girl," Blair said.

"I like working there," Amanda said. "And when it's quiet, I can get my homework done."

"How about parties, friends, goofing off?" Blair asked while Amanda set the table.

"Yeah, right," Amanda said.

"Is it my fault?" Blair asked. "If I didn't love you so much, you'd go have fun somewhere else."

Amanda leaned over and placed her fingers on her mother's lips. "Stop worrying about me," she told her.

"Could you bring me a glass of wine, sweetheart?"

The wine appeared, already poured and waiting. Blair took it from Amanda and grinned. When Amanda turned back into the kitchen, Blair closed her eyes, squeezing them tight. Not pain. Just too much noise in her head.

"Do you eat lunch by yourself at school?" Blair asked.

"Why?"

"I'm curious. I hated lunch at school. It was the most miserable time."

"I read a book," Amanda said quietly. "It doesn't matter."

"It does matter, sweetheart," Blair told her. "You need to talk to someone."

"I talk to you."

Blair watched Amanda in the kitchen, moving from pan to bowl to silverware drawer to stove, her hands always moving, every gesture as graceful as a dance.

"You're not lonely?" Blair asked quietly.

"No, Mom. I'm fine. I hate school. OK? But work's fine and then I come home."

"I know," Blair said.

"Dinner," Amanda announced, presenting the pan with a grand swoop of her arm. A perfect omelette.

"Bravo," Blair said. She was a chef; her daughter had learned well. And she shared with her the appreciation of good food.

Amanda slid the omelette onto Blair's plate.

"You eating?" Blair asked.

"Lasagna," she said. "I told you."

"How many nights will you work?" Blair asked. She tasted her omelette while they talked.

"It's up to me. I can match the nights you work so we can be home on the same nights."

"I might quit the restaurant," Blair said, though she hadn't thought about that yet. Her mind was racing through too many things—money, illness, leaving her daughter, and now this idea: leaving her work.

"Quit cooking? Why?"

"Burnout. I'm exhausted."

"Since when? What are you talking about?"

Blair got up from the table. She turned, looking for somewhere to go.

"I've got to pee," she said, heading into the bathroom.

She shut the door behind her and leaned back against it. Pressed hard against the spot where her mole had been, under her bra strap, the mole that scraped and bled and healed and scraped and bled.

Until finally she showed her doc during a routine physical and the good doctor cut the mole, tested the mole and pronounced her dead on arrival. Melanoma. Advanced stage. *Why the hell didn't you do anything about this?*

Because I was busy. Because I've got a daughter and a crazy job and not enough money. Because I don't pay attention to the details.

"Mom?"

"Coming." She flushed the toilet and splashed water on her face. Opened the door. Sat down at the table. Knew that Amanda was watching her. She had told the doc, "I can accept dying. For me. But not for my daughter. She's got no one else."

"The omelette's delicious," Blair said, staring at it.

"You had a doctor's appointment this afternoon," Amanda said.

"You don't miss much. You're a pain in the butt."

"My specialty."

"Yeah, I had a doctor's appointment."

"And?"

"I've got some bug. Some virus. The doctor wants me to take a break from cooking for a while."

"What is it?"

"A virus. I just need to rest some. And I need to eat omelettes. That's the magic cure."

Blair picked up her fork and started eating. Her stomach was rototilling and she could barely swallow her food. Amanda still watched her.

"You're lying," Amanda said.

"I'm not lying," Blair barked. "Don't accuse me of lying. I'm sick. You think I'm happy about it? You think I want to stop cooking after all these years?"

Amanda's chair banged back against the wall and she was gone. The door to her room slammed shut just as the chair clattered to the floor. Blair pushed her plate away and dropped her head to the table.

The good doctor had said, "Do you have family?"

"No. My parents died years ago."

"There's a support group at the hospital."

"I don't need a support group," Blair had said.

"You're not alone in this," the doctor said. "You have to think about your daughter."

"That's all I can think about." Blair had walked out. Leaving prescriptions for pain that would come. Phone numbers for people who would tell her how to cope. Pamphlets that would describe how she would die.

She walked out and kept walking, from the Haight to the Mission, from bar to bar, drinking a shot of tequila, moving on. When she met the man with the deep voice and the soft touch, she was numb enough to go home with him, numb enough to make love until they slept, numb enough to forget Amanda. Until she woke up.

She picked up her fork and took another bite of her omelette. Her hunger was gone. She drank her wine. Hours of tequila, sex and pot and still she couldn't turn off her brain.

"Amanda?" she called.

The door flew open and Amanda appeared.

"What?"

"I'm sorry I yelled. I hate being sick."

"What's wrong with you?" Amanda asked suspiciously.

"I told you." Blair drank the rest of her wine. "A goddamn virus."

"What kind of virus?"

"I don't know. I don't understand their mumbo jumbo. I'm tired, that's all. Maybe it's that fatigue thing. Where you can't get out of bed."

"I've never seen you not get out of bed."

"Speaking of which," Blair said, pushing back her chair and turning toward her daughter, "you have school tomorrow. It's past midnight. Get your sorry ass in bed."

Amanda walked up to Blair, leaned over and kissed her on the top of her head. Like a blessing.

"'Night, Mom."

"Good night, sweetheart. I love your omelette."

"That's two lies in one night," Amanda said, heading back into her room and shutting the door behind her.

• • •

Blair heard Amanda rattle around in the kitchen early the next morning. She didn't move. Chronic fatigue syndrome. Wouldn't that be nice? Too tired to care. She listened to the noise of Amanda's morning routine: *Now she's getting the milk; now she's pulling her cereal from the pantry; that's the cabinet for the bowl, drawer for the spoon. See. She doesn't need me.*

Where does a kid live when she's sixteen and she's an orphan? No way she's going to an orphanage. Does she stay here in the cottage, take her books and head to school, come home and make herself dinner, go to bed, wake up, take her books and head to school?

Blair buried herself deeper in the bed, smothering the sounds of Amanda surviving without her. When she came up for air, the cottage was silent—Amanda was gone. And somehow Blair slept.

Until she heard the door open and thought, *She's home; I've slept all day.* No, an hour had passed.

"Amanda?" she called out tentatively.

And for the first time she thought: *It's an intruder, a rapist, a madman. He'll kill me. Hot damn. I won't have to spend so much time dying after all.*

But still, there was the problem of Amanda. *How could the best thing in my life,* Blair thought, *become the worst thing in my life? My daughter.*

And then another door opened, her own bedroom door, and the madman stood there in the form of her landlord, Casey.

"What the hell are you doing here?"

"Checking up on you."

"I don't need checking up on. And you didn't knock."

"I have a key."

"You don't have a right to use that key. Unless there's an emergency."

"I'd call this an emergency."

"You're horny every day. What's new with that?"

"You're dying."

"That's got nothing to do with your being horny."

"Thought maybe you'd want to forget about your troubles."

"Casey," Blair moaned, but she pulled back the covers, and he walked toward her, throwing off his clothes on the way.

Casey was tall, skinny, balding and bearded, a caricature of an aging hippie. But he loved sex, almost as much as he loved drugs, and if he wasn't high on anything other than pot, he was a wonderful lover. So Blair let him in her bed from time to time—though he asked too often and stayed too long.

"Get a girlfriend, Casey. Get a wife," she said, looking up at him.

"You're beautiful," he said. He reached down and stroked her arm.

"For about another minute."

She wasn't beautiful, but men found her exotic or sexy or something—it had proved true through all the stages of her life. Now, at forty-two, she was still fit, probably because she walked back and forth to work, ate little because she spent so much time around food, and seemed to be in motion all the time—even in the small spaces of her restaurant kitchen or tiny cottage. She was dark, her hair cut short but untamed, with loose curls that framed her face and fell across her eyes. Her features were all a little large—her eyes wide, her nose long, her lips full—and though she saw the faults in that when she looked in the mirror, men saw a kind of lush, ripe territory they wanted to explore.

"You contagious?" Casey asked.

"No. Climb in."

"You hurt anywhere?" he asked, sliding into bed beside her, curling his body around hers. His hands started moving over her skin, sending little shock currents through her.

"Not anymore," she murmured, moving closer, breathing him in.

"What is it, Blair? What's wrong with you?" he asked, moving over her body, their legs tangling, their breath finding the space in the crook of each other's neck.

"Not enough sex," she whispered.

He pushed himself down in the bed, drawing lines with his tongue over her full breasts, between them, down along the flat slope of her stomach. When he buried his face between her legs, she moaned and felt herself open—her legs, her chest, her heart. And then she was crying, but he didn't notice, so he kept sucking her, and her legs wrapped around his neck so that he wouldn't stop.

When she came, she pushed him over and climbed on top of him, sliding his cock inside of her, not waiting for his rhythm, his desire, his need. She rocked against him, pulled away, her body lifted, her head thrown back. She was still coming.

Then he sat up, pushing her back, so this time he was leaning over her, plunging into her, hard, so hard that she thought he might break her, and she wanted him to go further, to make her body hurt from so much feeling. And suddenly he pulled out of her and grabbed himself in his hand and let himself come all over her stomach.

She looked at him. He had his eyes closed, and his mouth spread across his face in a sweet smile. Stoned. He was probably stoned at nine o'clock in the morning.

He opened his eyes and looked at her. "You're crying," he said.

She shook her head.

"We should do that more often," he said.

Again she shook her head.

He lay down next to her, upside down in the bed.

"Go away, Casey," she said.

"Give me five minutes, darling. Just let me lie here next to you."

"Five minutes," she told him. "Then go away and never come back. I don't want to do this anymore."

He leaned up on his elbow, gazed down at her.

"Did I hurt you?"

"Not enough," she said. She closed her eyes, rolled away from him. "Please," she said, her voice hard. "Go."

She kept her back to him while he stood, put on his clothes, moved toward the door.

She waited, turned away from him, until she heard him leave.

When the door clicked closed behind him, she lay in bed for a moment, contemplating sleep. But she thought about the cancer in her body and felt heavy, weighed down by so many black cancer cells, pressing her into the mattress. She pushed herself upright and began to tremble.

She would die. She would die before her daughter finished high school, before she finished growing up. Before she found boyfriends, lost boyfriends, chose careers and changed them again, found new cities, new homes. Blair would die, and someone would take her place in the kitchen at the café; someone would move into the cottage; Casey and Perry would find other women to love for a moment or two. But no one would step in as Amanda's mother. No one would love her daughter with the same passion, the same joy.

Blair forced herself out of bed. She needed to stop the shaking in her body. She threw on a kimono, went into the kitchen to put up water for tea. The kettle wobbled in her unsteady hand. She remembered a moment in her childhood—she had watched Hitchcock's *The Birds* one evening; she might have been eleven or twelve—and she woke in the middle of the night, screaming. Her mother was in her room before she herself was fully awake, the screams just beginning to subside. Her mother held her, quietly, stroking her head, waiting until Blair mumbled something about the black sky of birds. "Shh," her mother said, holding Blair, letting her fall back to sleep in her arms. *I need someone to hold me,* Blair thought.

Her parents were killed when Blair was twenty-six. They had taken their first real vacation, a fishing trip to Mexico, and chose to drive to Baja because flights were so expensive. The police said they must have been lost, to have ended up in such a godforsaken town in the middle of the mountains. A couple of teenage boys stopped their car, robbed them, and when Blair's father had a heart attack, the boys panicked and shot Blair's mother. They stole $345 and the old Buick, leaving the couple in a ravine at the side of the road.

Blair thought about her parents, guns pointed in their faces. Was her mother holding her father, who would have already fallen to the ground? Was her father already dead, her mother already mourning him when the bullet pierced her own heart? Or had her mother been shot first, and her dad's heart stopped cold at the thought of life without her? Did either have time to think about death? Did they die instantly? Were they lucky to die so quickly, with so little time to spend contemplating death?

A policewoman came to her apartment in SoHo, where she was living at the time, where the latest boyfriend had just moved out, where she had just learned that she was pregnant, that morning, and already she had an appointment for an abortion at the clinic in the Village. "I'm sorry, sugar," the cop said after telling her about her parents' deaths, and Blair had looked at her, confused: *Why is she calling me sugar? My mother called me sugar. Did she know that?* The woman repeated the story to Blair, as if she hadn't heard enough the first time, and still she couldn't react, couldn't make sense of any of it. Until the policewoman left, and Blair crumbled.

Blair found things to do to keep herself busy—collect her parents' bodies in Oakland, find a cemetery, bury them, sell their house, give away their belongings. And when she was done with it all, she was still pregnant, still aching with grief.

I want my baby, she decided.

She never went back to New York. She found an apartment in Berkeley, a waitressing job, a day-care center. When she yearned for her parents, she gathered Amanda in her arms instead. She was the grown-up now. She was the mother.

Over time, when she thought about her parents, her memories shifted in her mind, like pieces in a kaleidoscope. They reformed themselves, reorganized, rewrote her history. She had only hazy memory of the fights with her father when she was a teenager—about the way she dressed, her politics, the pot she smoked, the bad boys she dated. She forgot her anger at her mother for sending her to private school on a full scholarship—her mother thought she would belong to this other world but instead she inhabited its shadowy fringes. Blair remembered, rather, cooking with her mother, fishing with her father; she remembered their sweet love for each other and how she felt blessed when she heard the horror stories of everyone's parents' divorces. At home, she was safe. And when the world proved to be dangerous, she secluded herself in the cocoon of her childhood home.

Now she needed her mother, her father. She stood in the middle of the kitchen in her own cocoon, this tree-house cottage, and listened to the wail of the teakettle.

Chapter Two

When the phone rang, Luke was startled, forgetting he had a phone, wondering where it was and whether, if he picked it up, he would remember what to say. *Hello. How are you? Fine, thank you.* He had to remember that—the niceties of civilized behavior.

The phone rang a fourth time and he pulled it out from under the overstuffed chair, dragging along a sock he had lost months before.

"Hello," he called into the phone, like an old man leery of technology.

"Bellingham," the voice said. "You're a hard man to find."

"Who's this?" Luke asked. He fell into the chair and let Sweet-pea rest her chin on his knee. The dog, too, had been unsettled by the ringing phone.

"Harrison Driver," the man said. "Reese Academy." The guy paused, then raced on, giving Luke a chance to move through his memories. "We were on the basketball team together senior year. I went out with Trish Keller after you broke up with her."

"Right," Luke said, though he had no clue. Who remembers this stuff?

"So, you're a hermit, huh?"

"Something like that," Luke offered.

"Didn't like fame?" Harrison asked.

So that's what the press had offered.

"Something like that," Luke repeated.

"Well, hey, man. I can imagine it. Head to the mountains. Leave the adoring fans clamoring for more. J. D. Salinger did it and people would buy any piece of shit he wrote now just to get him back in the world."

"What can I do for you?" Luke asked. He reached for the glass of bourbon on the table next to his chair.

"Class reunion. Numero twenty-five. Can you fucking believe it?"

Luke didn't answer.

"So we're planning a reunion. Class party. Raise money for the school. Find out what the old girlfriends look like now."

"I'm sorry, Harrison—"

"Having your name on the committee list would be a good thing. For the school. For the class. Hey, you're a success, man."

Luke drank, finishing the warm bourbon in the glass.

"I can't imagine there aren't plenty of success stories. You don't need mine."

"There's money. Shitloads of money. Silicon Valley and all," Harrison said. "But you're Hollywood. You're Mr. Academy Award. You're also a goddamn golden boy."

Luke laughed. He was sitting in the middle of a five-hundred-square-foot log cabin with his dog, a few articles of clothing, a few pots and pans. He hadn't seen anyone except the guy at the market and the woman at the Lookout Bar in three months. He read books, made furniture in the studio out back, hiked the hills with Sweetpea. A goddamn golden boy.

"I can't help you, Driver. Sorry, man."

"Come to one meeting. Tomorrow night. At Coco's Café in the Mission."

"I don't get out much."

"Come see Trish," Harrison said. "She'll be there."

"Give her a kiss from me," Luke said, and hung up the phone.

And then as if three months of solitude hadn't cured him, he imagined a scene in his mind: He'd find Emily in the kitchen and come up behind her, placing his hands on her shoulders. Would she flinch? When did she stop responding to his touch? Did he miss every clue, every signal?

"I got a call," he'd say. "High school reunion. Twenty-five years. How the hell did that happen?"

Would she stir the sauce for the salmon, not hearing him, not feeling his hands on her shoulders, as if she were already gone, disappeared, a ghost to him? Or would she turn to him, trace the lines in his face, kiss his lips, whisper, "My old man."

She was ten years younger than he was, twenty-three to his thirty-three when they married, thirty-three when she walked out of the screening of his latest film and never came back.

"Do you want to go?" she'd ask.

"No. Yes. Aren't they always awful?" He'd lean toward her, smelling the lemon scent of her thick hair.

"Depends what you're looking for."

"What am I looking for?" he'd murmur, burying his face in the back of her neck, pressing his lips against her warm skin.

"You tell me," she'd say, pulling away, walking away, walking out, never coming back.

Dinner, he thought. *Sweetpea first.*

So he got up from his chair, walked to the food bin, scooped out a bowlful of chow. He turned toward the kitchen with its small oven and mini-refrigerator. A couple of shelves of canned soup, pasta, cereal. He reached for the bottle of bourbon instead.

He drank quickly, then picked up the phone.

Dialed information. San Francisco.

"Do you have a listing for Emily Peck? I don't know where. Anywhere."

When the operator told him no, he said, "Try everywhere else in the world." Still, there was no listing. Emily wouldn't make it so easy. She never made it easy.

He picked up a book, tried to read, tossed the book aside.

He picked up the phone again and dialed a number he knew by heart—still—even though he hadn't dialed it in months.

Dana answered, first ring, out of breath, as if she had been waiting for his call. He sighed, his heart suddenly heavy in his chest, and then realized: He was expecting his wife.

"Dana," he said finally.

"She's not here," Dana said.

"I know."

He remembered the first weeks after Emily left him—he called Dana daily, twice daily, hounding her: "Where's my wife? Why did she leave me?" She politely took his calls, politely refused to answer. Until he gave up and headed to his cabin in the woods. Three months of silence hadn't helped his anguish or his search for answers.

"I won't tell you anything."

"I know."

"Good." He could hear her breathe deeply. "How the hell are you?" she asked.

"I'm fine. Thank you."

"Bullshit."

"Well, let's keep it simple."

"You ever coming back?"

"Back to what? San Francisco? My old house? My old life?

Making movies and making love with my wife? What exactly are we talking about?"

"Back to life. Let's start with that," she said, sounding already weary.

"I don't know," he said, his voice softer. "How the hell are you, Dana?"

She paused for a bit and he waited. "I'm pregnant."

He smiled. "Weren't you and your sister going to do that at the same time?"

She didn't answer. He felt a stone in the deep center of his stomach.

"Was there another man?" he asked quietly. "Just tell me that."

"No."

"No there wasn't, or no you won't tell me."

"No, Luke."

"Right. Then I don't know. Good luck. Or something. Tell her—"

"I won't tell her anything," Dana said quickly. "She doesn't want to hear from you."

"Why?" Luke said, and then he couldn't say anything more. He knew he'd be crying if another sound escaped his lips.

"She was lonely, Luke. You have no idea."

He put the phone back on the cradle.

Lonely. A scene came to mind as if lifted from a screenplay. He's sitting at the desk, writing. It's evening, and the fog's rolling in over the city, tucking them in for the night. Emily's stretched out on the couch in his office, reading, sipping a glass of wine. Sweetpea's at her feet. Luke's happy she's there while he's working in the evening. The work is going well. And then she picks up the phone to call Dana, starts talking about something foolish—a dress she saw in a shop on

Fillmore. He stops typing, turns and stares at her, not needing to say more, and she gets off the couch, taking the phone and her glass of wine with her, out of the room. She slams the door behind her. End of scene. Did he make love with her that night? Did he promise her a weekend in Mendocino, no work to distract him?

Does your wife leave you without a word of explanation because she's lonely?

"Come on, Sweetpea," he said, and the dog leaped to her feet as if waiting for months for this moment.

Luke grabbed the keys to the truck and walked out the door. He had vowed he wouldn't leave the cabin until he was rid of Emily in his mind. But maybe he was wrong—he had to find Emily to get rid of her.

• • •

An hour later, he turned up the street toward his house on Potrero Hill. He pulled into the small space in front of the garage and stared up. No lights. No life. He had left three months before, locked the place up and hadn't been back.

It was dusk and the reflections of the setting sun cast an amber glow on the house. Haunted. Maybe he'd find his own ghost knocking around the old place. "Hey, Luke, my man. I was wondering where you'd gone. Left your soul behind, didn't you?"

Luke opened the car door and fumbled with his keys.

Maybe she'd been back. Maybe she was back, living there, out for a run, back in a moment.

He dropped the keys, picked them up, almost got knocked down by a wild Sweetpea, tearing out of the car and up the steps of the house. Home. Poor old dog.

He followed Sweetpea up the steps and stood awkwardly at the front door. Ring the bell? No.

He turned the key in the lock and the dog nosed the door open, tore through the entrance in a blur. Barking. Howling. She had been so quiet for so many months in the woods. Luke could hear the tapping of her footsteps as she raced through the rooms of the house.

"She's not here, my dog," Luke whispered. "Not anywhere."

He pulled the door closed behind him and looked around. The vestibule was bare—no jackets slung over the antique wooden bench, no hats thrown on the mantel. The place looked heavy, coated in a layer of dust, sunk into itself somehow.

The living room was elegant, spare, sophisticated. He felt like a stranger seeing it for the first time. *Cold,* he thought. *Did I ever like this room?* Emily always led guests into the living room—he preferred to have everyone stand around the cozy mess of a kitchen. Everyone. Their lives were always crowded with friends, business associates, people dropping in, staying, parties full of people who never went home.

Once, he and Emily had come home from a screening, drunk, amorous, and had landed on the black-and-white-striped couch to make love—or to finish what they had started in the car on the way home—and when they were done, exhausted, stretched across couch and rug, a pair of hands had clapped for them. Dana. Sleeping off her own drunk on the opposite couch.

"You do that very well," she said.

Emily had smiled sleepily, turned her head away from her sister's stare. Had Emily known she was there?

Luke had not missed the social whirl of their lives while holed up in the Santa Cruz Mountains. That had been Emily's sphere. To ward off loneliness? How many nights had he quietly escaped a party going on in his own living room to sit undisturbed at his computer for an hour or so? To live with the characters in his scripts instead of the characters in his house, Emily had once accused.

Luke walked through the living room and on to the kitchen, turning on lights as he passed through rooms, scaring off ghosts and memories.

Automatically he looked at the refrigerator, as he had for days after she left. When she walked out of the screening for *The Geography of Love* that day, three months ago, she had stopped home, packed a bag, left a note. She had posted the note on the refrigerator door, and he had left it there, dangling like a mere shopping list from a penguin magnet: *Buy milk, leave your husband.*

He didn't have to read it again, but he would. For days he had stood in front of this note, written on paper from the pad kept by the phone, artfully rimmed by dancing lions. She loved lions. She left him, framed in lions. He read, drank another bourbon from the full bottle he found in the liquor cabinet, read again, hoping this time to find more, to discover a code that he had missed the first three thousand times through. But drunk or drunker, the words were the same.

I'm sorry. I couldn't do this any other way. I'm leaving. Don't try to find me. It might not mean much, but I did love you. Em.

Em. As if the intimacy transformed the rest of the words into a love note: *Off for a run. Take off all your clothes. Meet me in bed. Em.*

He pulled the note off the refrigerator, jammed it into his pocket. The poor penguin magnet clattered to the ground. He kicked it across the room and it disappeared under the dishwasher.

Sweetpea howled from upstairs.

"Coming, girl," Luke called out, his voice echoing in the hallways.

He ran up the stairs, heard whimpering from the bedroom. He didn't want to go in there, didn't want to be so close to that empty space.

"Come on, girl. I'll get you a treat," Luke called from the top of the stairs.

The dog didn't fall for it. Luke headed into the bedroom.

Sweetpea was trying to stuff herself under the bed, moaning from the strain.

"Get out of there, old girl," Luke said, going to her side and pulling her back. He leaned down and scanned the underbelly of the king-size bed. A slipper. Emily's slipper.

Luke reached for the furry thing and passed it on to his dog, who snatched it between joyous lips.

"Lucky you," Luke told her, half-smiling.

And then he was crying, tears covering his face faster than he could wipe them off with his flannel sleeve.

"Let's get out of here, girl," he said, but Sweetpea had plopped herself down at the side of the bed—Emily's side—and was happily chewing on the slipper.

It was then Luke noticed the difference, noticed how the room had changed since he had left it three months before. The top of the dresser was bare, stripped free of jewelry box, photographs, comb and brush. He threw open drawers, now empty of lingerie, of T-shirts and tank tops, of bathing suits and running clothes. He pushed the closet door open—dresses, shoes, pants, blouses, gone. When she had left him, she had filled a suitcase, perhaps. Not much more. And he had waited for her to come back—if not for him, then at least for her clothes. Now she had done that. When? A week ago? Months ago? Had Dana called her, wherever she was hiding, on the day he left town? Told her the coast was clear. Come and get it.

The emptied bedroom was somehow more real than the note on the refrigerator door. What did it mean that she left without a word? That she couldn't talk to him, fight with him, make up with him?

He remembered a rip-roaring fight. Six months ago, the director of *The Geography of Love* had invited Luke to work with him in L.A., on the set—but Luke was already writing a new script and didn't want to be distracted. Emily begged him to take her to L.A., to let her watch production, go to parties, take lunches. He hated all that and chose to live in San Francisco, away from Hollywood, so that he could do what he did best—write. When he turned the director down, she was furious. She raged, accusing him of being selfish. This was his career, wasn't it? he countered. She left the house, slept at Dana's for a night, came back the next morning and they fell wearily into each other's arms. Her mouth at his ear, she had murmured, "I know you. I won't ask again."

So why, in the end, had she left without an argument? *Tell me you're lonely,* Luke thought. *Tell me what you need. Scream it, cry it, slam doors in my face. But don't leave me like that.*

He sank down on the bed. *I need a slipper to chew on,* he thought. And he rolled over, his head on her pillow. Still, after all these months, he could breathe her in.

• • •

An hour later, he awoke, feeling drunk and hungover at the same time. He dragged himself into the shower, found fresh clothes to wear, poured himself another bourbon. He needed food, but he could wait for that.

Sweetpea didn't want to follow him out of the house—she was home now, dragging the slipper from room to room.

"Stay here, girl," Luke told her finally. "I'll be back." What he wanted was to head to his cabin in the woods and never return. First he'd talk to Dana. Then he'd fetch Sweetpea and flee the city.

He drove across town to Pacific Heights. Dana and her husband lived in a pink Victorian, tucked between a sky blue Victorian and a mauve Victorian. Suddenly San Francisco seemed candy sweet, and Luke wondered how he had ever loved the city. He rang the doorbell and glanced at his watch, 9:45 P.M. Saturday night. And he knew when the door opened that he'd be falling into a Geller dinner party, the last place on earth he wanted to be.

Brady answered the door, clapped him on the back as if thrilled to see him. The bastard had never liked him. He was a big, once-handsome man, now ruddy from too many martinis and burly from business lunches and three-star dinners. "Just in time for the main course, Luke," Brady said. "Come join the gang."

"No," Luke said, holding ground despite the man's insistent pressure on his arm. "I just need to talk to Dana. For a minute. I'm not staying."

"We're in the middle of dinner. A few other couples here, nothing fancy. You'll join us, talk to Dana later. It's been—what?—months. We're dying to hear what you've been up to. My friends would love to meet you."

Of course, Luke thought. *Show me off.* For years Brady had shown no interest in him or his writing—until Luke had won an Academy Award. Suddenly he mattered in the world Brady inhabited.

"No, Brady. Just get Dana," Luke insisted.

"Who's there, dear?" Dana's voice called out.

"Luke," Brady said, and Dana appeared in the hallway. "You were right. He's back in town. Tell him to join us."

"No," Dana said. "He doesn't have to do that. Go ahead, Brady. Let me talk to him."

Brady shrugged, clapped Luke's shoulder, pecked Dana's cheek, moved on down the hall. Luke could hear uproarious laughter spilling out of the dining room. *We would be there,* he thought. *Emily and I. Would we be enjoying ourselves?* Luke couldn't remember.

"I can't help you," Dana said quietly. "I told you that."

He looked at her. She was tall and elegant, hair swept up into some sort of chignon, a rope of pearls gracing her long neck. She was a dark version of blond Emily, and the resemblance pulled at Luke's heart.

"I just want to talk to her," Luke said.

"She's gone away. You won't find her."

"My God," Luke said. He saw her hand move down across the swell of her belly. "Look at that." He reached his hand out—wanting to touch her—and he saw her step away. He dropped his hand.

"She wouldn't leave you when you're pregnant," he said. "She'd stay close."

Dana shook her head.

"How many months?"

"Four," she said. "Please go, Luke. I have nothing to offer you."

"Your husband offered dinner."

"My husband's an idiot. You know that." She finally smiled.

"You look good," Luke said.

"You look like shit."

He ran his hand across his beard—it was easy not to shave in the mountains.

"I like it," he told her. "Makes me look like someone else. I look in the mirror and I'm always surprised. Who the hell is that? And damn if I can't figure out the answer."

"Are you going back to your cabin?"

"Not till I find her."

"Let her go."

"I tried," he said. "It didn't work."

He turned and headed down the tall steps leading toward the street. He could hear the shrill laugh of someone in the dining room and the echo followed him all the way to the car.

• • •

Sweetpea wouldn't leave the house on Potrero Hill. Luke was too tired to fight with her—"One night, that's all," he warned the dog, and then settled in on the big bed.

When he woke once in the middle of the night, he reached out for Emily—something he never did in the single bed at his cabin—and then he pulled himself out of bed, stumbled into the bathroom to find a sleeping pill, or two, and lay awake, for hours, listening to his snoring pup, waiting for unconsciousness.

He thought about falling in love with Emily, an almost effortless, cool slide into life with her. She did the graphics for his film publicity, *Pescadero*—an ice blue sea, a strip of flat white beach, a girl lying alone in the sand, curled on her side. When he met her, he told her the poster was perfect, and when she smiled at him, so obviously pleased and surprised and just a little shy, he asked her to dinner on the spot. Within days they were living together. He would wake up in the middle of the night and watch her sleep, amazed by her beauty and his luck. When he met Dana, she said to him, "So, you're the guy who treats my sister like a princess."

"Is that a good thing?" he had asked.

"As long as you know that she's not," Dana had said. Sisterly concern or jealousy? He was never sure.

And now, in the middle of the night, with some vague scent of Emily still on her pillow, he conjured up memories of their marriage. An argument about having children—she wasn't ready, she insisted, year after year. An argument about canceling a vacation in Italy—he wasn't finished with his script, and no, he couldn't work while riding a bicycle through vineyards. An argument about his Academy Award speech—why hadn't he mentioned her?

His legs tangled in the sheets. He was hot, half awake, restless, and he reached for water on his bedside table. To quiet his mind he lay back down and imagined a scene. He had finished work for the night. The writing had gone well. He walked quietly into the bedroom, where Emily was already sleeping. He undressed and slipped in beside her. She turned toward him, smiling. "I've missed you," she whispered.

"God, I miss you," he told her.

"Shh," she said. "Don't wake me. Make love to me. As quietly as you possibly can."

He stroked her body while she slept. He climbed on top of her and entered her and they moved together as slowly and sweetly as the tug of the ocean.

• • •

He woke after noon, though he vaguely remembered letting Sweet-pea out into the backyard to pee sometime in the early morning. He was groggy and miserable. He dragged himself into the shower and stood there, hot water beating down on him. In the corner of the stall he saw a razor, Emily's razor. He picked it up—strawberry blond hairs caught under the blade. He tossed the razor across the bath-room, and it landed squarely in the wastebasket.

He found coffee in the kitchen, found the coffee press stashed away somewhere. It seemed that Emily had left most of the kitchen things. Well, he did most of the cooking. But when he pressed the coffee, he thought of mornings when he prepared breakfast for her and brought it to her in bed, and he cursed her for not having packed up every goddamn thing in the house and taken it with her.

Sweetpea followed Luke around, from room to room, as Luke searched for winter clothes to take back with him to the cabin. Evenings were cold in the Santa Cruz Mountains. The dog was whimpering—she knew they were leaving. "Where the hell did she store the ski clothes?" Luke muttered, throwing open closet doors, pulling down storage boxes.

One large box fell on him, then tumbled to the floor. A carton marked TAHOE. Taped and retaped. They skied once or twice a win-ter—she liked it more than he did.

He tore open the box and found what he was looking for: gloves, scarves, down vests, heavy sweaters, long underwear. Emily's were there, too—she had forgotten to clean out her own stored clothes. He picked up a ski sweater and held it to his face. It smelled only of cardboard—there was none of her sweet smell here.

And then, in a moment, he was throwing things wildly from the box: goggles, which crashed against the wall, hats—ridiculous hats—which made him ache for her face in front of him now. At the bottom of the box was a ski ticket for Squaw Valley. He picked it up, wiping at his eyes. On it was scrawled a phone number, a San Francisco number that he didn't recognize. In Emily's handwriting. And under it she had written, *Just tell him: I'll be home tomorrow.*

Luke stood, leaving the mess of the hallway strewn around him, and walked into Emily's study. She was a graphic designer, had worked from home the last couple of years. Now the study was empty of portfolios and drawings and artist materials, and even her framed work—the posters for his films—was gone from the walls. He sat at her bare desk and picked up the telephone.

A year ago, they had taken their last ski trip. To Squaw. With Dana and Brady. Emily had been miserable, said she had a project and a deadline and too much pressure from the client. They went home a day early. *I'll be home tomorrow.*

He dialed the number. A man answered.

"I'm calling from PacBell," Luke said. "I'd like to tell you about some new services—"

"It's Sunday, buddy. Leave us alone." And the man hung up the phone.

Luke didn't recognize the voice.

Luke raced from the house and into his truck, tucking the ski lift ticket into the back pocket of his jeans.

• • •

"You're imagining things," Dana said.

Luke had caught her walking out her door and had followed her into her car and off to the farmers' market. Now he seemed to be serving as some sort of grocery boy, carrying baskets full of produce that she bought at each stand along the way.

"Just listen to me," he insisted. "She wrote it down on her lift ticket. Gave it to you. It said: 'Just tell him: *I'll be home tomorrow.*'"

"I don't know what you're talking about."

Luke raced to keep up with her as she tossed a bag of tangerines in his basket, then moved on to a stand of Asian vegetables.

"You do, Dana. You would know. She told you everything."

"There wasn't anything to tell. Who knows what that stupid lift ticket means. It could mean anything."

"It means she was having an affair."

Dana stopped and turned toward Luke. They watched each other for a moment. She seemed about to say something—then she shook her head.

"Would it be easier to imagine she left you for another man? That some other man lured her away from you? Is that better than thinking that you lost her all by yourself? Then yes, I called that number. I said, 'She'll be home tomorrow.'"

Luke stood, in the middle of the marketplace, not speaking, not moving.

Dana looked around, embarrassed, as if watching for spectators. "My God, you're a fool." She turned away from him, grabbing handfuls of purple eggplants and bok choy.

Luke left her baskets on the ground, turned and walked away.

• • •

By the time he made it back to his car in Pacific Heights, then across town to Potrero Hill, it was almost six in the evening. Sweetpea needed a walk. Then he needed food. He was about to prepare something to eat from the cans in the pantry when the phone rang. He should remember to disconnect the phone, he thought. He should remember to sell the damn house, he thought.

"Luke?" the voice asked.

"Speaking."

"Trish Keller. From Reese? The good old days?"

"Trish Keller," Luke said, climbing onto a bar stool at the kitchen counter. "How the hell are you?"

"I'm OK. Old. Like all of us, I guess."

"You're not old, Trish. You're always seventeen."

"Yeah, then you better not come to the reunion meeting tonight."

"What meeting?"

"I heard you were coming."

"How?"

"Harrison Driver. I got your number from him. I tried the number he gave me at your mountain cabin first. Then I called here."

"Oh, Christ. Harrison Driver. I forgot about that."

"You're not coming." Her voice lowered with disappointment.

"I don't know. No. I'm not coming. I don't even live here anymore. I'm leaving in five minutes."

"You could just come by and say hello before you head out of town."

"You live in San Francisco? Last I heard you were in Boston. Married. To a fucking banker or something."

"No, the banker fucked me," Trish said, and laughed. "Divorced now. I don't know where I live. I'm out visiting Ruth Vargas—she convinced me to go to this shindig."

"If I come, can we ignore everyone else and just talk for an hour or two?"

"Oh, God. You haven't changed."

"No, I'm not seducing you. I'm just curious. Twenty-five years is a long time."

"Then come," she said, and she sounded shy. Trish was never shy. "I'd love to see you again."

Luke looked over at Sweetpea, shrugged his shoulders. "Guess I could use real food before I head out. What time? Where?"

"Now," Trish said, laughing. "Coco's Café. I'm heading out. Called you 'cause I got scared."

"You? Scared? Why would you be scared?"

"We don't always turn out the way we're supposed to," she said.

"I'm walking proof," he told her. He pawed at his beard. Luke Bellingham, mountain man.

"You'll come?"

"I'll come," he said.

"Thanks."

She hung up and he turned back to Sweetpea. "Lucky dog," he said. "You get to stay here one more night."

He poured himself a bourbon, went into the bedroom to find clean clothes, poured himself another bourbon, went into the bathroom to shave, decided against it, poured himself another bourbon. By the time he left, he knew not to drive. He found a cab and headed to the restaurant, though he couldn't remember one good reason for going there.

• • •

He made his way awkwardly through the crowded tables, looking desperately for someone who looked familiar. The noise level was deafening, and over the cacophony of voices, he felt, rather than heard, the insistent pounding of something that must have been music. He kept maneuvering around chairs and people and waiters, and still there were more tables, more unfamiliar faces. The walls and ceiling were painted burgundy and seemed to close in on him.

Someone—a waiter?—directed him upstairs, where he saw a long table and guessed that must be his group, though he didn't feel like he belonged to any group in the world, much less one sitting in this ridiculous restaurant. Aqua chairs? Black plates on a black tablecloth? He stopped for a moment, looking at them all, thinking about fleeing to his cabin.

"Luke!" someone called, and he saw a woman at the end of the table stand, and then everyone turned to look at him. He didn't know the woman—heavy, middle-aged—still didn't recognize the faces of these people. But he smiled, headed toward the standing woman, offered an elusive nod to everyone else.

"I saved you a seat," she whispered, taking his arm and pulling him down next to her. She planted a kiss on his cheek. "I knew you wouldn't recognize me. One of the reasons I didn't want to come."

He looked at her, saw Trish hidden somewhere inside the extra flesh. His heart ached for her, and he leaned over and kissed her, threw an arm around her.

"God, I'm glad you're here," he whispered back to her.

"Bellingham," a voice boomed, and Luke sat up straight, as if caught passing notes in class.

"My God," he mumbled, "I feel like I'm back at Reese again. Getting in trouble before I open my mouth."

The few people around him snickered—a guy reached over and slapped his back. "Good to see you, Luke."

Luke had no clue. "You too, man."

"You're late, Bellingham," the big voice boomed again, "but at least you're here. We'll settle for an appearance. That's what stars do, I heard. Appear at night."

Luke peered at the man at the head of the table—some pompous ass he would never want to know but probably did at some point.

"That's Harrison Driver," Trish whispered.

Luke shrugged. "You went out with him?"

She lifted her eyebrows. "Never. Did he say that?"

"If we could have your attention, Mr. Bellingham," Driver called.

"Yes, sir," Luke said, and saluted. A few people laughed.

Driver talked about the reunion and the need to raise money for the school, and Luke tuned out, scoping the crowd. Rich people, but he was used to that. San Francisco was full of them. But these were rich people who had always been rich—even back when Luke was at Reese during the hippie era, they had trust funds to support their drug habits, their trips to Peru or India, their lofts in Manhattan or San Francisco after college. He recognized a few of them, but they were all middle-aged. Funny, he never saw himself as middle-aged.

He turned back to Trish. "Do you remember these people?"

"Most of them. So should you. You slept with most of the women."

"I did not."

"At least half of them. That's Erica Bodine at the end of the table. You dumped me for her."

Erica Bodine was gaunt and elegant, bejeweled and scowling.

"I'd never pick her over you," Luke told Trish.

"Don't seduce me," she told him.

"Why not?" he asked. *Seduce,* he thought for the first time in a long time. *Sex.* Yet all he could yearn for was the deep sleep that good sex promised.

"Mr. Bellingham," Driver called out. "I'd like your attention for a moment."

"Can I get a drink?" Luke asked.

Driver gestured to a waiter who then appeared at Luke's side.

"Bourbon," Luke ordered. "Double."

"We thought we could use your power and influence," Driver called, and Luke began to slip down into his seat, "to invite some stars to this gala—make this a kind of Hollywood happening."

There was a murmur of excitement from the crowd.

"Sorry, Driver," Luke said. "I'm not happening at the moment."

"Leave him alone, Harrison," Trish called out. "This isn't about movie stars."

"This is about giving back," Erica Bodine said loudly, eyeing Luke.

"Do I owe her something?" Luke whispered to Trish.

"It was hard for all of us to get over you," Trish said softly.

Awkwardly Luke stood. "Listen, Driver," he said, then looked around the table, surprised that in his drunkenness he had put this particular fantasy into action. Everyone was listening. "I don't write films anymore. I quit. I don't know people anymore. I dropped out. Consider me a fallen star. *Pfft.*" He gestured with his closed hand—a long, slow descent from on high—until his hand dropped to the table and opened, with nothing inside.

There was an awkward silence. Finally Luke sat and Trish put her hand on his arm.

"Then I've got the perfect job for you," Driver said, and he looked immediately pleased with himself. "Finder of Lost Souls."

"Let's get out of here," Trish said, pushing back her chair.

"Wait," Luke told her. "What's that?" he asked Driver.

"We've got a list of alums who have dropped off the face of the earth. They don't support the school. They don't send in notices of the births of their children or their business promotions for the school magazine. We'd like to find them. Where are they? What are they doing?"

"Maybe they don't want to be found," someone said.

"Maybe they don't want to give money," someone else said.

"I'll find them," Luke said. He felt a surge of energy, a kind of rush that filled his chest and cleared his head. "Give me that list. I'll find the Lost Souls."

Driver riffled through some papers, found his list, and passed it on down the table to Luke.

"Now let's go," Trish whispered urgently. "I hate this."

"I'm the goddamn King of Lost Souls," Luke said loudly.

"Luke," Trish said, even louder.

"We're out of here," he said, and stood, bowing gallantly to the crowd, downing his drink and following Trish out of the restaurant.

• • •

Trish pulled her car up in front of Luke's house. They could see Sweetpea peering out the living-room window.

Luke looked at Trish, reached out his hand and stroked the side of her cheek. "Anyone in his right mind would take you to bed," Luke said.

She held his hand to her cheek, smiling. "Go on," she said. "Get out of here."

"Remember how cocky we were? How invincible?" he asked. He remembered a moment during his high school years, one Sunday, when he was high from beer and marijuana and decided to walk across a railroad bridge that spanned high above a rocky bend in the river. There was no safe edge along the tracks on the bridge—if a train had come, he would have dropped to his death or been crushed by the train. But a train didn't come—he crossed the bridge, lazily, unhurried, while his friends cheered him from the other side. He had never expected trains or runaway wives to derail him.

Trish nodded. She looked wistful, and in the shadow of the streetlight, Luke could imagine for a moment that she was forty pounds lighter and years younger. No, she was a woman now. Still beautiful. She let his hand go.

"I've got a son in high school," she said. "He's a terrific kid. But he's a geek, a nerd. He doesn't get invited to parties; he doesn't get phone calls at night. I see the clusters of pretty boys and girls at school when I pick him up every afternoon—and I hate them for their charm and their beauty."

"He'll be OK when he gets to college."

"But four years of misery is a long time," she said. "Did we know a thing about those kids?" She peered at Luke in the darkness of the car. "We were the popular kids. We went to every party; we had every boyfriend or girlfriend we wanted. Were we cruel? Did we just breeze on by those miserable kids on the fringe?"

Luke put his head back on the seat, stared out at the streetlight, half lost in the fog. Did he breeze on by? He remembered the confusion at his parents' divorce and the unbearable pain a year later of his father's death; he remembered the fear of too many pressures, too many dreams in his heart.

"Was it so easy for us?" Luke asked.

"I wasn't prepared for the rest of life," Trish said. "I thought I'd always win the guy, win the prize, win the race."

They were quiet for a moment. Luke could hear Sweetpea barking impatiently from inside the house.

"We weren't so invincible, were we?" Trish asked.

Luke turned toward her and shook his head. He ran his fingers through his hair. He had spent so much time thinking about whether Emily had been happy. Had he been happy? Christ, did he even know the answer to that?

"I'm leaving first thing in the morning," he said. "Otherwise I'd—"

"Please, Luke. Go to bed."

He leaned toward her for a kiss, then opened the car door and headed out.

"Don't forget your list," she called, and he turned back.

"King of Lost Souls," he said, and offered her a half smile, reaching back for the paper.

"Good luck," she told him, and she took off down the block.

When the car turned the corner, Luke felt a pang of loss or regret. For not urging Trish to stay? For the passage of time that had changed her so much? Or his own glory days, long gone.

• • •

Luke sat with a bourbon and his list of Lost Souls in the overstuffed chair next to the bed. He didn't want to get into bed. Sweetpea was sleeping next to Emily's side, curled around her slipper. Luke was beyond tired, beyond drunk. He would sit and drink bourbon for the rest of his life, he decided.

He didn't recognize all the names on the list. His class had been small—only seventy students, but still there were a couple of unfamiliar names. There was one surprise—George Hansen, class president, suck-up extraordinaire—why the hell would he lose touch? Wouldn't he be sending in those promotion announcements for each school bulletin? No, Luke wasn't going to find George Hansen. He couldn't really be a Lost Soul.

Blair Clemens. When Luke saw her name on the page, he sat up; his heart somersaulted in his chest. It was her story that had inspired *Pescadero.* He only knew hints of the true story. The mystery had intrigued everyone—what had happened to her that night at the beach. Everyone talked about it for a year or two and then, like all scandals, it was replaced by one more current, more thrilling. But somehow her story had haunted him, and years later he wrote a movie, trying to imagine what had happened to Blair Clemens and her boyfriend that night.

He never knew Blair. She was a real Lost Soul. Blair had floated somewhere above the class for all four years she had been at Reese. Luke remembered her as pale and ethereal, soft and unfocused, cool and untouchable. She wore long hippie skirts, gauzy peasant blouses, feathery earrings. Her hair swooned around her head. A real hippie chick when most of them were just playing dress-up. Her voice was too soft in class to really hear, so the teachers stopped calling on her. She always had a kind of smile on her face, as if she knew things no one else knew.

Lost Soul? No, maybe she was the only one who wasn't lost. The rest of us were desperately looking for something she had, Luke thought. *But we didn't even know what it was.*

Of course Blair Clemens lost touch with the school. She was a scholarship student, one of the few. She wasn't academic—or maybe she was so smart she didn't need to be academic. She didn't play sports or go to parties. She wasn't going to do things that needed to be bragged about in the school bulletin. *What was she going to do?* Luke wondered. *Win an Academy Award, marry a beautiful spouse?*

Lost Soul? I'll find her, he decided. *I have to find her.*

He picked up the phone, called information.

"Blair Clemens. Anywhere in the world." Easier to look for someone he didn't know than try to find his own wife. He'd start a missing persons bureau soon, he thought.

"I have a listing in San Francisco," the operator said.

"You're kidding," Luke said.

"Would you like that listing, sir?"

"Yes, ma'am."

And he wrote the number down on the list of Lost Souls. Could it be that the school never even tried to contact her? Or more likely, that she never returned their calls.

He looked at his watch. Ten-thirty P.M. He decided Lost Souls usually stay up late.

He dialed the number.

"You've reached Blair and Amanda's place," the answering machine told him. A husky voice, deeper than he remembered. Had he ever talked to Blair? Probably not. He could remember looking at her—she would look back, never turn away like the other girls. It always unsettled him. *Who is she? What does she know?*

"Leave a message." He was about to hang up when he heard the phone pick up, and a far breathier voice say, "Hang on. I'm here. Sort of." A long pause while the phone banged around. Then, "Hello."

"Blair?"

"Who's this?"

"You won't remember me. I went to Reese."

"Forget it." She hung up.

Luke smiled, drank his bourbon. He should have hung up when Driver called him. But then again, he wouldn't have had this—the search for Lost Souls.

He called back. Got the answering machine again. This time he left a message. "Hi. This is Luke Bellingham. I did go to Reese—but hey, I'm not asking for money. I don't know what I'm asking for. I just want to talk to you." He had run out of things to say to her machine. "I'll try you again. Another time. I'm leaving the city tomorrow. I just thought we could talk for a few minutes. . . ."

And then the phone picked up.

"I remember you," she said.

Chapter Three

Blair remembered his beauty. There weren't many beautiful boys in high school. Most grew in lumpy solids, big around the top or bottom, unformed in the face. But she remembered Luke as tall and lanky; he moved with remarkable grace. He had high cheekbones and the same shoulder-length hair that most of the boys wore, but his was wheat blond and as thick as a girl's. She remembered green eyes.

"I'm surprised," he said now, on the phone, arriving in her cottage by disconnect—a voice, a memory, a tug to the past just as she was dreaming about dying. She was swimming, underwater, a common dream for her, but when she wanted air, she found herself sinking deeper, water pressing down on her from above, as heavy as hands. She answered the phone to escape the dream. *Where the hell is Amanda at ten-thirty at night?*

"Why?" she asked.

"I don't think we ever spoke," he said.

"We did," she told him, sitting up in bed now, her head clear of the thick waters in her dream. "You asked me once if I was wearing underwear. You were drunk. We were at a party at Chris Martin's house."

"You didn't go to parties," he said.

"I went to that one."

"What did you say?"

"I told you I never wore underwear."

"Under those gauzy skirts," he said, and she could tell he was smiling.

"Now I'm surprised you remember," she said.

And then they were quiet for a moment and she liked that—a man who could pause, take a breath.

"Why are you calling?" she finally said.

"You're lost," he said, and then he laughed. "Or so Reese Academy thinks. I offered to find you."

"Last time they called me for a donation, I told them I was moving to Alaska with no forwarding address," Blair told him. "Why are you doing this?"

"I don't know," he said. "I mean, I know why they want you found. Contributions, loyalty, that sort of thing."

"Forget it."

"I'm not asking for that."

"What are you asking for?"

"I don't know. I can't go to sleep. And my dog wants a walk. Where do you live?"

"Nowhere near you."

"How do you know?"

"Because you're probably rich. I'm not."

"I bet you're doing a hell of a lot better than I'm doing right now," he said. Blair smiled at that.

"I don't think so, Luke Bellingham." She started to hang up and then heard him speaking again.

"You've never met Sweetpea," he said.

"The dog."

"Not just any dog."

"I'm sure."

"You can ignore me. Just take Sweetpea for a walk. She's been alone with me in the woods for months. She could use a fresh face."

"And what would you do?"

"Walk next to you."

"Now?"

"I might leave tomorrow."

"Back to the woods, I assume."

"This is Sweetpea's last chance."

"Thirty-five fifty-eight Lucas Street. In the Haight. I'm in the cottage in back. Don't come in. I'll meet you out in front."

Then she hung up.

"Damn," she said to herself. She crawled out of bed and threw a sweatshirt over her nightgown. She found a pair of jeans on the floor and pulled them on. The nightgown was too long to tuck in so it hung over the pants. "Gauzy skirts," she muttered, suddenly furious with herself. She had avoided all the Luke Bellinghams for four torturous years in high school. They were smooth and slick, while she was caught in the muddled mess of adolescence. They were trust fund babies; she was a fisherman's daughter. They knew the rules; she was making it all up as she went along. Why had she answered the goddamn phone? If she hadn't, she would have been dead by now, drowned by watery hands.

The door flew open and Amanda stood there, a wild smile on her face.

"I got a raise," she said. She twirled around in the doorway, then stopped and peered at her mother, her head cocked sideways.

"You're looking very attractive," she said.

Blair looked down at her ridiculous outfit and shrugged.

"I'm going to walk some guy's dog."

"Who? What? Now?"

"Don't ask," Blair said, giving her daughter a peck on the cheek. "Congrats on the raise. You were working?"

"All night," Amanda said.

"It's Sunday?" Blair asked. "I was sleeping. I'm completely jumbled."

"Maybe you dreamed about someone's dog?" Amanda suggested.

Blair walked into the bathroom connecting the two tiny pine-walled bedrooms. Even the bathroom was miniature, painted rose, the only hanging lamp covered with a plum-colored Japanese lantern. She brushed her teeth and eyed her pink self in the mirror. Bedhead. She ruffled her hair, but she had fallen asleep with it wet and there was nothing she could do about it now. *Who cares what I look like,* she thought, and threw the toothbrush at the mirror.

"What's wrong with you?" Amanda asked, watching her from the doorway.

Blair walked up to her daughter and put her arms around her. "I love you, my sweet girl."

Amanda pulled back a little and peered at her mom. "Is this dog-walking thing something permanent? Like you walk this dog and never come back?"

"You never know," Blair told her, grabbing the hat from Amanda's head—a purple derby—and pulling it over her own mess of a head. She walked to the door and then looked back.

"I'll remember you fondly," Amanda offered.

Blair curtsied, holding her nightgown out away from her jeans.

"The dog might be scared," Amanda said.

Blair blew a kiss and left the cottage, closing the door behind her.

Sure enough, a dog sat waiting at the end of the path. She looked around—not a Bellingham in sight. She knelt down and the big dog loped on up to her, sniffed around. *Good, it's not a licking dog,* she thought. She checked the dog tag: *Sweetpea.* Handsome in a mutty sort of way. Soulful eyes. Part shepherd, part something she couldn't identify. Lots of sweet in this Sweetpea. And the softest black-brown coat she had ever felt.

She looked around, eyeing the bushes, the garbage can, the side of the garage. "Where is he, girl?" she whispered.

Sweetpea nuzzled closer.

"Lonely, are you? Hmm. What a concept." Blair stood, looked around once more, called out: "You can come out now, Bellingham. I'll walk your damn dog."

He stepped forward, out of some darkness, and stood before her. Older, craggier, shorter hair, some mess of a beard on his face. Were those the same soulful eyes?

"Meet Sweetpea," he said, his voice almost a whisper.

"We met," she said. "Now we walk."

He stepped aside and she passed him, noticing that he was even taller, not just a boy who grew sooner and better than all the other boys, but a boy who kept growing.

He walked a half step behind her.

"You had blond hair," he said.

"No, I didn't."

"You were tall," he said.

"No, I wasn't."

"You look wonderful," he said.

She stopped and he almost bumped into her. Sweetpea knew to pause at her side.

"OK," she said, almost looking at him. "That's enough of then. This is now."

"I'm talking about now."

"How do you put up with him?" she asked Sweetpea, and they started walking again, and when they turned the corner, the streets were finally filled with people. Blair realized she was nervous. Was this a date? She didn't do dates. She occasionally met a guy in a bar, went back to his place for a bout of lovemaking. More often she stayed home on her nights off, hanging out with Amanda. There was something odd about a boy calling, inviting her for a walk. It seemed downright adolescent.

They walked, Blair holding Sweetpea' s leash, the dog brushing gently against her leg. Luke was there, somewhere, a half beat off, and whenever she looked back to see if they had lost him, he was always still there, and he looked ridiculously pleased with himself or her or his dog or something she couldn't figure out.

"Would you like a drink?" he asked, leaning toward her as they walked.

"I'm just walking the dog," she told him.

"Maybe the dog would like a drink," he said.

She had been walking quickly, as if trying to get somewhere. Sweetpea was panting.

"Your dog's out of shape," she said.

"It's the people," Luke said. "They're scaring us."

She stopped again, midsidewalk, and looked around. This was her neighborhood. The Haight. There were groups of people gathered at doorsteps, in front of bars, at street corners. They were shabby and tired and drugged. Most were twenty or younger—the age of Luke and Blair way back when. A kid—was it a boy or a girl—was it young or old—asked them for money and Luke pulled coins out of his pocket, pressed them into the person's palm.

"There's a café on the corner. We can get a table outside," Blair said. She rubbed Sweetpea's ear and the dog seemed happier. "You've been in the woods too long," she muttered.

They followed her to the café and she took a table on the sidewalk, under the striped awning. Sweetpea immediately squeezed under the table and sat by her feet. Blair liked the feeling of the dog's soft fur against her ankles.

Luke sat across from her.

"You're staring at me," Blair said. "Stop that."

"I was sure I remembered you. You're completely different."

"You didn't remember me. You made me up. Invented me out of thin air."

"No," he insisted, leaning toward her. "I remember those gauzy skirts. And the way you smelled. Like fire."

"That's all," she said. "It was all gauze and incense. Nothing of substance."

"I think you're wrong," Luke said.

The waiter saved them, offering menus and eyeing Luke. Blair was used to being ignored by most of the men in San Francisco, who only needed a woman to complain to about the men they loved. Luke didn't even notice the waiter's appreciative stare.

"Can we get a bowl of water for the dog?" Blair asked, but there was no dog the waiter could see. "Under the table. Believe me," she added.

"And two beers?" Luke asked, watching Blair, who nodded.

"On a night like this, there's nothing better than beer," she said when the waiter reluctantly pulled himself away from the Luke show.

"What's a night like this?" Luke asked, leaning forward.

"Hot," she said. "It's a hot night."

He smiled.

"I'm talking about the temperature," she said.

"Me too," he offered, still smiling.

"On a night like this, where would you normally be?" she asked. The dog snuggled closer and she tucked her feet under the soft fur.

"I've never had a night like this before," he told her.

Blair took her hat off and ruffled her hair. Luke looked enormously pleased.

"It's my daughter's hat," she explained, placing it on the table between them.

"You have a daughter," he said.

"She's sixteen."

"My God."

"We are old enough, you know."

"I know. I was doing other things."

"What things?"

"Writing screenplays."

"I never go to the movies," she told him.

"Good," he said.

"So why do you write films if you don't think it's worth doing?"

"I guess I'm trying to make it something worth doing. Or I used to. I don't do that anymore. I don't do much of anything anymore."

"What do you do that's not much of anything?"

"Three months ago, I changed everything I knew about my life," Luke said, sighing deeply. He leaned toward her, his elbows on the table. "I moved to a cabin in the woods. Alone. I don't talk to anyone for days at a time; I don't write a word. I undid my life." He paused as if surprised by what he had said. "You know what happened?" he asked Blair quite seriously, as if he were thinking this through for the first time. "Now I don't know what my life is. Who I am."

He looked at her, wide-eyed, and then he leaned back in his chair and offered an embarrassed smile. "I'm talking too much. I'm not much of a talker. I've been inside my own head for too long."

"It's OK," she said. Luke Bellingham? This was nothing like what she would have imagined. "What do you do all day?" she asked.

"I read. I walk in the woods. I build furniture."

"Sounds like a lot to me."

"But no one else knows. It's like that old question. If a tree falls in the forest and no one hears it, does it make a sound? I'm in the forest. No one sees what I do. No one buys it. No one throws openings for me."

"Lucky you."

Luke leaned back, taking a deep breath.

"I haven't felt good in a long time. It's nice to sit here with you."

She looked at him, squinting her eyes as if to see him more clearly. Again he was serious.

"Thank you," she said, ridiculously. *Thank you?* She felt confused, as if she were in one of his movies and no one had given her the script.

"On a night like this, I could fall in love."

"Don't bother," Blair said. "I'm dying."

She immediately regretted it, cursed herself for ruining a good time. When was the last time she had a good time with a handsome, straight man? She looked down at the table, thought of saying, "I'm only kidding. I like you; let's start over." And she thought, for a terrifying moment, of dying. She imagined the black sea pulling her down—not a nightmare, but something very real. She heard the words as Luke Bellingham might hear them and felt her pulse pound in her head.

The waiter arrived. Blair looked up, though she knew her face was flushed, her hands on the table now trembling. The waiter carried a large mixing bowl and ceremoniously filled it with water from a pitcher. He kept eyeing Luke, hoping to charm him. But Luke watched Blair. The waiter offered the bowl to Blair, as if she were the dog.

"Thanks," Blair said, her voice weak. She placed the water at her feet and felt Sweetpea shuffle into drinking position, then heard the sloppy sounds of her tongue lapping up the cold water.

"I'll be right back with the beer," the waiter told Luke.

"We'd appreciate that," Blair told him.

When the waiter left, Blair finally looked at Luke. His face was dark, his mouth twisted as if searching for words he couldn't find.

"Forget I said that," Blair said quietly.

She looked away—at a streetlight, blinding her as if she were looking into the sun. Then she looked at Luke again, at his face, which hid nothing, and she got up from the table, tugging her feet out from under Sweetpea's body, mumbling, "Bathroom, be right back." The dog whimpered, or maybe it was Luke, but she grabbed her hat as if she were leaving, so Luke stood, reaching out to her, his hand on her arm.

"Don't go," he said.

"I shouldn't have said that. I'm sorry."

"Don't be. Please. Sit with me."

Sweetpea whimpered again.

"Thank God it's the dog making that pathetic sound," Blair said. "I thought it was me."

"Stay," Luke said.

"You've spent far too much time alone with a dog," Blair told him.

But she sat and Luke breathed deeply and then the waiter arrived at their side, bearing beer.

They drank, and kept drinking.

"What is it?" Luke asked.

"Cancer," Blair told him. "It's nothing."

"Don't do that," Luke said.

"You know," Blair said. "It's the old tree-in-the-forest thing."

Luke shook his head. "You have a daughter," he said. "She'll hear the tree falling."

"Damn you," Blair said, and this time she left, too fast for Luke or Sweetpea to react. The purple hat and the swirling aqua nightgown disappeared into the streets of the Haight.

• • •

The next night, Blair walked the ten blocks or so to her restaurant, Café Rex. It was her night off—she worked Tuesday through Saturday—the place was closed on Sunday and Daniel suffered a night back in the kitchen on Monday. She was the chef of the tiny restaurant, having taken over from Daniel Marks, the chef/owner of the restaurant, a year ago. She had trained with him for seven years, long enough to gain his trust, to let him step out of the kitchen and spend his evenings in the spotlight instead of behind the camera. She never thought she'd step out—especially now that she was queen of the kitchen.

I will lose that, she realized. *My work, my world.*

They'll be winding down, she thought, looking at her watch, hurrying toward the restaurant. She loved the end of the evening, when the waiters slowed down, when the last of the diners lingered on, usually drunk, sometimes ordering yet another dessert just so the meal wouldn't end. Back in the kitchen they'd have opened a bottle of wine by now—it was Daniel's theory that they should all know the wine list well enough to sell it. And they'd have turned on a CD—probably some alternative-rock group that the twentysomething waiters loved. The noise would keep them going until the last of the diners left the restaurant.

Blair wanted to stand in the kitchen and watch Daniel—somehow that made sense tonight. She'd just stand back and watch.

She walked around to the back of the restaurant and heard the music blasting, felt the rush of adrenaline when she entered the kitchen and saw the blur of Daniel doing four things at once: stirring, sautéing, dicing, arranging it all on a plate so it looked as fine as it would taste—damn, the man was good. Meanwhile, Manuel scrubbed the dishes, while Philippe reached back for that last entrée, and Rianne swept through the door with six plates balanced on her arm and demanded, "What the hell are you doing here, Blair? Go home, go to bed; you look like shit, girl." Finally Daniel turned and saw her, smiled and pulled out a stool beside him.

"Sit," he said. "I'll teach you a thing or two." Which is what he'd been saying for years.

"I love you, Daniel," Blair said, perching on the stool and planting a kiss on Daniel's shoulder. When her lips touched the cotton of his chef's jacket, she held them there, closing her eyes, not wanting to move away. *I need you,* she could say. *Save me.*

"Don't break my concentration," Daniel muttered. He threw sliced potatoes back on the grill, tossed them a couple of times, layered them on a plate, flipped the salmon next to them, spooned the sauce on top. He wiped the edge of the plate clean with his apron.

"Why are you here, my lovely lady?" he asked, presenting Blair with dinner.

Blair began to cry.

"Eat first," Daniel said. "Philippe, get her wine. We'll talk when you're done."

The music got louder. Blair felt that she was in the kitchen and not in the kitchen, as if she were fading as she sat there, and the whirlwind of activity went on around her, would keep going on around her. Rianne fought with Philippe about stealing table seven: "He isn't gay; I know he isn't gay. Once in a while a man could pay attention to me around here." Philippe rolled his eyes and sliced chocolate cake, poured on the raspberry sauce and slithered back to table seven.

"He'll be gay by the time Philippe is done," Daniel told Blair.

"I hate this city," Rianne complained. "When was the last time you had sex?" she asked Blair.

"Couple of days ago," Blair said. "Now ask when the last time was I had love."

"Oh, who cares about love," Rianne wailed.

Philippe charged in. "Your table's waiting for the check, Rianne."

She stormed out.

"What's wrong?" Daniel whispered.

"I'm quitting," Blair told him, staring down into her plate. She hadn't eaten. But she held her plate on her lap, hoping hunger would come.

"You can't quit," Daniel said flatly. "You'll work till you're too sick to work. Right now, you're doing just fine."

"How did you know I was sick?" Blair asked, stunned. She looked at Daniel.

Daniel was trying something new in the pan, swirling things together, creating new smells and flavors and textures. He never looked at Blair.

"I've lost enough friends to AIDS," he said. "I know what it looks like."

"I don't have AIDS," Blair said wearily. Though she had worried about that long enough. Every lover seemed to have had a gay lover at some time in his past.

"What is it, darling? Some new exotic disease? Or one we've all grown so tired of?"

"Melanoma," Blair told him.

Daniel glanced at her quickly, then looked away. She saw him wince. *He knows what that means,* she thought.

"So you're not contagious," Daniel said, swirling the pan on the stove. "You've still got time. You're still walking. And you'll walk that skinny ass of yours into my kitchen every afternoon at five o'clock. Got that?"

Rianne flew in, dropping plates next to Manuel's growing pile, downing her glass of wine while swallowing a pill. For the first time Blair envied the girl her energy.

"You headed up or down tonight, Rianne?" Blair asked. The girl took something most nights—to sleep or to party.

"Up. I'm going dancing. New club south of Market. Wanna come?" She did a little shimmy and shake to the blaring music.

"No thanks. Another time."

Philippe pushed through the doors and dropped his plates in the sink, where Manuel slapped his hand. "Other side, hombre," Manuel told him, lifting the dirty dishes into the dirty dish sink. Manuel slapped Philippe as often as he could. Blair thought he still hadn't managed to get him to bed, though.

"Philippe, I've got a question for you," Blair said.

"Ask. And if you're not eating that, I'll take it. I'm famished."

Daniel shot Blair a look and she picked up her fork, starting to nibble at the plate of food on her lap.

"You're a film buff. Do you know Luke Bellingham? I think he writes screenplays."

"Won the goddamn Academy Award," Philippe told her. "*Pescadero.* Amazing film. A friend of mine worked on it."

Blair smiled. "I went to school with him," she said. "A million years ago."

"Did the movie man have the hots for Ms. Chef?" Philippe asked.

"I was invisible," Blair told him. "It's a good thing. Being invisible. I might just try it again."

A day ago, she had blurted out, "I'm dying," like a fool. She had run away, like a coward. She had liked him, like a teenage girl.

"Eat," Daniel said; Blair had left her fork lingering on the plate.

"Don't tell them," Blair said quietly when the waiters left to finish clearing in the dining room.

"I don't want to lose you," Daniel said so softly that Blair could barely hear him.

She looked up from her plate. He was standing in front of her, looking at her, lost without a spatula or pan in hand. Her heart caught in her throat.

"Don't," she told him. "I'm not ready—"

"You'll keep working, then," Daniel said. He whirled back around to face the stove.

"For a little while."

"I love you, Blair," Daniel said, though his spoon swirled in the pan, his hand reached for some herbs on the shelf, and his finger dipped and tasted the latest sauce creation.

"I know you do," Blair told him.

Over the years they had developed their own sort of intimacy—Blair talked to Daniel about her daughter and about her lovers, and Daniel talked to Blair about food. He was the most private man she had ever known, but he listened well. And he gave her his true heart—the kitchen in his restaurant.

But this is another universe, Blair thought—*the prospect of death. How do you talk about that? How do you even begin to think about that?*

"So who's Luke Bellingham?" Daniel asked.

"Just a guy," Blair said. "I didn't know him then. And I don't know him now. I'm invisible."

• • •

In the morning, when Blair woke up and looked outside, she discovered Sweetpea sitting on the front porch of the cottage.

"What's that? A wolf?" Amanda asked, peering out the window at her mother's side.

Blair opened the door and let the dog in. "She's nicer than she looks," Blair explained. "Don't let her owner in."

"Who's the owner?"

"Some guy."

"Some guy who drops his dog off in the morning? What are you, the dog walker?" Amanda asked. She scooted down and cuddled with Sweetpea, who buried her nose in Amanda's armpit.

"Yes," Blair said, pleased. "I'm the dog walker."

"Can I come?" Amanda asked. "I don't have class until ten."

"Absolutely," Blair told her. "Let me get dressed. We'll take her to the beach."

She left Amanda and Sweetpea in the living room while she went back to her room to find jeans and a sweatshirt. When she returned, Amanda was standing on the front porch, the dog waiting expectantly at her side.

Blair called out to her. "If you see the guy—you know, the owner—tell him to go away. He can pick up his dog when I leave for work at four-thirty."

"How am I supposed to know who the owner is?" Amanda called back.

"He's cute," Blair said. "Or something."

"Oh, God," Amanda moaned.

And then she returned with a note, attached to Sweetpea's leash, tied to the bottom rail of the porch.

Sorry about the other night. Sweetpea wants to spend the day with you. So do I, but I'm not as bold as she is. I'll come back to get her later this afternoon. Have fun. Luke.

"Who is this guy?" Amanda asked, reading over her mom's shoulder.

"Nobody. A guy with a cool dog. Let's get out of here."

They borrowed Casey's car—he left the keys under the floor mat and Blair figured this was one of the perks of fucking the landlord—and drove to Crissy Field, Sweetpea perched between them on the front seat.

When they walked on the beach, Sweetpea ran ahead, ran back, ran in circles around them, crazy with dog joy. Amanda found a stick and tried teaching Sweetpea to fetch, but the dog wanted only to rub her soft fur against their legs and to run at their sides.

They walked at the water's edge, letting the dog splash in the gentle lap of the tide. There were other morning beachcombers and plenty of dogs, but Blair felt as if she were wrapped in the fog with her daughter, protected from the rest of the world.

"So why was he sorry?" Amanda asked.

"Who? What?"

"Sweetpea's dad. The guy who wrote, 'Sorry about the other night.'"

Blair walked for a moment, considering. Which part was he sorry about? Misremembering her as tall and blond? Being a golden boy who dreams women out of thin air and then they appear, falling in love with him on the spot? Or did he say something about her dying and leaving a daughter behind?

"If something ever happened to me," Blair started, then stopped, almost stumbling over Sweetpea, who seemed to back up into her. So she looked at her daughter and tried to shake the thought out of her head, then picked up the pace so that Amanda had to half-jog to keep up with her. "If I died . . . a car accident. A drive-by shooting. Something crazy. Who would you live with? I mean, there's Daniel, I suppose, and there's a couple of teachers you like—"

"Mom? Mom! Stop! What are you talking about?"

"Just thinking about it. I mean, people write wills and figure this stuff out and I've never thought about it, but I mean, it could happen to anyone, and you're almost old enough to be on your own, but you're still a kid. You're my kid; I mean, no one else could raise you or anything—"

"Mom! Stop!"

Blair stopped. Sweetpea sat at her heels, panting. Had the dog understood all that and was now exhausted by it all? Blair watched the ebb and flow of the tide, thought about breathing like that, in and out, pulled by something much quieter than the noise in her own head. *I can't do this,* she thought. *If I tell her, then it's irrefutably true.*

"We'll talk about it later," she said.

"We'll talk about what later?" Amanda asked. She stood, hands on hips, unmoving.

"This idea. This question. I mean, it's an interesting question. We don't have family; you don't have a father; we don't have zillions of aunts and uncles to send you to in Omaha—"

"Omaha?"

"Someplace safe. Someplace to finish growing up."

"Mom?"

"I didn't sleep well. The guy. The dog. Weird dreams."

"Mom?"

"Yeah, yeah, keep walking."

So they walked, and Sweetpea circled round them, holding them close.

And after a while Amanda said, "I just asked why the guy was sorry."

"Right," Blair said. "The guy. I didn't tell you about the guy."

"Sweetpea's dad."

"Luke Bellingham. He made a movie. *Pescadero* or something."

"You're kidding! *Pescadero*?"

"You saw it?" Blair asked, looking back at Amanda, who had stopped in her tracks, dropped her jaw and was staring bug-eyed at her mother.

"Everyone saw it. *Pescadero*? We just studied *Pescadero* in my film class this semester. Mom, you know the guy who made *Pescadero*?"

"Wrote it. Keep walking. You're confusing the dog."

"How do you know him? This is his dog? This is *Pescadero*'s dog?"

"Luke's dog. What is *Pescadero* anyway?"

"It's named for the town on the coast. How do you know this guy?"

"Went to school with him. In the good old awful days. He was one of those good old awful boys."

"And he just appeared? At your doorstep? With Sweetpea?"

"No, he called. The school thought I was lost. He said he'd find me."

"Mom. Stop. Look at me. This is amazing. If Luke Bellingham wrote *Pescadero* then he's, like, famous. And we're walking his dog?"

"Yeah," Blair said, suddenly pleased. "We're walking his dog. We should be famous. The famous dog walkers of the famous dog of the famous man."

"So why was he sorry?" Amanda asked, rolling her eyes. It was a move she had perfected by the time she was seven. Blair had always known her daughter would be wiser than she was in so many ways.

Blair closed her eyes. She stopped walking and stood still, the world spinning around inside her head. *Tell Amanda. You've always been honest with her.* But not about something like this. When she opened her eyes, the world was still spinning.

"Sit down," she said, taking in great gulps of ocean air.

"Here?" Amanda asked.

"Here." Blair sat on the sand at the edge of the surf. Sweetpea fell into a heap at her feet. Reluctantly Amanda joined them.

People walked by; dogs sniffed Sweetpea and moved on; the clouds pulled past them in the sky. Blair was quiet. Amanda waited. Sweetpea perched her head on her paw, gazing at Blair adoringly.

"Do you think the dog speaks English?" Blair asked. "Like she'll report back to Mr. Hollywood everything we say?"

"Mom."

"I'm sick," Blair said finally. "I had a mole removed from my back and it might be cancer. It is cancer. They already did the tests. I'm screwed. We're screwed."

Amanda looked at her mother as if she were speaking a foreign language, one that she was inventing on the spot. So Blair reached out to her, and Amanda smacked Blair's arm away, hard enough to hurt.

"Amanda!" Blair said, rubbing her arm.

"There are treatments. Right? Like chemo and radiation and all that stuff. Right? It's just hell for a while and you lose your hair and then everything's fine. Right?" Amanda's voice was angry, defiant.

"Maybe. Please, baby. Let me hold you." Her daughter looked small suddenly, too small to be sitting in such a huge expanse of space—sand and sky and sea, dog and mother and so many words.

"What's maybe? Tell me what that means."

"It means that they don't know. Or they don't like it. This is one of the bad ones, the ones they're still trying to lick. Before it licks me."

And miraculously, Sweetpea got up, moved over to Amanda and plopped down again, this time with her head in Amanda's lap. Amanda fell over the dog and Blair heard sounds coming from one of them, small and weak sounds.

"My baby," Blair said, and her heart broke, hard and fast enough to feel it like a rupture in her chest, making her bend over, gasping for breath.

Amanda looked up and whispered, "Mom," and Blair moved over to pull her daughter into her arms. They cried the same way, the way they always had, taking big heaving gasps of breath with each sob. The dog buried her head between them.

When Blair's cries subsided, she smoothed Amanda's hair back from her face, wiped her face with her hand.

"We'll get through this," Blair said. "We'll be OK. We'll fight it, right? We're good at that. We'll fight the damn thing."

Amanda looked at Blair. "Don't lie to me about any of this. OK? I'm not a baby. I want to know."

Blair nodded. "You're not a baby, sweetheart. I know that." But she felt like she was still lying, promising her daughter a fight when the doctor had said there were no weapons to use against this monster.

Amanda looked around. "We're making a scene."

"Let's go. The dog is slobbering all over me."

They stood and headed back toward Casey's car. The air around Blair seemed changed somehow—it was now so cold that it burned her skin.

"Do you hurt? I mean, are you in pain?" Amanda asked quietly.

"No," Blair told her honestly. "I'm tired a lot. That's all. So, I don't really believe it, you know. Even now, walking on the beach, telling my daughter that I've got cancer, I think Luke Bellingham's making a movie about someone else's life, or that I'm in someone else's nightmare. Because none of it feels true. So, I'm not telling you lies; I'm just trying to catch up to the truth myself."

Amanda put her arm around her mother and pulled her close. They walked like that, quietly, until they reached the car and headed home.

• • •

Luke Bellingham was sitting on the front step of their cottage. He stood when they approached, then got knocked down by a racing Sweetpea. He scrambled to stand up again and offered Amanda his hand.

"Luke Bellingham," he said.

"I know," she said, shaking his hand. "I like your dog."

"Thanks. You look like your mother did when she was your age."

Blair watched the scene: handsome man wowing vulnerable girl, suitor wooing girlfriend's daughter, golden boy/man reminding the lost soul what she never had and never would have.

"You have no idea what I looked like in high school," Blair interrupted. "You never even saw me in high school. The other night you thought I was blond and tall. Today you think I was a redhead. And even if we like your dog, we don't need you coming around our house like you're trying to renew an old relationship. Well, that old relationship never existed."

Blair stormed past Luke and stomped up the stairs to the cottage. She slammed the door behind her.

And then she fell onto the couch under the front window and buried her head in her hands. *I'm dying,* she thought. *I just told my daughter I'm dying.*

• • •

By the time Blair dressed for work—in her white chef's jacket and checked pants, wearing her beloved red high-top sneakers—Amanda was off to her job at the café, and Luke and Sweetpea were long gone. *Back to the woods,* she hoped. *Wherever that is.* Montana? Wyoming? Far away from the Haight and her heart. Far away from Amanda, who had gone gaga at first glimpse. Who was angry at her mother for pissing off Mr. Hollywood. Easier than being angry at her mother for dying.

Blair heard the phone ring, let the answering machine pick up, didn't even wait for the message. *I'm outta here,* she thought, glad to be going to work, where she was always too busy to think.

She walked the ten blocks to the restaurant, early enough to be the first one there. Leon, the pastry chef, had left a note along with the pies and cakes he had created that day: *Blair, it doesn't matter that I'm nineteen. It only matters that I'm crazy about you. Yours, Leon.*

Leon had never met Blair. He came in the morning, early, and spent hours concocting his delicacies for the evening dessert. He left hours before Blair arrived and somehow he had begun the tradition of leaving her love notes with his raspberry tarts and his lemon soufflés. Blair wrote back every so often, leaving her notes in the bin of flour, telling him all the reasons he shouldn't love her.

Men kept inventing her. Leon and Luke.

She started her work routine, setting up the materials for her sauces and side dishes, checking the fish and meat delivery, putting everything in place for the fun and games to begin.

She was going to try something new today—a tuna tartare, too fancy for this little café, but she had seen the recipe in *Gourmet,* imagined its taste in her mouth, adapted the recipe for something spicier. And Daniel had OK'd the order for sashimi-grade ahi with the promise that she give him the first plate.

She found the tuna, wrapped and marked: *For Blair: Make it worth it. Daniel.* She smiled—Daniel loved what he had created, a food maniac who lay in bed at night dreaming up new versions of the same old thing. Funny, she hadn't thought about food for a while now. Since her last doctor's appointment? Or had she lost her appetite somewhere along the way and not stopped to notice? She was certainly losing weight—she had cinched her belt tighter today just to keep up her pants.

She unwrapped the tuna and smiled—it was beautiful, worth eating raw, worth wowing Daniel. Which was secretly still her ambition—to make the guy proud of her. She cleared her work space and gathered together the herbs and spices she'd use for the dish. She turned around to find her cleaver in its drawer behind her, and the room seemed to close in on her, space becoming narrower and tighter, light disappearing from the edges of her vision until her vision itself was gone and then she wasn't standing anymore. She was curled on her side on the cold tile floor and then suddenly her arms and legs were thrashing about, on their own, as if they weren't connected to her body at all. Her torso jerked forward and down, so that her head smacked hard on the tiles. She felt her legs convulse, kicking at something that wasn't there, her arms pumping the air as if fighting with someone. And then she blacked out.

When she came to, without any notion of how much time had passed, she thought first about the tuna, unwrapped, unrefrigerated, unmarinated. *Daniel will kill me.* And finally she realized she must be on her way to her own self-made death, here on the floor, chilled and numb. She knew she was wet, that she had peed and was lying in her own puddle. She was suddenly a sick woman, a dying woman, a woman who passes out in the middle of the day while trying to make tuna tartare.

She couldn't get up. Her legs were numb and her arms were weak. She tried calling out, but her mouth was dry and parched. If any time had passed, why hadn't Daniel arrived? And then she shuddered at the thought of Daniel finding her—he was so clean, so fussy, so elegant—he would hate the messiness of this spillage on his floor.

So she pulled herself across the floor to the edge of the counter and worked her arms up one of the cabinets until she could reach the telephone cord and then yanked at it, miserable, swatting and missing. Before she fell back to the floor, she tried once more and this time caught the cord and pulled the phone with her to the floor. It toppled over her, banging hard against her shoulder, then clattered to the floor. She picked it up. And then thought: *Who do I call?*

Amanda was at the café—she didn't want to call and scare her. She couldn't call Daniel, didn't want to be here when Daniel arrived. She didn't want to be anywhere but home, in her bed. Casey! She dialed his number, fumbling the phone and picking it up in time to hear his recording: "You know what to do and when to do it." She hung up. She didn't have friends the way other women had friends. She had her daughter, her boss and a hippie landlord.

She could call 911. She could tell them to come find her under the rotting tuna. But as much as she hated dying, she hated dramatic ambulance-wailing scenes.

Luke. Luke Bellingham, Hollywood star. Savior of dying women. She didn't need to fall in love with him after he saved her. She just needed a ride to the hospital.

She dialed information. Luke Bellingham. He'd be unlisted, she was sure. But the operator was telling her his number and she was dialing it with the one hand that still seemed to be working.

"Hello?"

"Luke. It's me. Blair."

She stopped to catch her breath and then remembered the last time they had talked, when she told him to disappear forever.

"Don't say anything," she said. "I need your help."

"You OK?"

"No. I'm on the floor. At the restaurant. Where I work. I fell. Or passed out."

"Give me the address. I'll be there."

• • •

She didn't remember the ride to the hospital or the first few hours of doctors and tests and rolling around on gurneys through white-tiled hallways. When she woke up, Luke was sitting in a chair beside her hospital bed. He had a magazine in his lap, but he wasn't reading it. He was watching her.

Blair licked her lips, trying for moisture, which didn't seem to come. Luke stood up and reached for a glass by her bedside. He placed a straw in her lips and she sipped at the cool water.

"Amanda," she finally whispered.

"I left a message on the door of the cottage," Luke said. "I told her to call my cell phone."

"Thank you," Blair whispered, and she knew she was crying, though she wasn't making any sound.

Luke sat on the bed at her side.

"Who can I call?" he asked.

"What do you mean?"

"Your friends. Boyfriend. Who can take care of you?"

Blair shook her head, fighting back more tears. Luke waited, watching her. He put his hand on her shoulder and she closed her eyes.

"Call Daniel," she finally said. "At the restaurant. My boss. Tell him what happened."

"Will he come here?" Luke asked gently.

Again Blair shook her head. "I don't want him here."

She felt Luke's hand on her cheek.

"You shouldn't be alone," he said.

"I know," Blair said, moving away from him, turning her body away from him in her bed. "I have my daughter."

"I can help," Luke said.

She didn't say anything. She stared at the curtain in the room, separating her from some other sick person, maybe another dying person. She heard voices, muffled voices, from behind the curtain.

Someone was crying. She closed her eyes, wishing herself anywhere else but here.

"Why would you help?" Blair asked gently.

"I don't know," Luke said. "Maybe I really have been in the woods too long."

Blair opened her eyes and turned toward him. She waited—she could see that he was working something through his mind and that he still had more to say.

"Maybe I'm getting tired of my own problems. I'd like someone else's for a while." He shrugged sheepishly, as if embarrassed.

"I don't want your help," Blair said quietly.

"Then I won't help you," Luke said. "I'll just hang out and entertain you."

Blair shot him a skeptical look. He was smiling, or almost smiling, and she had to look away again.

"I'm not really in the market for new friends or lovers. You know?" Blair said to the ceiling.

"I know," Luke said.

"So, thanks for the ride. I mean, thanks for helping out tonight. But that's all I wanted. A ride."

"I'll just wait here till Amanda calls," Luke said, his voice soft. She wouldn't look at him—didn't want to see the expression on his face.

"Fine," Blair said. "I might sleep a bit."

They were both quiet for a while and then Blair asked, "What happened to me? I mean, do you know? Did you talk to anyone?"

She felt Luke's hand on her arm but kept her eyes closed.

"You had a seizure. The doctor said that the cancer might have spread to your brain." He paused. The world seemed so quiet and all she could hear was the deep draw of breath from his lungs. "He'll be back later tonight. He'll explain it all to you."

Blair didn't say anything. She kept her eyes closed, waiting for her daughter to call, to come to her, to crawl in bed as if it were any long-ago night and Amanda had a nightmare and needed the comfort of her mother's body next to her. *But this time I'm the one who's scared,* Blair thought.

Chapter Four

Luke couldn't sleep. In the old days when he woke at two or three in the morning and knew that sleep would elude him for a couple of hours, he would head to his study to write. He'd pick at his foggy brain in a different way than he did during normal working hours—he'd push scenes in new directions, challenge his characters, re-envision his plot. He liked that slightly groggy state—it made him think differently, and then the next day, in the light of day, he would take his odd ideas and shape them into something usable.

Now he couldn't imagine writing. He couldn't imagine inventing characters and scenes and dramas. He wanted to escape from his mind, not to explore it. When writing, even if he was working on a script that was far from his own life, his own circumstances, the deeper he plunged into his characters' consciousness, the closer he came to himself. He became the serial murderer, the lonely housewife, the grandmother shoplifter, the young boy riding the trains. Now he wanted far away from inner life.

But he did think of his computer, still hooked up in his study, and he thought of a middle-of-the-night activity that jolted him out of bed. He would track down the phone number he had found on the ski ticket.

He walked into his study, a small sunroom in the back of the house with a view of the bay, now dark. He logged on, found a Web site he had heard about: a reverse Yellow Pages that would give you the address and name if you supplied the phone number. Unbelievable. Within seconds the screen displayed: MR. AND MRS. GRAY HEALY. An address on Laguna.

He didn't know the name. Had never heard Emily mention Gray Healy or his lovely wife. But she had asked Dana to call him from Tahoe. *I'll be home tomorrow.*

Luke remembered back to the trip, their last night at the hotel, her impatience with him when he tried to make love in the middle of the night. "I'm sleeping," she had said.

"But I thought you were stirring; I thought you were awake," he said, apologizing, still nestling close to her, pressing his penis against her thigh.

"If I'm awake, that doesn't mean I want to make love. If I can't sleep, it's because of the job I'm working on, the pressure, the deadline. I'm not waking up because I want you to climb on top of me."

She drew herself away from him. He stared at the curve of her back, cursing his stubborn erection. But he wasn't angry. He felt protective of her, sad that this new job was going so badly, concerned that she felt the stress of it so terribly. Fool.

The next morning they drove back to San Francisco and he remembered that she fled the house the moment they arrived, her portfolio tucked under her arm, promising to be home before dinner. Unless the meeting ran through dinner. Had it run through dinner? Was she wrapped in Mr. Gray Healy's arms ten minutes later, now urging his eager penis inside of her?

Luke wrote down the address of Mr. and Mrs. Healy on the ski tag, beside the note: *I'll be home tomorrow.*

He turned off the computer and headed back to his bedroom. If he wrote tonight, he would only produce pages of his own weak imagination: a story about a man who has been mourning the loss of his beloved wife and discovers her infidelity. Does this man now have to rewrite his own story? Does he have to take every one of his memories and twist them into something ugly?

• • •

A scene at the premiere of *Pescadero:* The wife is dressed in white silk, with her hair upswept, her neck long and lovely. The husband is tuxedoed and uncomfortable. They're ushered through the crowd and into the party, and the throngs of adoring fans cheer. The husband wants to flee. The wife begs him: "Please, I want this so much."

Cut to hotel room, later the same night. Tuxedo trimmings thrown over back of chair. The man wears only the black pants. He stands behind his wife, still dressed, who stares out the window.

"Why do you want this so much?"

"Because you give me so little."

She doesn't turn around.

The man puts his hand on her bare shoulder and her body stiffens.

"Don't touch me."

He turns and walks to the king-size bed in the luxurious hotel room. He lies down, exhausted. She turns and looks at him.

"Look at me," she says.

He looks at her.

"You're beautiful," he says.

She's crying.

"You don't see me," she tells him.

• • •

Luke finally slept, sometime toward dawn, and when Sweetpea nosed him out of bed a couple of hours later, he was ready to find Emily.

• • •

"Mrs. Healy?" Luke asked into the phone when a woman answered his call. He was standing in the kitchen, drinking coffee, staring at the ski ticket on the counter in front of him.

"Yes?" Her voice was small, unsure.

"I'm calling from Flowers on Fillmore. I've got a bouquet here for you and wanted to make sure someone would be home for delivery."

"Flowers? Oh. I'll be home till noon," she said.

"See you before noon," Luke said, and hung up.

He headed to the nearest flower shop, bought an impressive bundle of roses, wrapped it in a white ribbon, drove his truck to Pacific Heights.

Mrs. Healy lived in a modern stone-and-glass box of a house, the kind Luke hated, with a wall of windows on the top floor offering views out toward the bay. Luke rang the bell at the gate, and she buzzed him in.

He headed up the path to the door and rang yet another bell. She kept him waiting.

She opened the door and reached for the flowers without looking at him. The help. She turned the bouquet in her hands, looking for a card.

"Hey, where's the card?" she asked.

He looked at her. She was his age, early forties, dressed in running clothes with a bandanna wrapped around her forehead. The cuckolded wife? Perhaps. Emily was taller, blonder, finer-boned. Lovelier.

"No card," Luke said.

"Well, who are they from?" the woman asked impatiently.

"I don't know," Luke said. "Up to them to let you know. I just deliver 'em."

"You mean, they sent these with no card? I don't get it. You must have a record or something. Someone paid for the damn things."

"Cash," Luke said. "No record."

"A woman, right?" she said. Finally. Annoyed.

"Yeah," Luke said cautiously. "A woman."

"Did you see her?" she asked.

"I might have."

"Tall? Blond hair? Drop-dead gorgeous?"

"You might say."

"Fuck her," Mrs. Healy said. She dropped the roses to the ground and slammed the door in Luke's face.

Luke left the flowers on the doorstep and headed to his truck, feeling oddly elated, as if knowing lessened the pain of what he knew.

• • •

"Sweetpea," Luke said, climbing into the truck, "you've got a job to do, pal. Let's go visit Blair."

He had called the hospital and had been given the news that Blair was released that morning. He hadn't tried her at home, knew that she wouldn't talk to him, that his sweet dog would have to do the talking.

He drove to the Haight, pulled up in front of the driveway leading to the cottage. A man sat in a lounge chair on the unkempt lawn of the purple Victorian in front of the cottage. He was smoking a joint, reading the newspaper.

Luke ignored the guy, started up the path past him, toward Blair's cottage. On the other hand, Sweetpea, unfaithful Sweetpea, went sniffing.

"Nice dog," the guy called out, petting her.

"Thanks," Luke said. "Come on, girl."

"You a friend of Blair's?"

"You the guardian at the gate?"

"You might say that."

Luke stood on the path, eyeing the guy, who stroked Sweetpea and toked on his joint.

"Sweetpea! Let's go!" Luke called, more insistent.

"Blair's resting," the guy said.

"I'll let her tell me that," Luke said.

"But you'll have to wake her up so she can say fuck off. That wouldn't be very nice, would it?"

"Maybe she only says fuck off to you," Luke offered.

"Who the hell are you?" the guy said, though he didn't seem to care.

"A friend. Come on, Sweetpea. Let's go."

"My name's Casey. I'm the landlord."

"Right."

Luke hesitated a moment, then started toward the cottage again, deciding to leave Sweetpea with her new best friend. But Casey called out, "The lady is resting."

"So you said," Luke told him. He kept walking.

Casey stood up and started toward Luke. "Listen, buddy. I *am* the guardian at the gate. And I'm telling you not to bother her."

"And I'm ignoring you," Luke said, and kept walking.

Until he felt Casey's hand on his shoulder and he swung around, knocking off the hand, knocking the guy off balance and onto the ground.

"What's your problem?" Casey said, working himself upright.

"Right now, you're my problem."

Luke bounded up the stairs and knocked lightly on Blair's door.

She opened it in a quick moment and stood in the doorway, arms on her hips, glaring at Luke. She looked pale, thin, a little shaky—but her stance was defiant.

"What are you doing here?"

"Sweetpea missed you," Luke said gently.

"I tried to stop him," Casey called from below. "He hit me."

"I didn't hit him," Luke said. "The guy's asking for trouble, Blair."

"Maybe you're asking for trouble," she said.

"Can I come in? Just for a few minutes?"

"I told him you were resting," Casey called up.

"I'm resting," Blair echoed.

"Shut the fuck up!" Luke called back to Casey.

"You can leave now," Blair said.

"Who the hell is this guy?" Luke asked, and suddenly he was shouting. "Your landlord? Or your lover? What right does he have to interrogate me? Look at him. He's wasted. It's ten o'clock in the morning. Is this your goddamn boyfriend? What kind of life do you have?"

Blair slammed the door in Luke's face.

Luke stood there, feeling the reverberations through the soles of his feet. He didn't want to turn around. He didn't need some asshole pothead to tell him what an asshole he was.

So he'd make it worse. He knocked on the door again. And again. She didn't answer. Finally Sweetpea made her way up the stairs and stood at his side.

"Sweetpea wants to see you!" he called out.

And in a flash the door opened; the dog scooted into the cottage; the door slammed shut. *Make that three slams in an hour,* Luke thought. *Three slams and you're out.*

"Call me when you want me to pick her up!" he shouted, but he was sure no one was listening.

When he headed down the stairs, he saw that Casey was back in his lawn chair, joint in hand.

Luckily, the guy was decent enough to ignore him as he climbed back into his truck and drove away.

• • •

By six that evening, Luke had had too much to drink and not enough to do. Blair never called—so he was dogless as well as wifeless. In his muddled state he decided to go after the wife instead of the dog.

He drove to Healy's house and parked across the street. He wanted to see if the roses were still strewn on the front steps, but he couldn't get a glimpse of the house behind the imposing gate. He didn't know what he wanted, but he stayed there, stubbornly sitting in his truck for an hour.

He thought of his mother waiting for his father to come home, telling Luke they wouldn't start dinner without him, he'd be home soon. Luke would do his homework at the dining-room table—the light was terrible in his room and he liked the movement of his mother in the kitchen while he worked. But as the dinner hour approached and his father didn't show, his mother would begin calling people—his dad's secretary, his fishing pal, the clubhouse, the bar at the Lighthouse Grill. He was never at any of those places. Luke would look up from his math homework or his social-studies book and tell her, between calls, "He's fine, Mom. He'll be home soon."

"I know he's fine," she'd say curtly.

When Luke was twelve, his dad invited him on a Saturday sail—out to Angel Island for a picnic.

"Mom coming?" Luke had asked.

"Nah, she's got her things to do," he said vaguely. "I'm bringing a friend from the office. A real sailor."

The sailor was a beautiful redhead, Marian, who wore a sea green bikini and a matching green kerchief wrapped around her thick hair. Luke watched the two of them all day, moving carefully around each other on the small boat, Dad's hand softly placed on Marian's back while he passed by her on the way to the head, Marian's arm gently brushing across Dad's leg as she reached for the wicker basket of sandwiches. On the island Luke went for a walk by himself, and when he came back, Marian's kerchief was gone. He never saw it again.

The next week he told his dad, no, he didn't want to sail with them again. He had started a woodworking project in the garage with the new tools they had bought him for Christmas. He started spending weekends in the garage, away from the sea and his dad's boat. He labored for hours at his worktable, learning how to build with different woods, learning about objects of permanence, their shapes, their transformations. He never mentioned Marian to his mother and hated his dad for pulling him into the secret of it all.

A couple of years later, his father left his mother. *Did she know?* Luke wondered. He never asked her. Marian was around for a while, but then was replaced by other women, all beautiful it seemed.

When Luke and Emily threw parties, everyone seemed to flirt. They sat next to someone else's husband, someone else's wife, at the dinner table. They whispered into someone else's ear. They placed their hand on someone else's thigh. It was just fun, wasn't it? Dangerous fun. And there was a kind of thrill to taking each other to bed, husband and wife, at the end of the night.

Luke was startled when a car pulled up in front of him, and he sat up straight in his truck, peering at a long black BMW. The driveway gates opened to let Mr. Healy through. Luke glimpsed blond hair, a handsome profile, a loosened tie. And then the gates closed behind the car.

Still, he waited. He had nothing else to do.

He remembered one party, in L.A., just after he sold *Pescadero.* Hal Levy, a producer on the project, invited him to Malibu for the day, for lobster and champagne. Somehow, late in the summer evening, he found himself heading to the ocean for a swim. And then someone was next to him, her warm arm brushing against his own. Belle. Was she an actress or a screenwriter or someone's girlfriend? It didn't matter. He didn't recall talking to her—but at the edge of the surf, she stripped off her bathing suit and he watched her smiling. "Your turn," she said. He obliged. She was lovely and naked and he followed her out to sea.

They didn't make love; they swam. And after they were warm enough to slow their pace, they moved toward each other, exploring each other's bodies underwater. Someone yelled from the beach for Belle. They kissed, once, and Luke felt his heart ache with the kiss—not with desire but regret. Emily was home, in San Francisco. He was learning about Hollywood. Some lesson. He let Belle swim alone to shore and paddled around in the darkening sea for a long time before he made his way back to the party.

Did I love Emily so much, he wondered, *or did I need so desperately to believe in our marriage?* He had vowed so long ago to be a different kind of man than his father, to make a marriage that would last. Was that good enough?

He sat in front of the Healys' house for a half hour, when the gate opened again and the car backed out of the driveway. Mr. Healy. Hair a bit messed, clothes a bit askew. Wrestling match with the athletic Mrs. Healy? Luke pulled out behind him and followed him down the street.

He imagined the scene—Mrs. Healy raging, Mr. Healy fumbling for words and explanations. *Is it easier that Emily walked out on me and disappeared? Would I have wanted the chance to call her a cheating whore? Not my style,* Luke thought. *Emily knew that.*

He followed Gray Healy as he wound his way through the city. Heading toward Noe Valley. Luke felt his adrenaline kick in; he felt the rush of the chase, something he used to experience when a script neared completion or his agent told him about the deal that he was about to make. So why was the finished script, the finished deal never as satisfying? Why was he always let down, somehow, as if the chase were better than the catch.

Did he want, now, to catch Emily? Or should he stay like this, hot on the trail of something, for the rest of his life?

Gray Healy and his black BMW turned into a parking space, half a block ahead of him, and Luke had to act fast if he wanted to stay with him. He pulled into an alleyway and parked illegally, caught a glimpse of Healy turning the corner, left the truck and followed close behind.

Luke stopped at the corner, eyeing Healy in the doorway of the first house on the block. He stayed back, pretending to read a sign for yoga classes stapled onto the tree curbside. But in his peripheral vision he could see Healy extract a key from his pocket, insert it into the lock, turn the handle, enter the house. The door closed behind him.

Emily's house? Luke suddenly couldn't imagine Emily—here or anywhere. He knew what she looked like—yes, tall, blond, drop-dead gorgeous—but that was a picture, a still life of wife. Emily in this house was impossible to imagine. Emily greeting Gray Healy, asking: "What happened, darling? Why are you here? Oh, my God, she knows? No, I didn't send any flowers!" Luke couldn't run the film through his mind, couldn't write the scenes, couldn't hear the dialogue.

He stood there, on the corner, reading the sign for yoga classes, YOGA NOW, as if yoga were something to be insisted upon.

Healy was gone. Inside Emily's house. If it was Emily's house. It could belong to Healy's best buddy, Frank. A big, fat Italian guy who listened with avid interest to Healy's stories of lurid sex with the screenwriter's wife, egging him on all the time. Yes, Frank lived here, alone and miserable. And now, here was Healy, crying on his shoulder: "I ruined everything for the sake of sex."

Sex. With tall, blond and drop-dead gorgeous.

"Go for it, man," Frank says. "The wife? Who needs a wife when you can have Emily?"

Luke tore the yoga poster off the tree, dropped it in the street. He spun around, away from the house, and headed back to his truck.

Some big guy leaning out of a Porsche in the alley was screaming at him: "How the hell am I supposed to get out, motherfucker?"

Luke surrendered with a weak wave of his hand. He climbed into his truck and pulled out. The guy in the Porsche looked vaguely like Frank, the character he had just invented. When he was writing, this happened all the time—characters appearing in real life, edging too close to him. He liked Frank. He'd use Frank if he ever wrote again.

He drove past the house, took note of the address, the windows upstairs with lime-colored curtains. Emily would never choose those curtains.

Frank would not have curtains.

He had to get out of there. So he drove home, dogless, wifeless, hungover, as miserable as Frank.

• • •

Sometime in the middle of the night (but it was only eleven o'clock—he had been sleeping for what seemed like hours), the phone rang, and when he picked it up, miraculously, Blair was there, talking sweetly to him, as if in a dream.

"I love your dog," she told him.

"I know," he said. "How are you? How are you feeling? God, I'm sorry."

"Shh," she said. "Let me tell you about your dog."

"Tell me," he said. He didn't get out of bed, didn't sit up or turn on the light. He stayed in that blurry state, sure that light or too much motion could scare her away.

"Tonight I gave her salmon for dinner. Is that OK? Can she eat salmon?"

"It's perfect," he told her. "She should eat salmon for dinner for the rest of her life."

"Daniel came over and he brought me dinner and I shared it with Sweetpea because I couldn't finish it, which made Daniel happy; even though he hates dogs, he didn't hate Sweetpea—"

"Who's Daniel?" Luke asked, though he hated to interrupt her, but he hated more the idea of a man who was let in when he couldn't sit by her side, a man by her side, eating salmon for dinner, sharing it with Sweetpea.

"My boss. A man I love—"

"Your boyfriend?"

"He's gay. Christ. Everyone's gay."

"I'm not gay."

"Yeah. I noticed. Now listen. So Sweetpea charms Daniel, an impossible thing, no one charms Daniel except Daniel, and we all eat salmon, and then Daniel leaves and I lie down to rest and Sweetpea jumps in bed, cuddles up right next to me—"

"Which side of the bed?"

"What?"

"Which side of the bed? Left or right?"

"I'm on the right side. Why?"

"Go on."

"And she throws one paw over my waist. Like a lover. And she breathes her salmon breath in my ear."

"I know."

"Does she sleep in your bed?"

"No. Not for a while."

"You were married?"

"I was married. Sweetpea loved Emily. When Emily left, she stopped sleeping on the bed. She sleeps on the floor. On Emily's side of the bed."

"The right side."

"Yes, the right side."

"What happened to Emily?"

"I don't know. She just disappeared one day. I'm still trying to figure it out."

"You don't know why?"

"No. How can you think your life is good and then one day someone tells you it was all a lie?"

"Why was it a lie?"

"She walked out. Without telling me. In the middle of my happy life."

"She wasn't happy."

"And I thought we were doing fine. That's the lie I was living with, I guess."

Blair was quiet for a moment. Luke could hear her breathing in the phone and he pulled up his blanket, as if drawing her closer to him.

"Maybe you weren't paying attention," she said finally. Gently. As if she didn't want to hurt him.

Luke sighed. "I thought I wasn't one of those guys. My work is different. Writing makes you pay attention. But maybe I fooled myself. Typical guy dressed in sensitive guy's clothes."

"I've been meaning to talk to you about those clothes."

"What's wrong with my clothes?"

"You've been in the woods too long. You look like a mountain man."

"I didn't know I was going to stay in the city this long," Luke told her. "I thought I was driving in for the night."

"What made you stay?"

"The Search for Lost Souls."

"Mine or yours?"

"Touché."

"You found me. So now why are you staying?"

"My dog is missing. I can't go anywhere without my dog."

"Can she spend the night? I think I'll sleep better if she's here."

"Of course she can spend the night. I wouldn't think of taking her away from you."

"Thank you. She's kind of a comfort."

"You could ask a human being for comfort, you know."

"I'm not a very big girl about being sick."

"I noticed."

"And I don't have many friends."

"Why not?"

"Work. Raising a daughter alone. I never seemed to have the time or the inclination."

"Where's the father?"

"Beats me."

"Ancient history?"

"Real ancient. He was a cute guy I hung out with once; he moved on; I got pregnant."

"Does he know? That he has a daughter?"

"He wouldn't even remember my name. If I found him. If I cared."

"Does she?"

"We play a game. We invent fathers. We sit in a café and watch the guys go by and choose one to be Father for a Day. We invent his life, his loves, his fatherly habits. And we watch him disappear from our lives at the end of the game."

"She likes this game?"

"She loves me. I'm enough for her."

"How was she at the hospital?" Luke had left before she arrived—Blair had wanted it that way.

"Scared. Hiding it. Family tradition."

"Can I bring you breakfast in bed?"

Blair was quiet. Luke waited, but she didn't say anything.

"I didn't ask if you'd marry me. I asked about breakfast. Croissant. Coffee. That sort of thing."

"Why are you doing this?"

"I don't know." Luke waited a moment, thinking about it. He wished he were in his small bed at the cabin, not lost in the king-size bed of his old house. "I know you didn't see my movie. *Pescadero.* When you do see it, talk to me first."

"Why?"

"My wife used to say I was stuck in the past. And somehow you're a part of that past. Even if I didn't really know you."

"I don't understand."

"Neither do I. But you've haunted me somehow."

"It's usually the golden boy who haunts the outcast girl."

"Not this time."

"Don't fall for me."

"I'll do my best," he told her.

She was quiet for a moment, and Luke waited for her.

"Come by at ten," she said finally. "I want to sleep for a very long time."

"Good night, Blair. Kiss Sweetpea for me."

He could hear the sound of her kiss before she hung up the phone.

• • •

At 7:00 A.M. Luke was parked across the street from the house in Noe Valley, the house Gray Healy had run to the night before. Sometime in the middle of the night, Luke had decided that he was done searching for Emily, that he had found Blair, his true Lost Soul. Blair's soft voice had hummed in his ear all night, weaving through his own troubled dreams. But by morning his resolution had faded and he had fled his house before breakfast, before a shower, before finding something other than mountain man clothes to wear.

He waited for Emily to emerge. When they lived together, she always woke early, went to a yoga class or for a run before work. He couldn't make those assumptions anymore. She walked out on him, proving that he knew nothing about her.

He listened to music on the radio, changing stations impatiently with every lousy song. He felt irritable, angry at himself for stubbornly sitting there and waiting for her. He tried to imagine the scene: She walks out of the house and then what? He's furious, his anger exploding in words hurled in her direction? He's overcome with love, runs across the street and into her arms? Shouldn't he know this before he confronts her? Does he want to see her because he loves her or because he hates her?

He decided then: He loves her and he hates what she's done to him.

What did I do to you, he thought, *that made you capable of such cruelty?*

He remembered this: There had been an evening in fall a couple of years before, a surprisingly warm evening in the city, when he had finished work and then picked her up at her office—this was before she was working at home. They had walked along the Embarcadero, arm in arm, telling each other about the day. His was good—he was finishing the script for *The Geography of Love* and liked it. In his own life his father had died while out sailing with a neighbor's son, a boy who should have been Luke if Luke had agreed to sail with him every weekend. If Luke had been in the sailboat instead of in the garage, turning wooden bowls, destroying them, turning new ones. In *The Geography of Love* the father and son are so close that the son can hear the father's thoughts. When the father dies in a boating accident, the son's on board, and though he tries like hell, he can't save him. His father's voice stays in his head, but his own voice leaves him. Luke knew the young man would find his voice by the end of the script—he was writing for Hollywood after all. And as he told Emily on their walk, "I can rewrite my life. I can give my father a different son." She had said, "You can give yourself a different father."

She talked about a poster she had created for the arts festival, one that she was sure would win the competition, and at that moment she was happy because she didn't know that it wouldn't win, that like most of her work, it was good but not good enough. They had walked and kissed and walked some more.

When they got cold, they decided to stop at a restaurant, and suddenly they were ravenous for oysters and white wine, which they ate till they were giddy. Someone came by their table—an older woman they didn't know—and said, "Excuse me for interrupting, but you two are blessed, we can see that, sitting near you and watching you this evening." And the woman moved on, as if she had bestowed a blessing upon them.

After dinner they found a cab and headed home, and Luke couldn't stop touching Emily, her hair, her face, her bare arms, her narrow waist. "I am blessed," he told her, and she giggled, thinking he was teasing her when he was more serious than he had ever been in his life.

The door opened. Across the street. Luke held his breath. He thought of taking off quickly, before glancing toward the door even once. He thought of ducking, like a child, hiding on the seat until whoever was there would go away.

But he sat, frozen, and Gray appeared, dressed in a different suit, newly showered, hair slicked back, face smiling. He leaned back inside—to kiss her good-bye? To grab his briefcase? And then he closed the door and headed down the path.

Luke had never thought to see if Gray's car was still there. *I'm one helluva private eye,* he thought.

Gray Healy. Blessed? Certainly buoyant this morning, walking with a little lift between steps as if he had spent the night in the arms of a tall, blond and drop-dead gorgeous woman.

Luke was out of the car and heading toward the house before he made any decision. He reached the door in a second, without being conscious of having crossed the street or walked up the path. And his hand was knocking on the door, as if it were an independent thing, not his arm at all.

No one answered. He sensed someone inside, felt her presence rather than catching any glimpse of her or anyone else; he held his breath, hoping he would hear some movement, the drop of a curtain upstairs, the intake of breath as she saw him standing there.

There was no one at the window, no curtain falling back into place.

He turned and left, climbed into his truck, drove away.

He was shaking; he saw that now. In a rush he suddenly felt too much at once—fury, fear, anguish. He was confused, driving too fast through unfamiliar streets.

He thought of Sweetpea, of Blair, of the cottage in the back of the purple Victorian, and he turned toward the Haight, sped toward Blair, thinking: *Somehow, Blair will make me stop feeling like this.*

By the time he reached the Haight, his eyes were fogging, so he could barely see his way to a parking space. He knew Emily had been there, in that house, and that she knew he was there at the door. She had run away from him, and she didn't want him to find her. It took his breath away, as if for three months he had not quite believed it, not quite felt the heavy weight of it, and now it knocked him out, a wild punch in the gut, followed by a blast of pain.

He walked up toward Blair's cottage, thankful that her hippie landlord wasn't lurking.

He knocked lightly on her door, glancing at his watch. It was nine o'clock, an hour too early for her breakfast in bed.

"Come in," he heard her call out.

He walked in, walked down the tiny hallway to her open bedroom, stood in her doorway.

She was lying in bed. She looked at him and lifted her covers to invite him in.

He climbed into her bed and she held him, let him cry softly, without asking a question.

Chapter Five

She liked the size of him, the broad back in front of her own small torso on the bed, the way her arm wrapped around his flannel shirt and pulled him toward her, pressing him into her. She curved her legs into the back of his, somehow matching them—she was not tall, but her legs were long, and she could tell he carried his height in his upper body. She liked the heat of him, the smell of him as she pressed her face into the back of his neck.

She knew he was crying. That didn't bother her—there was something different about this man, something that allowed him this. And she liked forgetting about herself for a moment.

She didn't want to know why—she was sure it had something to do with the wife. Ex-wife? She didn't know the story and wasn't in any rush to find out. Life was complicated. This, on the other hand, a man in her bed, crying, seemed so very simple.

She was wearing a tank top and cotton pajama bottoms and she hadn't brushed her teeth and she had never even kissed this man. She had watched him, for years, when they were kids in high school. From afar. She remembered one day when she had cut class—probably Latin, which she hated—and had taken a walk to the creek behind the school to smoke a cigarette by herself. She saw two kids downstream, Luke and his girlfriend, Trish, lying on a wide, flat rock, idly touching each other, sometimes kissing. Luke's hand was stroking the girl's body as if that were all he wanted to do in the world.

Blair was mesmerized. This was a glimpse into another world. She had just lost her virginity with a boy from her neighborhood, a boy who had already dropped out of school and was working at the convenience store. They had gone to elementary school together, and then she had been whisked away from his world to go to the private school in San Francisco.

"Stop staring at me," she had said to him when she stopped in the store the week before to pick up cigarettes.

"You think you're too good for us," the boy had said.

"No, I don't," she had answered. He looked different from how she remembered him—darker, more mysterious, somehow older than she. The boys at her own school were so young and safe, it seemed.

"You're not," he had said. He never took his eyes off her.

"I know that," she had replied.

"Wait for me after work," he had said, daring her. "I close at eleven."

She was waiting for him in the parking lot at eleven, terrified, determined not to show it. He had a friend with a studio in the Mission and the guy would give them pot, he said. And a bed, he said. They took a bus to the Mission and found the friend's apartment, smoked weed with him and another girl, an older girl. Then the boy led her into the bedroom and fumbled his way into her clothes, into her body. She didn't stop him. She wanted to know what sex was. Now she knew. He drove her home, using his friend's old car, dropped her off at her house.

Had she proven that she wasn't any better than they were? Yes, she had certainly proved that. She never saw him again.

The boy on the rock by the creek, Luke Bellingham, knew something else about sex. She had seen it that day, had watched him touch his girlfriend, and she kept watching for an hour or so. When Luke and Trish left, without ever making love, Blair felt oddly sick, as if she had done something terrible. She never went back to school that day.

Now Luke was lying next to her. He didn't seem to care that she was unpopular or rude or dying. He pressed his body back against hers as if he had never needed anyone so intensely in his life. And she held him.

Finally, after some time had passed and his body seemed calmer, quieter, Blair whispered in his ear: "I don't see any croissants here."

So he rolled over, smiling, and took her in his arms, as if he had done this many times, curling around her, pulling her so close she felt the heat of his skin through his clothes.

"Thank you," he murmured.

His hands began to explore her body, over her pj's, following the contours of her shoulder, arm, waist, hip, thigh, then rounding up her back.

"You feel so good," he whispered.

"That's just because you've been sleeping with a dog for too long."

"Where is that dog of mine?"

"Amanda took her for a walk."

"Will she be back any time soon?"

"Too soon for you to get fresh with me."

"Damn," Luke said, and pulled back so he could see her expression.

"You OK?" she asked, watching him.

"Better," he said.

"You want to talk?"

"I did something really stupid," he said.

She reached up and smoothed his hair away from his forehead.

He looked at her. "Why didn't I fall for you in high school?" he asked.

"I was weird," she said. "I'm still weird, but now so are you."

"Thank you," he told her.

"What did you do? The stupid thing?"

"I tried to find my wife. I might have found her."

Blair didn't say anything, but she felt herself pull back a little, as if she needed some space between their bodies.

"No, don't go away." He held on to her.

"What happened?" Blair asked.

"I think she's having an affair. She's in a house in Noe Valley. The man went to her last night."

They didn't say anything for a while. Blair saw the pain in his eyes.

"Isn't that easier?" she finally said. "That she left you for another man? She might have even loved you the way you thought she did and then she found someone she loved more."

He shook his head. "I don't believe that," he said. "You wouldn't do that."

"How do you know what I would do?" she asked, pushing back from him and sitting up in bed. "I don't know anything about love. I'm the world's greatest failure at love."

"Have you been in love?"

"I love my daughter. I love Daniel. That's good enough for me."

"No love affairs?"

"Affairs. I can get a guy. I just can't get in love with a guy."

"Why?"

"Hey, wait a second. We were talking about you. If we're going to start talking about me, I want breakfast in bed."

Luke leaned over and kissed Blair tenderly on the mouth. She watched him and saw that he, too, watched her. He smiled when he was done.

"How do you like your coffee?" he asked.

"I'm not sure I want you to leave," she said quietly.

So he pulled her back to him, and she slipped down in the bed, into his arms, and this time when he kissed her, they opened their mouths and closed their eyes and lost themselves in the kiss. Their bodies wrapped around each other and then unwrapped, while their hands pushed up each other's shirts, sought the heat of their skin, fumbled around in clothing as if they were indeed high school kids fooling around for the first time.

They moved around each other, exploring new territory, skin and hair and muscle and bone. Luke kissed her collarbone, the nape of her neck, her ears, her face. His hands rode over her body as if her clothes had melted away, both of them feeling too much even through the thin cotton. She felt herself gasping for breath, and at one moment Luke asked worriedly, "Are you all right?"

"Shh," she said. "I'm wonderful."

He turned her over then and, with her shirt hiked up, he looked at her back. He ran his finger along the scar from where they had removed the mole, still raw, still awful-looking, she knew. He didn't say anything and she was glad for that. She felt his lips along the ragged edge of the scar.

She rolled over and held him to her, pressing the full weight of him onto her. He was solid, strong. She liked the earthy smell of him and breathed him in.

He found her mouth and they kissed. This man held nothing back. His urgency excited her, made her want him even more.

His hands moved down along the sides of her body and then he rolled over, pulling her on top of him. She sat up, straddling him, catching her breath. She was smiling.

"You're amazing," he said.

"I could almost believe you," she told him.

"You're too far away," he said.

She lowered herself onto him, and then they both heard Sweetpea's bark, the quick scramble of dog feet on the steps heading up to the front door. Blair shot up off Luke, off the bed, and dashed to her bedroom door, pulling it closed. She heard the front door open at the same time.

She leaned back on the door and saw that Luke was already standing, straightening his clothes.

"Damn," she muttered.

"Mom?" Amanda called.

"I'll be right out!" Blair yelled back.

Sweetpea knew Luke was there; she barked and scratched at the closed door of Blair's bedroom.

"Sweetpea, get away from there!" Amanda called. "Stop barking!"

Luke was composed, somehow, and he leaned over, pressed his mouth to Blair's cheek, nudged her to the side, and opened the door enough to slide out. He closed the door behind him.

Blair stayed where she was, leaning against the closed door, taking in deep breaths.

"Hi," she heard Luke say.

"You're here," Amanda finally said. She must have been standing in the hallway, blocking Luke's way.

"I came to visit."

"I can see that."

"And to get my dog."

"You got her."

They were quiet for a second. Blair held her breath, wanting to hear everything.

"Thanks for walking her," Luke said.

"My mother's sick," Amanda said.

"I know that."

"She doesn't need a boyfriend right now."

"Maybe you're right. I'm not sure."

"I'm sure. We're doing just fine without you."

"Amanda. You're sixteen. You can't take care of everything."

"Who said you can drop into our lives like this?"

Blair threw open the door and stood there, half-crazed from half sex, glaring at them.

"Amanda!" she said sternly.

Amanda turned and stormed into the kitchen.

Blair put her hand on Luke's shoulder.

"Bad timing," she whispered.

"I'll call you later," he said.

"You don't have to leave," she told him.

"Yes, I do," he said.

"I didn't get my croissant."

"I'll bring it to you another day," he said, smiling. He leaned over and kissed Blair, who reached up and touched his cheek.

Sweetpea scrambled to her feet and led the way out of the cottage. Blair watched them leave. She heard Amanda banging things around in the kitchen. She walked to the kitchen and stood in the open doorway.

"Nice manners," she told her daughter.

Amanda was pouring orange juice, freshly squeezed, into a glass. She handed the glass to her mother.

"I don't care," she said. "I don't trust him. Here, drink this."

"Wow," Blair said, taking the glass. "What a treat."

"You need vitamins and stuff. I checked on-line. There're some articles I want you to read. About treatments, alternative treatments. There's this place in Mexico—"

"Stop," Blair said, putting down her glass. "Amanda—"

"They have this great success rate. All these people were told by their doctors that it was too late for treatment and they go to this place in Mexico and they take this herbal stuff—"

"Amanda!"

"Drink your juice, Mom. We can talk about it later. I'll show you the articles."

"I don't want to talk about it later. I told you. My doctor agrees. No treatments. Maybe it's better this way, sweetheart."

Amanda turned away from her and started throwing things in a pot on the stove. "Oatmeal?"

"Amanda. Please. I'm not hungry. Come sit down and we'll talk about it."

Amanda threw the wooden spoon into the sink. She turned to her mother, her face dark with anger.

"So what are you going to do? Have sex? That's a great way to deal with this."

Blair turned away and sank into a chair at the dining-room table. "Sit down," she said.

Amanda left the kitchen, slid into the chair across from her mother. Blair saw that she was crying, though she didn't make a sound.

"I don't know how I'm going to do this," Blair admitted. "I've never done this before."

She looked at Amanda, who lowered her head. Blair reached out and lifted her chin, offering her a small smile.

"We'll do it together. We'll figure it out. But I'm not running to Mexico for alternative treatments."

"You could read the articles," Amanda said, her voice small.

"I don't think so, Amanda. I think the doctors are right on this one."

"I never heard of that," Amanda said, and she choked on a sob. "Everyone does chemo. Or radiation. Or something."

"Not with advanced melanoma. Not at this stage."

Amanda dropped her head onto her arms on the table and sobbed. Blair stroked her head. She felt her own tears streaming down her face.

"I don't know how to let you go," she murmured, but Amanda was crying too hard to hear her.

• • •

Blair made it to work later that day, exhausted before she began. Each day she felt more tired. And she knew she was losing weight, but she couldn't seem to do anything about it. She couldn't call in sick. There was plenty of time for that. And she needed to get out of the cottage. She needed to lose herself in the restaurant kitchen.

Daniel was standing in the back bathroom, door open, primping in front of the mirror.

"Why are you here?" he asked, turning around to face her. "Go home. They should never have let you out of the hospital if you won't stay in bed."

"I'm fine," Blair insisted, though she could see by the way Daniel was eyeing her that she didn't look fine.

"I can cook tonight," Daniel said. "I still know how to do that."

"Go wow them up front," Blair said.

"You're sure?"

"I'm sure."

So Daniel went back to fussing with his shirt collar in the mirror.

"You're gorgeous," she told him, walking past him to pick up her chef's jacket. She slapped him on the butt.

"I know," he said. "Every man in San Francisco is lusting after me." He turned and kissed her cheek.

"Why don't you have a lover, Daniel? Why aren't you madly in love with some hunk of a guy?"

"I don't believe in love," he said. "We're booked tonight. A party of ten, which I set up in the back corner, keep 'em out of everyone's way. Rianne said she was too hungover to work, so I told her to take one of her magic pills. Expect the worst."

He started to move through the kitchen doors, heading toward the bar, where he liked to set up, even before the bartender arrived.

"Why don't you believe in love?" Blair called after him.

"Waste of time," he muttered.

Blair followed him into the dining room. She had too much to do, but she had never had this conversation with Daniel before. Love was the untouched territory, the forbidden land.

"Why? How could it be a waste of time?"

"What is it, girl?" Daniel said, turning toward her, his expression pure exasperation. "Did you fall for the movie man or something?"

"No," Blair said sheepishly. "I'm thinking. You know. I've never been in love. And here you are. My best friend. And you've never been in love. What's wrong with us?"

"We're perfect," Daniel said. "Except you missed a button, dear."

Blair rebuttoned her jacket over her tank top.

"Answer me," she said, her voice stronger.

She looked up and saw that Daniel was looking at her, his head cocked to one side, his expression pained.

"Don't get weepy on me, Blair. I liked you much better when you weren't sick."

Blair rolled her eyes and turned away from him.

She marched back into the kitchen, where Philippe hovered over the chocolate sauce, his pinkie dipped into the brew.

"Get your hand out of there!" Blair exploded.

He pulled out the finger, plunged it into his mouth.

"Look out—she's in a foul mood!" Daniel called from the dining room.

"Screw you, Daniel," Blair blasted back.

"You guys are like an old married couple," Philippe offered, grinning a chocolate smile at her. "And that sauce is awesome."

"Does he have boyfriends? Does he even have sex?" Blair asked.

Daniel pushed the swinging doors open and stood there, glaring at them.

"It is none of your goddamn business," he said.

"I don't know anything about you," Blair said.

"You know everything about me," Daniel said. "Sex is nothing. Love is nothing."

"You really believe that?" Blair asked.

"I live for sex," Philippe tossed in. "Sex and chocolate."

"Shut up," both Blair and Daniel said at the same time.

"Phew. Whatever is going on between you two, just leave me right out of it." Philippe sashayed past Daniel and into the dining room to start setting up the tables.

Blair and Daniel glared at each other.

"I do like the movie man," Blair finally said. "Dumb, you know. I mean, what good is it?"

"No good," Daniel said.

"Right," Blair said, shrugging. "I knew that."

"And I hate the idea of your getting hurt."

She smiled at him, reached out a hand to touch his arm. "Is that why we don't fall in love?" she asked.

Daniel pulled her close to him for a hug. *He never does this,* Blair thought. But he pulled away quickly, straightening his collar.

"You making that tuna tartare tonight?" he asked.

She looked at him, her eyes wide open. "Oh, my God. It's wasted. All that sashimi-grade tuna."

"I made it," Daniel said. "Everyone loved it." He turned, starting back toward the dining room. "Ordered another batch for you. It's in the fridge."

"Thank you," Blair said, smiling.

She pulled open the refrigerator and found the ahi tuna, glad that she'd have another chance. Something to take her mind off everything.

Until Philippe banged back into the kitchen, looking for the napkins, and tossed off, "I hear you've got the hots for the movie man."

"Fuck you, Daniel!" Blair yelled out toward the dining room.

"Can't, darling," Daniel called. "I'm gay."

"I hate him," Blair muttered.

"So, tell me about the movie man," Philippe urged, napkins in hand, now perched on the pastry counter, beaming.

"You tell me," Blair said. "What do you know about him?"

"Everything," Philippe said eagerly. "*Premiere* did a small profile on him when *The Geography of Desire* came out a couple of months ago. He's married to a beauty. Not that you aren't a beauty. Well, you're not exactly a beauty. But you're interesting."

"I wasn't asking about me," Blair said. She pulled out a bowl and started working on the tuna tartare.

"You want to know about the wife?"

"Ex-wife."

"Maybe. Maybe not."

She glanced at Philippe, who was delighting in this. "What does that mean?"

"She ditched him. He went into mourning. He can't work without her."

"How would you know this?"

"I have a friend who worked on *Pescadero.*"

"Right. So he loves his wife. What else can you tell me?"

"He was at a screening of *The Geography of Love.* His wife walked out in the middle. He chased after her. By the time he got to the street, she was gone, never to be found again. His life is better than a goddamn film."

"Well, maybe he found her."

"If he did, then '*Au revoir,* Blair.'"

"Not necessarily."

"We're talking love of his life. The man went to the woods for a year after she disappeared."

"Three months."

"Is he writing again?"

"I don't know."

"Trust me. If he found the wife, he'll start writing again."

"Not necessarily."

"You're a dreamer, Blair. This is Hollywood. You're the Haight. There are about a million miles between the two."

"Philippe!" Daniel shouted from the dining room. "Are you gossiping all night or working?"

Philippe jumped down from the counter and pecked Blair's cheek.

"Good luck, *chérie,*" he said. "You'll need it." He started toward the dining room.

"If you know everything," Blair called after him, "tell me one thing."

Philippe turned back to her.

"Why is Luke Bellingham so successful? What makes his movies so good?"

"Because he knows about love," Philippe said, winking.

• • •

Blair was at the video store when it opened the next morning. She found *Pescadero*—his other two films were out.

"Great film!" the video clerk told her.

"Yeah, I've heard," Blair muttered.

She paid, threw the video in her backpack and headed home.

Her bones were so tired, they ached. *Damn this disease,* she thought.

It was Sunday and foggy and she didn't want to do anything but hole up in her cottage to watch the movie. Amanda was at the library, working on a history term paper, and Blair had the house to herself for a while. She bought a croissant at the bakery and thought about Luke in her bed: *I'll have breakfast in bed with him one way or another.*

At home she popped in the cassette, undressed, curled up under the covers, nibbled at her croissant and smiled at the opening credits. Written by Luke Bellingham. *My movie man?* she thought. *Ridiculous. High school Luke Bellingham with his sandy blond hair swept over one eye, his crooked smile, his long, lanky body, his gaggle of girlfriends? Or Luke Bellingham in my bed, his body now thickened, broader, his hair brushed back, his eyes staring so intensely into mine?*

He had asked her to talk to him before watching *Pescadero.* Why?

The front door opened and closed—she could hear it click shut.

"Amanda?" she called.

Her bedroom door opened and Casey stood there, joint in hand.

"Goddamn you," she said. "I told you not to let yourself in. You're my landlord, not my boyfriend."

"Ease up," he said. "Take a hit."

Blair pushed herself up in bed, clicked the video off with her remote control.

"No," she insisted. "Get lost. Beat it. I am not available for you anytime day or night."

"How ya feeling?" he asked, standing there, toking away.

"Are you listening to me?"

"You look better. You looked like shit when you got back from the hospital. You know they say pot is the best thing for chemo."

"I'm not doing chemo!" Blair shouted. "Get out of here. You're in my house!"

"It's my house," Casey said. "But you can live here as long as you want. What's Amanda going to do when you die?"

Blair threw back the covers and stood up.

"You're naked!" Casey exclaimed. "You were waiting for me!"

Naked, she started pushing him out, backward, toward the door.

"I will call the police. I will buy a gun. You may not come in here like this. I will never sleep with you again."

At last he was at the front door. She gave a final push, closed the door and locked it. She leaned back, panting.

"Just one more roll in the hay for old times' sake?" she heard him shout from the porch.

She slumped to the floor. So much for breakfast in bed with the movie by Luke Bellingham.

She threw on clothes, made herself a cup of coffee, finished her croissant, then decided to try again. She climbed into bed, clicked on the video.

The first scene showed a beach town at night, the color of everything a kind of blue-black, the sky charcoal. The camera panned a long stretch of white beach, the sand eerily fluorescent as it caught the light from the moon. The ocean was black, its roar thunderous. A young woman walked alone on the beach. She was unbelievably tall, pole thin, blondly beautiful. *His wife? No, Philippe would have said so. Maybe the man is just obsessed with the same woman, the same body type, the non-Blair of his dreams.*

And the front door opened again.

"I am calling the police," Blair yelled out. "I swear. You step one foot in this cottage and I'll bust your sorry ass."

"Good morning to you, too," Amanda said, standing in the doorway.

"Oh, God, I'm sorry." Blair pushed herself up in bed. "What are you doing home?"

"I finished my work."

"That's impossible. You said it would take days."

"I can do it at home."

"We don't have a computer. How are you going to do the research?"

"I'll make up the research."

Blair eyed her daughter, who stood in the doorway nonchalantly, swinging her backpack in front of her.

"You can't spend every minute with me," Blair said.

"You feeling OK?" Amanda asked.

"I'm fine. Really, Amanda. Go on back to the library."

"I don't want to. It's Sunday. I want to hang out with you."

"I could be sick for a long time," Blair said. "You have to live your life, you know."

"Or you could be sick for a short time. And then what do I do?"

Amanda started to turn away from her mother.

"Come here, sweetheart." Blair patted the bed next to her.

Amanda crossed the room in a second and slid under the covers next to her mother.

"So what did your new boyfriend do to get you so angry?" she asked.

"My new boyfriend didn't do anything. Casey was bugging me. And, for your information, I don't have a new boyfriend."

"What are you watching on TV?" Amanda asked.

A young man, bearded, long hair wrapped in a bandanna—Blair knew the actor was someone famous but couldn't place him—ran from behind toward the beautiful blond woman. She turned when she heard him, her expression terrified. But in a moment they were kissing. The guy had his hands all over her.

"A movie," Blair said. "I felt like being lazy this morning."

"*Pescadero,*" Amanda said, watching the screen. "You're watching *Pescadero.*"

"I don't need shit from my sixteen-year-old daughter just because I'm watching a movie that someone from my high school wrote."

"I don't like him."

"So you mentioned."

"I like his movies and all—"

"But?"

"I don't know. You want me to shut up so you can watch?"

"No. I can watch it later."

"I'll watch it with you," Amanda said. "I want to see it again."

"I'd like that," Blair said, propping up the pillows so the two of them could lean back against the headboard and watch together.

They heard a bark and a knock and Blair leaped from the bed, rushing to turn off the VCR and the TV, to get to the door, while Amanda lay in bed, grumbling.

"Did he move in and you forgot to tell me?" she asked her mother.

"Don't tell," Blair whispered. "I mean, about the movie."

"I hate him!" Amanda shouted, and slammed the door of her mother's room as soon as Blair headed to the front door.

Blair opened the door and Sweetpea bounded in. Luke stood on the porch, smiling.

"Not a good time?" he asked.

Blair shook her head.

Luke shrugged, still smiling. "You got company?"

"My daughter," Blair said. "Who needs some of me right now."

Luke nodded. "She's going to want a lot of you now."

Blair turned toward her own closed door and then back toward Luke. "Listen," she said quietly. "Tomorrow morning. I mean, if you want to. Breakfast in bed. That sort of thing."

"I want to," Luke said.

"Why?" Blair asked. "I mean, why me?"

"Everyone should get a second chance," Luke said. "I missed you in high school. Took me all this time to find you again."

Blair rolled her eyes.

"What time?"

"Eight. She leaves for school at seven-thirty."

"You sure I can't take you both out for lunch?"

"No. Go home. Go away. Go do something else."

"I started to write again," Luke said.

Blair looked at him, surprised. Her stomach churned. "Really?"

They heard the bedroom door open, and Luke leaned forward, giving Blair a quick kiss. "Tomorrow," he whispered, and started down the stairs.

"Your dog!" Blair called after him.

"Keep her!" he yelled back.

Blair closed the door and turned around, but the dog had already disappeared down the hall. She headed back to her bedroom, where the door was now open.

Amanda and Sweetpea were curled around each other in Blair's bed.

"There room for me in there?" Blair asked.

"Where is he?" Amanda asked sourly.

"I told him we were busy," Blair said.

"Really?" Amanda asked.

"Really. Move over."

Blair squeezed onto the bed with them. Sweetpea laid her head on Blair's feet.

"You still want to watch?" Blair asked.

Amanda jumped out of bed, popped in the videocassette, cuddled back next to her mom.

"I love you," she said as the movie started again.

"My sweet girl," Blair said.

"Shh," Amanda said, and they leaned back against the pillows to watch the movie.

The young woman and man on the beach walked silently away from the ocean and toward the dunes. They had their arms wrapped around each other and the wind whipped at them. The dunes were shadowed by the light of the moon, ominous mountains of sand.

They climbed a dune and at the top saw a kind of sand valley below, surrounded by more dunes. They ran, laughing, down the mountain of sand, and tumbled on top of each other on the sandy bottom.

"How old are they?" Blair asked, feeling the first nudge of unease. The scene was too familiar and yet completely strange.

"Shh."

"Are they kids? They're in their twenties, right?" she insisted.

"I don't know. Yeah. Stop talking."

They watched. The couple started to make love. The woman was suddenly timid, unsure. The man coaxed her along, urging off each article of clothing, covering her exposed flesh with kisses.

"Something's going to happen," Blair said, and pushed herself upright against the headboard as if bracing herself. Her stomach roiled.

"Quiet!" Amanda insisted.

Finally the couple was naked, the woman now easy in the man's embrace. The background music—a wailing electric guitar—pounded over the sound of the ocean. And on top of the dune, two men stood, watching them.

"Oh, my God," Blair said.

"Shh," Amanda repeated.

"Turn it off," Blair said.

Amanda looked at her mother.

"Turn it off," she repeated. She was looking away from the screen.

Amanda picked up the remote control and clicked—the screen turned to black.

"Mom?"

Blair pulled her knees up and wrapped her arms around them.

"She gets raped, right? He runs away?" Blair asked, her voice tight.

"Yeah," Amanda said. "You've seen it?"

Blair shook her head.

"Mom?"

Blair looked at Amanda, then down at her knees. "It happened to me."

They were quiet a moment, and then Blair sat up taller in the bed. "I never told you. I should have. I never knew when you tell your daughter a story like that."

"You were raped?" Amanda asked.

Blair reached out and touched her daughter's shoulder.

"Oh, God," Amanda said. Her eyes were full, ready to spill over.

"I never wanted you to know," Blair said. Her chest felt constricted—she had to push her words out as she talked. She wanted to scream—at Luke, for using her story and not telling her. *Why did he write a movie about me?* There was another scream inside her that she had lived with for so long—the rage that surged to the surface of her consciousness whenever she remembered that night. And suddenly, without preparation, she had to do what she had been unprepared to do for so many years: tell her daughter.

"I wanted you to be strong and independent," Blair finally said. "Hard to grow up that way when you know how brutal the world can be."

"Mom, you can tell me. I'm not a baby." Though when Blair looked at her, Amanda looked terrified, the way she did when she was very young and too scared to sleep alone in her room.

"I know that, sweetheart."

"What happened?"

"That," Blair said, pointing to the television. She remembered the beach, on the California coast. It was evening, the sun setting, the air getting cold, so she and her boyfriend, Wes, had wrapped themselves in a blanket she kept in the trunk of her car. She remembered the men—three of them rather than two—finding them while they were making love in the cove. She remembered the laughter of those horrible men and how she knew in that moment that something awful was going to happen.

Amanda stared at the blank screen.

"You mean, he knew? Luke Bellingham?"

Blair nodded. "The whole town knew. It wasn't such a big town. And no one keeps secrets."

"He used your story?" Amanda asked, stunned.

Blair shrugged, shaking her head in disbelief. *That's why he wanted me to talk to him first,* she realized. "What's the rest of the film about?"

"The guy," Amanda said. "The woman dies. Not right away, but after a while. And the boyfriend blames himself. I mean, he ran away and all. Did the guy you were with run away?"

Blair nodded. He had grabbed his jeans and had run, scrambling up the path that led away from the beach, away from Blair, who was tackled by the first of the men as soon as she struggled to stand.

"My God, Mom. *Pescadero* is your story?"

Blair tried a smile. "Apparently not. In case you didn't notice, I'm sitting here next to you."

"Were you beat up?"

Blair nodded again. When she screamed, one of the men hit her. And kept hitting her, every time she made a sound. Until she learned to let them do what they wanted, in silence. "Pretty badly. But my body healed. I was younger than the woman in the film. I was sixteen. Your age."

"How'd you go to school the next day? How'd you talk to your friends or your boyfriend after that?"

"I didn't. I never talked to my boyfriend again. He ignored me. And the rest of the kids were so awful that I stopped talking to all of them. It was like I was yanked out of childhood, and I didn't have anything in common with any of them anymore."

"Did they catch the guys who did it?"

Blair shook her head. The police knew that she had been naked on the beach with a boy—so maybe she had been asking for it, they suggested, ready for any man who came by. Maybe she wanted to be gang-banged by three drunken guys, out looking for a good time. Maybe she was a good-time girl with her contusions and her cuts and her torn vagina.

"So, if I ever worry about you too much," Blair said, "when it's late and you're not home yet, you know why."

"I'm careful," Amanda said.

"So was I," Blair said.

I had been careful with my heart, Blair thought. She had not had a boyfriend until she met Wes, and they had become friends, her first friend, another scholarship student, though one who moved well in the world of Reese Academy. When he kissed her for the first time, she let herself love him, knowing that this was so different from anything she had experienced before. They had made love twice in that cove, on other evenings, sneaking away from families and schoolwork—and Blair had thought, *Yes, this is what sex is; this is what love is.* Until the men found them, and Wes ran away.

"Is that why you never have boyfriends?"

"No. Maybe. Who knows? I don't trust the world very much, do I? This is why I never told you. I want you to believe in a better world."

"Are you mad at Luke Bellingham?"

"I don't know. I'll think about it."

"Maybe he always liked you."

"No. The whole town always wanted to know what happened. That's all it is. A mystery."

"What did happen to the guy who ran away? Your boyfriend."

Blair shrugged. She remembered passing him in the hall at

school—he'd look away, never acknowledging her. He hated her, as if it were her fault somehow. She hadn't escaped the way he had. She could barely remember his tenderness, his sweet adolescent love that had drawn her to him from the start. "He didn't even go for help. He told the cops he thought the guys would follow him. So he ran and hid in the bathroom at the parking lot for an hour or so. At school the story got out that he ran away. Maybe the kids gave him a hard time. I don't know. I wasn't paying much attention. He left the school after a year. Started over somewhere else, I guess."

"Did you want to kill him?"

Blair shook her head. "I went numb for a long time. It's hell, Amanda. Rape is like no other kind of violence."

Amanda put her head down on Blair's lap. Blair stroked her hair, and they were quiet for a while.

"If you fast-forward," Blair said finally, "I'll watch the rest of the movie with you."

Amanda looked up at her mother. "Really?"

"I might not want to watch myself die, but the rest would be OK."

And so they watched *Pescadero,* Luke's story about a man who ran from his girlfriend's rape and spent the rest of his life trying to find a way to live with his guilt.

"He couldn't have saved me," Blair said at the end. "My boyfriend. If he had stayed and fought. There were three of them and they were much bigger."

"He could have tried," Amanda said.

"No," Blair said. "He saved himself. He was seventeen years old—that was as much as he could do."

"Luke Bellingham thinks the guy should have saved you," Amanda said.

Blair looked at her, surprised. "You're right," she said, thinking of Luke sitting in the chair at the hospital, waiting for her to wake up.

"You're so smart," she said, putting her arm around her daughter and pulling her close.

"I'm sorry that happened to you," Amanda said, her head on her mother's shoulder. "And you were so young."

"I know, sweetheart," Blair told her, wrapping her arms around her. "I'm sorry this is happening to you."

Chapter Six

Luke sat down at his desk and looked at what he had written in the middle of the night. Half of a short story about a man who lives alone in the woods, sees only the regulars at the local bar, develops a friendship with the woman bartender. She wants more from him than he's ready to give. One night her daughter, a sixteen-year-old beauty, shows up, takes a table, works on her homework, asks the man for help with her math. He helps her, leans in close and smells her coconut suntan oil—she's a surfer and had been at the beach that day—he remembers his youth, his glory days. That night the bartender invites him home with her—he turns her down. And the next morning, the sixteen-year-old shows up at his door. He makes love with her.

Does he go back to the bar the next night? Luke would figure that out next. But he was pleased that he was writing again, for the first time in months.

Why had he written this story? Clearly, the Blair/Amanda relationship was on his mind. He didn't find himself drawn to Amanda—unlike some guys, he had never lusted after young girls. But there she was, living in that tiny cottage with her mother, both of them alluring in their own ways. He would write the fiction instead of feeling the lust. Keep himself out of trouble.

He had all afternoon to do nothing. Maybe he should head back to the woods, where he had his workshop to play in. He was in the process of building a table—an outdoor table where he could eat alone with Sweetpea. Maybe he should get out of his haunted house and go back to the place where he was able to forget.

He thought some more about the short story. Maybe the man already has a relationship with the bartender—the daughter seduces him. Or he seduces her—make him struggle with his own demons. Make the bartender someone he cares about—then his actions matter. Who is the man who could sleep with the girl? Can he create this character, enter his skin and live there, squirming for a while?

He'd write this out as a story, see if it was a screenplay—perhaps leave it as a story. He wrote short stories years ago, before he met Emily, before he tasted the success of *Pescadero.*

He tapped his fingers on his desk. He picked up the phone and called Mr. Gray Healy.

The wife picked up.

"Hello?"

"I'd like to speak with Gray."

"Who's calling, please?"

"This is an old high school friend. Peter. Peter Bullock."

"I don't know you."

"I've been out of the country."

"Right. Well, Gray's not home. He's away. For a while."

"Anywhere I can reach him? It would be great to catch up after all these years."

"No. Sorry. Can't help you. I'll tell him you called."

"You'll be seeing him then."

"No. I mean, when he gets back. Why don't you give me your number?"

"No. I'm moving around too much. I'll call him. When do you think he'll be back?"

"I can't tell you that, Peter. Call again in another lifetime, all right?"

And she hung up.

Luke typed on his computer: Husband finds wife shacked up with guy, then kills them both. End of movie.

He pushed himself away from the desk, suddenly desperate to get away from the house.

Once in his truck, he didn't know where to go.

Sunday afternoon. In the old days they would have gone to Dana's house. The only two sisters in the world who lived their lives as if they were still sharing a room with two twin beds with matching comforters. Except now, Dana had a husband and a baby on the way.

Luke remembered a scene: He and Emily were in bed early one morning. They made love, taking their time, ignoring Sweetpea, who poked her nose over the side of the bed, begging to be fed. When they were done, Luke wanted to fall back to sleep in Emily's arms, but she whispered, "Go feed Sweetpea so she leaves us alone." Luke padded downstairs, filled the dog bowl, let Sweetpea out into the backyard to pee. He was feeling lazy, happy, ready to fall back into bed and curl himself around his sleeping wife. When he returned to the room, he saw that Emily was on the phone, talking to Dana, sitting up against the headboard with the sheet pulled high over her breasts.

He felt oddly betrayed. He watched her for a moment. *This is my time,* he thought. By the time she got off the phone, he had determined not to be jealous—Dana was her sister, not a lover, after all—but churlishly he got dressed, made coffee and took it with him into his study to get to work.

Of course his wife needed more than what he could offer. A sister. A lover.

Luke turned the truck toward Pacific Heights. He'd drop in on Dana. Perhaps the new couple was there, sharing martinis and sob stories:

"Can you believe the asshole delivered flowers to Gray's wife?"

"Well, at least it got Gray out of the house—right, dear?"

And if she were there, what would he do? He still didn't know—couldn't write his own goddamn script past the first scene. Husband searches for wife.

He parked, walked up the hill to Pacific, saw Dana at her own front door, key in the lock, bag of groceries perched on one hip.

"Dana!" he called.

She looked back at him, smiled, shrugged, opened her door, entered the house, closed the door behind her. *Is Emily there?* He looked around for her car, a yellow Miata. None in sight. No black BMW parked curbside.

He marched up to Dana's door and rang the bell.

No one answered.

"Open the goddamn door!" he shouted.

The whole neighborhood seemed to hold its breath—*God, it's quiet out here on a Sunday,* he thought.

"Dana! Open the fucking door!"

He pressed his thumb on the bell and held it there, felt its vibration up his arm like an electric shock.

Finally the door flew open and Dana stood there, hands on hips, scowling at him.

"Go home. Go away. Leave us alone."

"I found her," Luke said. "In Noe Valley. Don't do this to me, Dana. I know where she is, why she left. Tell her to talk to me. Tell her I just want to talk to her."

Dana's face softened. "I'll tell her," she said.

Luke turned and walked down the steps and along the path. He heard the door close behind him. He kept on walking, past his truck, and on down the hill toward the marina. He wished Sweetpea were at his side. He walked as far as he could, to the edge of the bay, and he sat there, watching the water, the fog, the few brave sailboats and windsurfers, until he was numb with cold.

• • •

Sometime in the middle of the night, Luke woke up, stretching his arm out toward the side of the bed as if Emily were there, just out of reach. They used to sleep curled around each other, turning over in the night and curling in the opposite direction. It had taken him so long to learn how to sleep alone. And now, he was forgetting again.

Three-twenty A.M. He threw on jeans and a flannel shirt and got into the truck and drove to Noe Valley. There was no parking place near the house—her house?—and so he circled, slowing as he passed the house each time. The lime curtains were closed; the lights were out. Of course.

Luke remembered a scene: Emily home from a meeting with a client, discouraged. He stood in the doorway of her studio, watching her drop her portfolio onto the floor by her drawing table. "They don't like what I've done. I've got to start over."

"You're good," Luke comforted her. "You'll come up with the right image for them."

"It's so easy for you," Emily said under her breath, as if Luke wouldn't even hear.

"It's not easy for me," he told her. "I work so damn hard."

"I can't do it," she finally said, beginning to cry. "I can't get what they want."

"Quit," Luke told her. "Tell them you don't want the project."

Emily glared at him, her eyes dark. He remembered the look: It was something close to hatred. For succeeding? For creating the life they had dreamed about?

"Maybe I'm just not good enough," she said.

"For what?"

"For you."

"Emily." He walked toward her, wanting to wrap her in his arms. She turned away from him.

"I adore you," he said, standing behind her, his arms at his sides.

"I know that," she told him. But she kept her back to him and finally he turned and left, closing the door behind him.

Luke sat in his truck at four in the morning and wondered about the kind of love that made someone flee.

After fifteen minutes he saw the lights go on in the house next door; a face at the window was peering at him. He hauled out of there before the police got a late-night call about some deranged husband trying to lure his wife from the arms of another man.

• • •

At home he sat at his desk and opened the file of his new short story. The man makes love with the young girl. Before she leaves his cabin, she asks him to come to the bar that night. Recklessly, he goes. He's feeling invulnerable, like a kid who can get away with anything.

The bartender knows. Her daughter has told her, has used the information to hurt her. She ignores him for a while, slamming down his drink, hurling comments about him to the other regulars. But then something happens—something to make him face her.

Luke stopped writing, stared at the screen. *I hate the bastard,* he thought. *I have to go deeper, find out what drives this man into the arms of a sixteen-year-old. Perhaps his own glory days.* The man imagines himself young, handsome, his life filled with young girls. He can forget for a moment his recent divorce, his work failures, his wish to drop out of life. He's become someone he once was.

Do I miss my own glory days? That's absurd, he thought. He was supposed to be living his glory days with Emily, with his own career success. But why did he feel something with Blair that he had been missing for a long time?

Luke pushed his chair away from the computer, rubbing his eyes. Maybe he should be writing something far removed from his own life, something that didn't demand so much from him. He'd surprise his fans with a space thriller or a born-again Western. He'd write porn films under a pseudonym. Or he'd haul his ass back to the woods and build furniture for another few years.

• • •

He slept, finally, for a couple of hours, waking with just enough time to shower, dress and dash off toward the Haight. Fresh croissants in hand, he knocked timidly on the door of the cottage. He heard Sweetpea's bark, was glad of her presence as Blair's protector in the cottage, a place that seemed vulnerably perched on the edge of this dangerous neighborhood.

The door opened; Sweetpea rushed out and back; Blair stood there in the doorway, an odd smile on her face.

"Good morning," Luke said without confidence.

"You're here," she told him.

"You're surprised."

"I didn't sleep well last night. By morning I figured I had probably just invented you."

"Why couldn't you sleep?"

"Bad dreams."

Blair was looking at him, her head cocked to one side. He waited.

"I dreamed I was in a movie. On a beach. Except the things that were happening to me in the movie were really happening to me."

Luke felt his stomach twist. He watched her face. Her eyes bore into his, watching for his reaction.

"Are you upset?" he asked.

She raised her eyebrows. "Hard to live through it again."

"I never really knew what happened."

"I know," Blair said. "I didn't die."

"I noticed," Luke said. "I'm sorry, Blair. Using your story was a lousy thing to do."

She shook her head. "I don't know. It's interesting. You invented my life."

"No. You're still a mystery. I couldn't begin to understand the hell you went through. I took the coward's route. I could only get close to the guy who ran."

"I don't blame him, you know."

"Then you're truly a mystery."

"I blame the guys who raped me. Wes had nothing to do with it."

"I know."

"Why did you choose to tell his story?"

Luke shrugged. "Guys are supposed to protect their loved ones. But I don't know—all my life, I wasn't very good at it. My mother fell apart after my dad left her—and I just stood by her side, doing nothing. My dad died during a sailing accident when I wasn't there, when I couldn't save him." Luke paused for a moment, looking away. "I think a lot of guys think they would save their girlfriend. And a lot of guys would run."

Blair reached out and touched Luke's cheek softly, then let her hand drift back to her side.

"Can I come in?"

Blair stepped aside and let Luke enter. She closed the door and turned toward him.

"You feeling OK?" he asked.

"Do me one favor," she said. She was wearing her pj's—a pink tank top and yellow-flowered boxer shorts. Or maybe they were her real clothes—he wasn't sure.

"Name it," he said.

"Just for now—this morning—let's pretend I'm not sick. I don't have cancer. We never heard of cancer."

He nodded.

"Thanks," she said. She took the bag of croissants from his hand and started searching for a plate.

"Leave it," he said, taking the bag and putting it down on the table.

He put his hands on her shoulders and pulled her to him. She was hesitant, unsure. He wrapped his arms around her—she seemed so small to him—and he felt her let herself go, sinking into his chest.

He lowered his head and breathed in the smell of her hair—something fruity, perhaps orange or peach shampoo? He ran his hand through her hair and buried his face in it.

Her hands started exploring his back and he liked her touch, firm, solid—*Let me know you,* her palms seemed to say on his skin.

He pulled her back and looked at her, saw her face so open to him and he leaned down to cover her mouth with his own.

"Bed," she murmured when he released her, and she led him there, holding his hand tightly.

"Let me undress you," he said.

He lifted off her shirt. He lowered himself to his knees and kissed each breast. He heard her sigh.

He pulled down her boxer shorts. Her waist was small, her hips wide—she was all curves and he was delighted, expecting someone so much thinner, slighter, less womanly.

He ran his hands over her warm skin. She made a noise and he looked at her, surprised. She was watching him.

"I'm not used to this," she said quietly.

"Sex?" he asked.

"Sex, I'm used to. This is something else."

He smiled up at her.

"This is what you deserve," he said.

She closed her eyes, and he saw her smile as his hands ran over her body.

He stood up and began unbuttoning his shirt.

"My job," she said.

She worked her way down the buttons, her tongue running a line down his chest.

"Luke Bellingham," she whispered. "The cutest boy in the school. And this morning he's mine."

"Blair Clemens," Luke said. "The mystery girl. And I get to discover her mystery."

She had worked off his pants and pressed herself up against him, reaching around to hold him tight.

"You are the mystery," she told him. "What brought you to me?"

"I need you," he said; without understanding his own words, he somehow knew they were true. He felt something inside him opening up, something that had been tightly closed for a long time.

He lay down on the bed with her, their bodies wrapped around each other, their tongues and hands exploring every inch of skin.

When they made love, it was long and slow and sweet, and Luke saw that she had tears in her eyes.

"I could love you," he whispered when they were done, lying in each other's arms, breathing each other in.

• • •

Luke drove home after breakfast and a shower and a walk around the neighborhood with Sweetpea. He left Sweetpea with Blair.

"Can I come to your restaurant?" he had asked.

"Yes," she said, pleased. "You might have to give a few autographs. One of the waiters knows your movies."

"No autographs," he said. "This would be your show. I'd love to watch you work."

"You can't do that," she said. "Daniel would die if anyone entered his kitchen. But I will feed you. I will fatten you up for tomorrow morning so we can work it all off again."

"I can come back tomorrow morning?"

"If you eat well tonight."

He drove home smiling. He had used her shampoo—peach—and felt like he was taking her smell home with him.

When he pulled onto his street, he saw the yellow Miata sitting in the driveway. He stopped the truck where he was, until the man in the car behind him blasted his horn.

He drove on, pulling in next to the Miata.

He sat in the truck, waiting. He had been waiting for this, for Emily, and now he couldn't move, couldn't open his door and set his feet in motion.

He saw the curtain move in the bedroom—beyond it, he thought he glimpsed her hair, that long sweep of blond hair, and then the curtain closed again, trembling, the way he was.

He pushed the truck door open and forced himself out.

At the door he paused. *Do I knock? Use the key?* And then it opened, and Emily stood there, looking at him.

They didn't speak for a moment. He saw that her hair was longer, perhaps blonder. She was wearing a sweater he didn't recognize, a pale blue cashmere sweater, and he thought: *Gray Healy bought her that. I should have bought her that sweater.*

The jeans were the same, her old worn Levi's. She wore black boots that they had bought together in New York last year. She had forgotten to wear earrings—she always said she felt naked if she went out without earrings.

"I like the beard," she said finally.

He moved his hand to his chin, as if needing to remind himself: *Beard, months gone by without her, I've changed.*

He couldn't find any words, though they all raced through his mind crazily, as if he could choose any one: *I love you; I hate you; go away; stay.*

"Where's Sweetpea?" she asked after a moment.

"At a friend's," he said.

"I miss her," Emily said.

"You can't have her," Luke said.

"I wouldn't ask for her," Emily told him.

"Then why are you here?"

"Dana told me you wanted to talk to me. You found my house. I can't hide. I don't even want to hide." She was so calm. But then he saw that her eyes were tearing.

"Then why did you disappear like that?"

"It was the only way I could leave you," Emily said.

"What does that mean?"

"You would have convinced me to stay."

"No, I—"

"Yes, Luke. You could talk me into anything."

He stood there, in the doorway, and realized that he couldn't quite catch his breath. He felt as if he had been running for miles and then had stopped suddenly, without winding down.

"Can we talk inside?" she asked.

He nodded. She turned away from him and moved down the hallway.

He thought, oddly, of running away. Of turning and hopping into his truck, of fleeing. "It was the only way I could leave you," he'd tell her years from now.

He walked into the house and pulled the door closed behind him.

He looked down the hall and she was gone. Had she been there? Had he written her dialogue, given her stage directions, then whisked her out of the story line?

She would have walked into the living room—he knew that. And he stood there, still catching his breath.

"Are you coming?" she called out.

"Yes," he said, and that got him moving again.

He stood in the entrance to the living room. She was at the window, looking out, as if still waiting for him to come home. He watched her profile and saw that her shoulders were raised, as if she were cold. Was she scared? Did he still know her so well? Or did he know nothing about her?

"How long?" he asked.

She didn't turn around.

"I don't know what you're asking," she said. She wrapped her hands around a glass of water.

"How long were you having an affair?"

"I didn't leave you because I was having an affair."

Finally she turned and faced him. Her eyes were tight, as if she were peering into the darkness.

"I didn't ask that. I asked how long you were having an affair with Gray Healy."

"I met him right before I left you."

"Weeks before? Days?" Luke's voice was getting louder. He

moved toward her and she seemed to flinch, step back. He had never hit her—surely she didn't think he could do that now.

He walked to the couch, sat in the middle of it, watching her.

"Does it matter?" she asked.

He didn't answer.

She stepped toward him and then sat in the chair across from him. She had never sat there before, in years of living here. That was the chair for a guest. Her place was next to him, curled into him. She sipped her water.

"Do you love him?" Luke asked. It wasn't a question he had considered until it was out of his mouth. He wanted to take it back, rewind, rewrite, respeak.

"No," she said quickly.

"I don't know how to do this," he finally said. "I don't know what I want to know." He saw that her chin was trembling, and he remembered how hard she could cry when she let go.

"Gray Healy has nothing to do with it," Emily said. Her voice broke, and then she got up, walked away for a moment, turned back. "I should have been able to leave you without running to someone else," she said, her face wet, her voice uneven.

"What does that mean?"

She didn't answer. She started walking in circles, around the couch, around the chair.

"Please sit down," he said gently.

She sat across from him again.

"I felt like a little girl in a grown-up marriage," she told him. "It was bad enough when it was just about our age difference, but then you hit the big time and I was still trying to figure out what to do with my life."

"I don't care about whether or not you're a big success," Luke offered.

"I care, Luke. And I'm not. I dabble in art; I dabble in some silly affair. I don't even run away like I mean it. I never left San Francisco."

"You were in the house in Noe Valley the whole time?"

Emily nodded. "Remember that time you told me I don't take risks in my art and that's why I wasn't winning prizes?"

Luke remembered the argument. He was helping her with a competition she had entered for an AIDS-awareness organization that wanted to reach out to street kids in the Haight. She was creating posters that were too clean, too white, too old. He pushed her on each attempt, urging her to try something she had never done before. Finally she had exploded: "You wish I were someone else."

"No," Luke had told her. "I'm just suggesting that you think like someone else." But even then, he wondered for a moment if it wasn't true: if he hadn't wished she could not just think bolder, but be bolder.

For a quick moment Luke thought about Blair, and saw her lying next to him in bed, after making love. Her face open, staring back at him. He reached for Emily's glass of water and took a long drink.

"I took a risk," Emily said, and she looked shy about it, her voice wavering. "I moved out. I thought about going to New York or to Paris. But I was so scared. I couldn't imagine leaving both you and Dana at the same time. I've never been on my own. Isn't that terrible? So I hid out in San Francisco. And I hated every moment of it."

"Why?"

She shrugged. "First I didn't leave the house. I thought you'd find me. I was scared someone would see me and tell you and that you'd come after me."

She looked up at him, and he saw how vulnerable she was.

"You're scared of me," he said sadly.

"I was scared of being without you."

"You had Gray Healy to comfort you."

"I didn't have Gray Healy. He belongs to his wife."

She stood up, circled the couch again.

He waited. She came back to the chair and fell into it.

"And then Dana told me you had left town. Headed to the hills. I was free. I started to go out—to classes, to meet Dana for lunch. And I kept coming home, calling out to you as if you were working on the computer in your study and you'd come out in a few minutes and wrap your arms around me."

"I don't understand."

"I missed you. Terribly. You took care of me. I wanted you to stop taking care of me, and then when you weren't there, I felt so damn lost."

Emily lowered her head and her hair hung over her face like a curtain.

She looked exhausted. He remembered putting her to bed after parties, helping her out of her clothes, tucking her in, lying next to her and stroking her back until she was deeply asleep.

"I needed to grow up," she said as if envisioning the same image in her own mind. A child.

Luke shook his head. "You didn't have to leave me to grow up."

She winced as if he had struck her. "I sat in that theater at the screening for *The Geography of Love.* The film was brilliant—I knew it would be. I stopped watching after a while and looked around the audience. Everyone was stunned, amazed. And I couldn't stand what would happen next—the way they would gather around to praise you and fight for your attention and they'd talk about the next big project and I'd stand somewhere on the side, watching the circus, feeling invisible. It was so easy for me to disappear that I thought I'd try it—I'd just disappear."

"I didn't want any of that," Luke said, leaning toward her. "Emily—"

"Listen to me," she insisted. "For once."

He leaned back into the sofa. This, he remembered. Her accusations: "You don't listen to me; you don't take me seriously; you think I'm a little girl."

"I'm listening," he said.

"Maybe you didn't say it," she said, her voice calmer. "But I knew better than you knew. How I disappointed you."

He shook his head.

"Then maybe I disappointed myself. Does it matter?" She glanced at him, then looked away. "Do you know what I thought?" she asked. She was looking out the window—he didn't answer her. "I thought that by having an affair—by sneaking out and going to hotels, meeting in dark restaurants—that I'd become a more interesting person. I was doing something so adult, so illicit." She turned and looked at him, her expression pained. "Isn't that sad?"

"Emily," he said softly.

She turned and walked out of the room. He waited to hear the front door slam, for the Miata's engine to turn over, for the car to back up and speed away. He waited for her to be gone forever. Another forever.

But the house was quiet. Finally he heard a cabinet door close in the kitchen.

"There's no food here," she called out. "Not one goddamn thing to eat."

He pushed himself out of the couch, walked slowly into the kitchen to find her. He had the odd sense of watching the scene as it was happening—as if he or someone else had written it long ago and finally some director was urging the actors to get through the scene, no matter how hard it was.

He remembered Blair in her bed, surrounded by her green velvet blanket, and he could smell the jasmine that grew outside her window and he could feel the lush heat of her body and he could taste something like oranges on her skin.

He leaned into the doorway and watched Emily. She was throwing open cabinets, banging them closed, rifling through the boxes of staples in the pantry.

"How do you live here?" she asked. She started throwing boxes away—sugar, salt, flour, pancake batter.

"I don't live here," Luke told her.

She stopped what she was doing, held a bag of peanuts in her hand and faced him.

"Why did you come back to the city?" she asked gently.

"I thought I had given up on you," he told her. His voice was quiet, strange even to his own ears. "But I couldn't."

She dropped the bag of peanuts, missing the garbage, then kicked it across the floor as she walked toward him.

He opened his arms, and she fell into them.

"I'm so sorry," she said, and she let herself cry finally. He held her for a long time, and she pressed her wet face into his chest. He kept his mouth on the side of her head, close to her ear, pressed in a kiss.

• • •

Luke opened the door to the café and stood there a moment, unsure of where he was or what he was doing. Suddenly he felt drunk, as if he had stumbled through the streets of the city to get here.

A pretty waif of a woman, bare-armed and tattooed, put her hand on his arm.

"You OK?" she asked.

He stood up straighter. "Fine," he said. "Hot, that's all."

It was cold outside, the city socked in by a damp fog. She eyed him.

"You by yourself?" she asked.

He couldn't understand—why was she asking? And then he looked past her, at the dining room, and he realized she was a waitress or a hostess and was doing her job.

"I'm looking for Blair," he said.

"You the movie man?" she asked, wide-eyed.

Luke shrugged. "I guess."

"I've got your table," the woman said eagerly.

"No, I'm not eating. I just have to talk to Blair. To tell her that I can't stay for dinner."

She looked at him oddly.

"Don't screw with her," she said.

Luke closed his eyes. "I know." He opened his eyes and looked at her. She was peering at him—he had become a member of that awful species: men.

"She's cooking," the woman said.

"Can I go back there? Just for a minute."

"Daniel will kill you."

"I was warned. This will only take a minute."

"That's what they all say."

"What's your name?" Luke asked.

"Rianne. Don't hit on me."

"I'm not going to hit on you," Luke said, smiling. "You're a friend of Blair's?"

"Everyone loves Blair."

"I know," Luke said. "Or I can imagine."

"Daniel's out. If you go back now, you may survive. As long as you're not fucking with Blair."

"Thank you," Luke said.

He passed Rianne and walked through the restaurant. The place was crowded, noisy, every person at every table dressed in black or leather or both. Luke felt old and decidedly unhip. A male waiter checked him out as he passed—the guy winked when he saw him push through the door into the kitchen. Someone else who loved Blair.

She didn't look up. She was at the stove, midstir, her cheeks flushed. He thought of her body under him, his body riding over her, her eyes locked into his, paying such close attention. He turned away, thought of leaving, heard her gasp.

He looked back at her.

"You scared me," she said. "I didn't see you standing there. The ghost of Luke."

"I could stand here and watch you all night."

"I would like that," she said, smiling. Her face full of the smile.

"Keep working," he said because she was motionless, her wooden spoon dangling over the pan, the sauce in the pan beginning to bubble.

She stirred, still happy.

"I saved you a table."

"Emily came back."

She kept her head down and worked quietly. She chopped herbs and stirred them into the sauce. She tasted. She added more herbs. She moved to the next burner, turned it lower, added cream to whatever was in the pot.

Leaving Luke to say something. "Listen. Blair. I don't know what this is. I need to give it some time, maybe a couple of days."

Blair kept focused. Pepper in the pot, add some fresh basil. Taste. Move to the next burner.

"Get out of here."

"I can't just send her away. We spent ten years together. I can't make sense of this. I'm falling for you, and my wife wants—"

She looked at him. Her face was twisted in anger. "Get out of here!" she said louder.

Luke walked out. He walked past Rianne's glare. He pushed through the door of the restaurant and then stood outside, in the middle of the sidewalk, unmoving.

Now he could go home. Not to the cabin in the mountains, alone with his dog and his dark thoughts, but back to the old house at the top of Potrero Hill, with Emily waiting for him. If he had waited for this for so long—and he had, hadn't he?—then why couldn't he keep moving? Blair. He wanted to be back in her arms, in her bed, and when they finished making love, he wanted to begin again. *That isn't good enough,* Luke told himself. *All men want that.* His father went from redhead to blonde in search of that. Luke had always promised himself that he wanted something different—marriage, even if it was hard, commitment, even if it meant sacrifice. Yet he stood paralyzed on the sidewalk outside of Blair's restaurant when he was supposed to hop in his car and head home.

Blair is dying, he reminded himself. How much of a fool could he be to fall for a woman who was dying? With Emily, he had all of it, the past ten years and the next ten. Growing old together. And they could do it better now—both of them wiser for the experience of the past three months.

He started walking slowly to the Miata. He had taken Emily's car—it was easier to park. He climbed in and sat there, in the dark, without starting the car. He could smell stale cigarette smoke—Emily didn't smoke. He looked at the odometer. She had put on a lot of miles in a few months.

He didn't know anything about those months. She had asked, "Can I stay with you?" And he had answered, "Yes."

• • •

When he got home, Emily had made dinner. She had found pasta and a can of tomatoes to make a sauce. *Someone must have taught her to cook,* Luke thought.

I've gone from one woman cooking to another, he thought. And he imagined Blair cooking all night after he left, feeling the way she would feel. *How could I have left her like that?* He felt sick, his stomach twisted in knots.

He opened a bottle of wine and poured them each a glass.

He pulled out plates, forks, knives and glasses. He filled them with water, hers with no ice, and set the table, where they always sat, he by the window, she in the chair to his left. He thought of sitting down to dinner in Blair's restaurant, the waiter serving him the food she had promised. He should have stayed. He should have told Emily: "No. It's too late."

He thought of Emily setting the table for Gray Healy in Noe Valley, just a few miles away.

"You rented that house? In Noe Valley?"

"I saw you circling the other night. You're crazy."

"Is that why you're back? Any man that crazy in love is a man to hang on to?"

"No. That's not why."

"Tell me why," Luke said, finally sitting heavily in the chair. She handed him his plate of pasta.

"I don't know," Emily said.

"That's not good enough."

"It might be all I can offer you. I can tell you a million things: I got lonely; I missed you; I missed Sweetpea; I wanted our life again. I'm pregnant."

Luke looked at her. She was staring at him straight on, unsmiling. He looked down at her stomach—the cashmere sweater was long and full—he couldn't see if her belly was round.

"Whose baby?" he asked.

"Yours," she said, still looking at him.

"How do you know?"

"I wasn't sleeping with him."

"Ever?"

"Then. It's your baby."

"How do you know? Goddamn it!" Luke shouted and stood up, knocking the chair back behind him.

Emily closed her eyes and gripped the sides of her chair.

"I wasn't sleeping with him then," she said quietly. "I'm three and a half months pregnant. I left before I knew. Three months ago."

"How can I believe you?"

"You just have to. Please, Luke. Sit down."

He stepped toward her and saw her flinch again. Why the hell was she afraid of him? "I'm not going to hit you. Did Gray Healy hit you?"

"No, Gray Healy did not hit me."

Luke sat down.

"I need to know," he pleaded. "About the baby."

"Then believe me," she said.

He held her eyes. "Why did you keep it?" he asked.

"I never considered otherwise."

He had wanted a baby, their baby, and he had tried to talk her into it for years. She wasn't ready, she said. And kept saying. She was too young, she wasn't yet established in her career. She always had a reason for putting it off. Luke remembered the promise that Emily had made with her sister.

"Who got pregnant first?" Luke asked. "You or Dana?"

"She's two weeks ahead of me."

"And you're back because you decided to have this baby—and you thought you should raise it with its father?"

"No. I told you that was only one of the reasons."

"If I hadn't come looking for you, what would you have done?"

"I was ready to come back. And then you showed up. Outside my window in your green truck at four in the morning."

Luke walked away from the table. "Why don't I believe a word you say?"

"Because I hurt you," Emily said.

"And now, you're back."

"If you want me back."

"With a baby."

"Your baby."

"So you say."

"Stop it, Luke. Just believe me."

"What did you tell Gray Healy?"

"I don't have to tell Gray Healy anything. Gray and I made love every so often. We met right before I left and I liked the idea of something so casual that had nothing to do with marriage."

She sipped her water, keeping her back to Luke.

"Go on."

"I was wrong. Nothing's casual."

"I could have told you that."

"Maybe I needed to learn it on my own."

"And now what do you want?"

"I want you."

• • •

Luke heard a dog barking—in his dream? He was wrapped around Emily—or was it Blair? Was that Sweetpea? Where was he? He turned over and she stirred—it was Emily beside him in the bed;

he was home in San Francisco; the dog barked into real life—and he looked at the clock. Six twenty-five A.M.

Sweetpea barked again. But Sweetpea was at Blair's, something he hadn't yet worked out. How was he supposed to get her back?

The doorbell rang. The dog barked again. He turned on a lamp.

Emily sat up, looking at Luke as if terrified. *All of the ghosts we bring to bed with us,* Luke thought. *I'm not Gray. I'm not anyone else—was there anyone else? I'm the man who drove my truck in circles around your house.*

"I'll go see who it is," Luke said. "Go back to sleep. It's much too early."

She slipped down in the bed, sleeping immediately.

He pulled on his boxer shorts and padded downstairs. *Blair doesn't know my address,* he thought.

He looked through the door's window and saw a girl. It took him a couple of seconds to make the shift from girl to Amanda, who was staring in the window at him.

He grabbed a coat he had hung on the rack earlier in the day. Now he looked completely ridiculous, coat hanging just below his boxers, bare legs showing below the coat. He opened the door.

"Fuck you," she said.

"Amanda—"

"I knew you were awful. I knew my mother shouldn't trust you. She doesn't fall in love, you know. This isn't one of those things she does all the time. I bet you do this all the time."

"Come in and we'll talk. I'll put real clothes on."

"I have school. I don't want to talk."

"Then why are you here?"

"To bring back your dog. I wish you'd never brought your dog into our lives."

Amanda looked like some odd combination of high school girl and biker chick. She wore knee-length jeans, black boots, red hair wild around her small face, a backpack heavy with textbooks. Her tank top revealed a tattoo—ROVE—rove?

"Keep Sweetpea for a while," Luke said.

"Who's going to keep Sweetpea for a while?" Emily's voice floated down the stairs.

In an instant, Sweetpea shot past Amanda and Luke at the door and raced up the stairs, barreling into Emily. She was standing at the top of the landing, a flannel bathrobe wrapped around her. Sweetpea seemed to twirl in circles at her feet.

"I'll explain later," Luke called up to her, but she was already walking down the stairs to join them.

"Listen, Amanda," Luke said. "I'm sorry. I never meant it to be like this."

"I said I'm not interested in talking," Amanda said.

Emily arrived at their side.

"Who's this?" she asked.

"Amanda," Luke said. "The daughter of a friend. Amanda, this is Emily."

"His wife," Emily said.

"That's hot," Amanda said. "His wife."

She turned and walked away. She hefted her backpack.

"How are you getting to school?" Luke called out.

"None of your business," she called back.

"Hang on, I'll give you a ride," Luke yelled to her.

She kept walking.

"Goddamn it," Luke said.

He grabbed the truck keys at the side of the door and started out after her.

"Where are you going?" Emily called.

"I'll be back."

Luke jumped in his truck and started down the street. Amanda began to run.

Luke pulled up beside her.

"Get in," he called out the open window.

"Go away."

"Come on, Amanda. I'll take you to school."

"Someone's going to arrest you for trying to kidnap me."

"Amanda."

She stopped, and he stopped the truck beside her. She glared at him.

"Go away," she said.

"Please."

Amanda looked around, then climbed onto the seat.

"Where's the school?" Luke asked.

"Portola and O'Shaughnessy," she said.

He headed off, down the street.

"How'd you find me?" Luke asked.

"You're in the stupid phone book," Amanda said.

"How'd you get here?" Luke asked.

Amanda didn't answer. She stared straight ahead.

"You walked, didn't you? You must have woken up at four."

Amanda shrugged.

"Sweetpea's not going to be very happy," Luke said. "Never seeing you again."

"She's a dog," Amanda said.

"You need money?" Luke asked.

Amanda shot him a look.

"I'll pay you thirty bucks a day to walk Sweetpea. You take the bus from school, take her for a walk for an hour, and I drive you home."

"Why?"

"Sweetpea got attached."

Amanda didn't say anything. Luke drove. *I got attached,* he thought. *But you're not my daughter. And my wife is pregnant.* He turned on the radio to a news station.

Amanda reached over and turned the knob to a rock station, then leaned back in her seat.

"Why'd your wife come back?"

"She's pregnant," Luke said.

Amanda looked at him, surprised. "And you want the kid?"

"I don't know," Luke said. "Of course I want the kid. I don't know if I want the wife."

He knew as soon as he said it that he wanted the kid. That he'd take back the wife. That somehow they'd stumble through some new version of life together for the sake of this child. He thought about his father for a moment—and he remembered this: His father came into the garage one Sunday while Luke was making a bowl on his new lathe. His father asked what he was doing and Luke looked at him, surprised by his sudden interest. "It's really cool," he told him. "I'm not very good at it, but I'm learning how to turn a bowl."

"I'm leaving," his father said. "Marian—you met Marian on the boat that day—she and I are going to live together in Sausalito. I told your mother already."

Luke kept his hands on the warm wood and felt it breathe into his skin. After a moment or two his father turned and left.

Amanda was quiet while Luke drove. Her foot beat out the rhythm to the song.

They pulled up in front of the school. There were kids hanging out on the steps—they looked like street people, homeless, wasted.

"What's your school like?" Luke asked.

"Just like your pretty prep school," she said.

"Right."

Amanda opened the door.

"Come over at three-thirty," Luke said.

Amanda hopped out of the truck and slammed the door without looking back at Luke.

He watched her walk up the steps of the school. She didn't talk to anyone. She walked through the front doors. Luke remembered Blair, a completely different version of this girl, walking the halls of his school, not talking to a soul.

• • •

When Luke unlocked and opened the door to his house, he saw Emily sitting on the floor, Sweetpea in her lap, licking her face.

Fickle dog, Luke thought. *Choose your woman.*

"Sorry about that," Luke said.

"Who's the girl?" Emily asked.

"I told you. A friend's daughter. They got attached to Sweetpea."

"A girlfriend?"

"Someone I met a few days ago. Someone I fell for, because my wife had left me."

"And now what?"

"You tell me."

"I get to make all the decisions around here?" Emily asked.

She pushed Sweetpea off her legs and stood up.

"You're the one carrying our child," Luke said. "Your child. Someone's child."

Emily turned and walked toward the kitchen. She put a pot of water on the stove and pulled the coffee beans out of the freezer.

"Our child," she said.

Luke stood in the doorway watching her. In the middle of the night he had rested his hand on her belly, now slightly rounded. He kept his hand there for a long time, willing it to be his own.

"Or Gray Healy's."

"Fuck Gray Healy."

"That's your job."

The glass coffeepot slipped from Emily's hands and crashed to the floor.

"Don't move!" Luke shouted. Emily was barefoot—already a line of blood appeared at the top of her foot where a piece of glass landed. She stood frozen in place, glass shattered around her feet.

Luke ran to the closet and pulled out a broom. When he turned back to Emily, he saw that she was crying.

"Are you hurt badly?" he asked.

"No," she said, shaking her head.

"Scared?"

"Of you," she said.

"Why?"

"You've never been mean to me before."

"You've never left me before."

"I'm back, Luke. Can't we start from there?"

"No," he said.

He leaned down and picked up the largest shards of glass, starting with the one in her foot. It was not a deep cut, leaving only a trace of blood on her white skin. Luke touched the cut, then wrapped his hand around her thin ankle.

"I need you," he heard her say.

"Now," he said.

"Always," she said so quietly, he could barely hear her.

He stood and brushed the glass into a paper bag. "Let me clean up," he told her.

Chapter Seven

Blair left the doctor's office and stopped at the first water fountain in the clinic to swallow a Vicodin. She didn't need one, at least not for physical pain. *Psychic pain,* she thought. *I deserve a dozen.*

The doctor had suggested a very experimental form of chemotherapy. Not that it would help. Her words, not his. His words were long and complicated, but when she asked him to translate, he said she was going to die.

Fuck chemo, she said. Not in those words. She was oddly polite to the good doctor, as if good manners would get her good results. An extra year to live. Maybe he handed out years like lollipops at the end of the visit.

Well, at least he was handing out Vicodin.

She'd top it off with a scotch. There was a bar around the corner from her cottage that was open and safe. Weird guys, weirder women, but they didn't bother anyone. She didn't want to be bothered.

She walked from the clinic through the heart of the Haight. *How many people are dying here?* she wondered. *Certainly many of the homeless souls must be signing off soon. AIDS, drug overdoses, street rot.* Two well-dressed women passed her on their way into Starbucks. *Breast cancer? Crossing the street and getting hit by the bus next week?*

Who do they leave behind? Who cries for them? Who has to put together a life without them?

She thought briefly of Luke, of his body wrapped around hers in bed, and she pushed the thought away and reached in her pocket for another Vicodin. Kept it tucked in her hand to take with her first splash of scotch. Like a rabbit's foot, wrapped in her palm. *Wish me good thoughts.*

A woman with no legs begged from an open alleyway. Blair put the Vicodin in the woman's cup, smiling conspiratorially at her. She pulled another out of the bottle in her pocket for herself. She'd just have to call the doctor tomorrow. Tell him the pain is extraordinary.

"Why don't I have much pain, Doc?" she had asked.

"You will. You're lucky."

"Lucky," she had said, and he apologized.

Poor choice of words.

"I've been lucky," she told him. "In life. I've got one helluva kid."

He nodded, knowing too much. Knowing the helluva kid was going to have a helluva shitty experience. Coming soon to a theater near you.

"You'll need someone to take care of you at the end," the doctor had said. Gently.

"I can take care of myself," she had countered.

"Not then," he had explained. "No matter how tough you are."

She winced. Tough girl. A lifelong occupation. She wasn't about to give up a good thing just because the going got rough. Though she remembered the months after she was raped, when her mother quit work, though they could barely afford it, and stayed home with Blair, urging her out of bed, back to school, back to life.

"There's hospice," he told her. "Why don't you read these brochures, and we can talk about it next time."

"How soon until I can't take care of myself?"

"We don't know. We can't tell you that."

She remembered visiting a friend of Daniel's a few weeks before he died of AIDS. He was bedridden, covered with sores. She couldn't breathe in his room. He and Daniel told bad jokes for an hour while she sat beside Daniel, holding his hand, trying not to cry. Tough girl. Maybe she was never any good at being tough. Once her parents died, she just didn't have any other choice.

She thought of Luke again, his hand running along the side of her body. Who falls in love with a dead woman? She must have been a fool to let herself believe that he wanted more than good sex. To let herself want more than good sex. *Screw you, Luke Bellingham. And your dog, your movies, your sweet kisses.*

She turned the corner and beelined for the bar. One-thirty P.M. She'd join the other derelicts in a good afternoon stupor.

When she opened the door of the bar, she couldn't see a thing in all of that darkness. Then her eyes adjusted and she could make out a man huddled in the corner of one booth, too lost to notice her entrance. The bartender—a young goateed guy with eyebrow, nose and lip piercings—nodded at her and wiped the bar clean, waiting for her order.

"Scotch, double," Blair told him.

"I don't know you," he said, eyeing her.

"You now know everything you need to know. Scotch. Double," she repeated.

"I'm on it," he assured her.

She swallowed the second Vicodin with the scotch. She hated waiting for the edges to blur. She drank quickly, urging on her high.

Her high was low. *I'll turn into a maudlin drunk,* she thought. *Misty-eyed at the prospect of my own demise.* She remembered one other time she had contemplated death. After the rape, after the three men had fucked her and beaten her, they left, thinking she was dead. She had feigned unconsciousness, then found it a better place to be. Her eyes closed, her senses numb, she eventually lost time and place—but not memory. She could open her eyes and begin her life again—with a rape, with a ravaged body, with a ruptured heart. Or she could die—and surely she must have been close. As she lay there, thinking but not feeling, she felt it would be so easy to slip on over to the other side.

But somehow she opened her eyes. Bugs crawled over her bloody body. She felt nothing. She pushed herself up, found a blanket to wrap around herself, began to move slowly to find someone to help her. And as she moved, she began to feel—the pain in her limbs, in her vagina, in the center of her soul. *Why not die?* she had wondered later, for weeks, lying in her bed, unwilling to get up and get moving. *Why not?*

Amanda.

She ordered a second scotch. Double. She was seeing twos of everything: Vicodin, double scotches, women in Luke's life.

Screw his wife, too.

He'll be screwing his wife tonight, while I sleep alone.

The bartender slid a bowl of peanuts in front of her. She was suddenly ravenous. She ate handfuls of the stuff and then looked up, saw the bartender looking at her.

"I didn't eat lunch," he said. "If you want, I'll get us both a couple of sandwiches from the deli next door."

Blair shook her head. "I'm fine."

"You don't look fine."

"I'm drunk, and I'm hungry. Big deal."

"Listen. I offered to help out with the hungry part. Come to think of it, I'm helping out with the drunk part, too. Might as well let me offer a full-service operation here."

"I'm not sleeping with you," Blair said.

"Good," the guy said. She couldn't look at him—her eyes seemed to catch on his lip piercing and stay there. Was that a stud in his tongue, too? "What do you want on your sandwich?"

"Ham and cheese. Mustard. Chips if they have them."

"They have them."

The bartender picked up the phone and called in two orders. When he hung up, he poured himself a beer.

"OK," Blair said, "so you're my guardian angel. I could use one."

"What else can I do for you? I don't pay bills, so just forget about that wish."

"How many wishes do I get?"

"Only one. Make it good."

"Well, it's tricky," Blair said. "I'm gonna die. Cancer. Let's not get into it."

She checked his expression—he just listened.

"You'd think I'd want life. Long life. Kill the cancer. But, I don't know, I never counted on long life. I never counted on much of anything. I kind of floated through most of my time here on earth."

He waited, not pressing her. She drank the rest of her scotch.

"I want to take care of my daughter for the rest of her life," Blair said finally. "She doesn't need much caretaking. She's the most independent kid in the world. But I don't want her to go it alone. I want to be there. Watching from the sidelines."

"Maybe you will be," he suggested.

"You mean Heaven," she said, shaking her head. "Doesn't do it for me."

"Maybe part of you lives on—in her."

"Not good enough," Blair said.

"Maybe you've already taken care of her enough. She'll be OK for the rest of it."

Blair looked up at him, lifted her glass and clinked his beer glass.

"A wise man," she said.

The door of the bar opened, and light spilled in, surprising them. Blair looked toward the light and saw a young kid carrying a bag. He tossed it on the bar and high-fived the bartender. Then he left, and when the door closed, they were cloaked in darkness again.

"Do you do this for all your customers?" Blair asked.

"Only the really fucked-up ones," the bartender said.

Smiling, he pulled sandwiches out of the bag and placed Blair's in front of her.

"Eat," he told her. "It'll do more for you than wisdom."

"I give in," Blair said. "I'll have sex with you."

He laughed and shook his head. "You need sleep, not sex," he said.

"Luke. I need Luke," she murmured.

"Who's Luke?" he asked.

"Too late. I only get one wish."

Blair ate the sandwich, the most delicious sandwich she had ever eaten. The bartender served her a Coke, and they shared the chips. Before she left, she leaned over and kissed him lightly on the cheek.

• • •

Outside, the air was terrifyingly bright, as if the ozone had burned away. Blair found sunglasses in her backpack, and she still squinted. She walked unsteadily toward her cottage. The Vicodin was kicking in, taking her someplace softer in the world.

Casey sat outside in his lawn chair, sunbathing.

"I met an angel today," Blair told him.

"I could use an angel," Casey said. "What does she look like?"

"She's a he," Blair said. "Don't you do anything? I mean, all day. You just sit here."

"I'm a lucky guy," Casey said.

Lucky, Blair thought.

"When I die, can Amanda still live here? Can I figure out how to pay you for the next year and a half until she goes to college?"

"It's too nice a day to talk about death."

"Answer me, Casey. Can Amanda live here?"

"Yes."

"Good. Now I'm going to bed."

"Can I come?"

She looked at him. She thought of Luke; she thought of the heat of their bodies together. "Yes," she told Casey.

He followed her into the cottage.

"When are you going to die?" Casey asked. He was already undressing, dropping his clothes on the way into Blair's bedroom.

"Is there anything you care about?" Blair asked. She watched him a moment, standing in the doorway.

"Sex," he said.

"Is there anyone you care about?"

"The woman I'm having sex with."

"Is life that simple?"

"I wish it were," Casey said.

He flopped back on the bed and sprawled across Blair's bedspread in his tall, lanky glory. His penis lay languidly across his thigh.

"What happened to you, Casey?" she asked.

He ran his hand through his thinning hair. She could imagine him twenty years ago, handsome, his eyes clear, his body strong.

"You mean, how did I get so sexy?" he offered, grinning.

"Something like that."

Blair watched him. He sat up in bed, so exposed and so unselfconscious.

"I don't know. The girls love me at night. And they leave me in the morning."

"It's the girls' fault?"

"Would you want to marry me?"

"Not on your life," Blair told him.

"Exactly."

"And all you want," Blair said, moving toward him, pulling off her tank top and dropping her jeans to the floor, "is a wife."

"A wife. What a thought. I'd take a wife. As long as she loves sex," Casey said, watching Blair.

"My angel wouldn't sleep with me," Blair told him.

"Angels wouldn't be very good in bed," Casey assured her. "They're too airy, too ethereal."

"Unlike you."

"I'm made of earth and fire."

"I don't know anything about you," Blair said. "I don't know where you come from or how you live without money or who your friends are."

"You know my body," he said, smiling at her.

"What is it, Casey? Why do you love sex so much?"

She walked toward the bed, sat on the edge, rested her hand on his penis. He sighed.

"Lie down on top of me," he said. "Cover my body with your own."

She lay on top of him. He closed his eyes, and a smile spread across his face.

"Who are you imagining I am?" she asked.

He kept his eyes closed.

"You're part of me."

She pressed her body onto his.

• • •

Blair was trashed when she got to work. The Vicodin, alcohol, sex and sleep had pulled her too deep, too far from the confines of her body. Hours later, her hands were still shaky, her movements in the kitchen awkward and ungainly. She'd reach for a pot and watch her hand follow moments later. She moved to place the salt back on the shelf and watched it drop before it even reached the shelf.

"Go home," Daniel said. "You need to rest, darling."

"No," Blair told him.

"You're screwing things up. I'll take over," he insisted.

"No," she told him. She urged her fingers to wrap around the whisk. "See," she said. "I'm fine." The eggs splashed around the bowl.

"Pain?" Daniel asked.

"No!" she barked. "I can't feel a goddamn thing!" she yelled. And finally she started to cry.

"Go," Daniel said, his hands at her waist, moving her from the heart of the kitchen to a stool in the corner. "Sit here," he instructed her gently. "Cry, for Christ's sake. Scream. Yell. Just promise me you won't cook."

"I won't cook," Blair whimpered.

Daniel kissed her forehead. "Rest," he whispered. He moved into place at the stove. When Philippe entered the kitchen with an armload of dirty dishes, Daniel called out to him, "I'm cooking. Take over the front. We're through the first seating anyway."

Philippe shot a look at Blair, blew a kiss, flew back out to the dining room.

"I'm sorry," Blair murmured.

"What's up?" Daniel asked.

"Luke went back to his wife," she said.

"Oh, Christ," Daniel said. His fingers flew from pot to pan to bowl. "Luke Bellingham never left his wife. She left him."

"I know," Blair said. "I just thought—"

"You thought he fell in love with you?"

"You don't have to say it like it's impossible to imagine."

"It's impossible to imagine."

"Why?"

"Do I have to tell you?"

"Yes."

"You're odd. Your life is odd. Your daughter is odd. Your cottage is odd. Luke Bellingham lives in the center of the world and you, my dear, inhabit the fringe."

"I'm exotic."

"A belly dancer is exotic. You are odd."

"I heard you. Stop saying that."

"And, though I hate to say this, you're dying."

"There is that."

"I will love you until your last day. Isn't that enough?"

"No," Blair said, and she saw that Daniel looked at her quickly, then away. "Yes, of course. I'm a fool."

"No doubt."

Blair was quiet a moment, watching Daniel work. When he paused for a minute, he must have felt her attention because he turned and looked at her.

"What is it?" he asked.

"Luke gave me a taste of something I didn't even know existed," she said; her voice was so quiet, Daniel had to lean close to hear.

He nodded. "I know, darling."

"I could have died without knowing I was missing anything," Blair said. "But now, I know. Kind of a shame, isn't it?"

Again Daniel nodded.

"Tell me how you'll grow old," Blair said.

"This is it," Daniel said. "The restaurant. I'll grow old right here. I'll be standing here in my bathrobe stirring the sauce."

"I never imagined the rest of my life," Blair said. "How did I live like that? I have dreams for Amanda. But for myself—I don't know. I wanted to have a good day. Pretty limited, don't you think?"

"Not if the good days add up," Daniel said.

"You know what I'll miss," Blair said to Daniel's back. She waited till he turned from the stove and faced her again. "Amanda's life. That's what twists my heart."

Daniel nodded. She saw that his eyes were wet.

"Go on," she said. "Don't let the sauce burn."

"I don't need lessons from you," he said, getting busy again.

She sat quietly for a moment. And then she said, "I guess I'll miss the rest of my own life, too."

Daniel nodded, tossed mushrooms in a pan, added some herbs. In another pan he sautéed a couple of fillets of sole.

"I'll miss the rest of your life," Daniel said.

"Sweet friend," Blair said. She got up from the stool and walked over to him. She pressed a kiss into his back. "I'll go for a walk," she said, her voice stronger.

She unbuttoned her chef's jacket and tossed it onto the stool, then wandered out into the night.

• • •

Blair walked home. She trudged up the stairs of her cottage and heard music blasting from within. Hard, raunchy rock music. *Amanda,* she thought. *That's what I need. Not sex or romance or work—I need my daughter.*

She threw open the door and saw Amanda in the middle of the living-room floor, surrounded by books and notebooks. She looked up for a moment, scrunched her face and went back to whatever she was studying.

"Hello, my wonderful girl," Blair said as she walked over the mess.

"I hate physics," Amanda mumbled. "Why aren't you working?"

"I got fired."

Amanda looked up at her, horrified.

"Just for one night," Blair explained. "The doc gave me something that made my hands shake. Doesn't make for a good chef."

"What did the doctor say?"

"He said you should study physics. It will get you far in life."

"Mom."

"He said nothing. Gibberish. Meaningless drivel. Did you deliver Sweetpea to Mr. Hollywood?"

"Yes."

Blair poured herself a glass of wine and took it with her to the couch in the living room. She sat, watching her daughter in the middle of the room.

"What did he say?" she finally asked.

"Nothing."

"Amanda."

She stopped working and looked at her mother. "Tell me what the doctor said."

Blair put the wineglass down on the end table—it wobbled and the wine sloshed around in the glass. She put her hand on top of the glass, steadying it. "He said it will get worse soon."

"What does that mean?"

"Pain, I think. We might need someone here to help out."

"I can do everything."

"I know you can, sweetheart. We still might need someone from hospice to help out."

They were quiet a moment. Blair sipped her wine.

"Did you ask about other treatments? Alternative treatments."

"No, sweetheart," Blair said. "It's too late for all that."

Amanda kept her head down as if studying. But she didn't turn a page or take a note.

"How can you concentrate with the music on?" Blair asked.

"What will I do?" Amanda asked. "If you die."

"You'll stay here. I asked Casey. You'll finish school. Go to college. It's only a year and a half away."

"Am I allowed to? Live alone?" Amanda still didn't look up from her sprawl of books on the floor.

"I don't know. I don't care. No one's taking you to an orphanage, that's for sure."

"I don't like Casey," Amanda said.

"Casey won't bother you. You'll be here alone."

They were quiet a moment, with some kind of acid rock blasting from the stereo. Blair liked the music, felt somehow lost in the wail of the guitar, the pounding of the drums. She could imagine Amanda a little less alone because the cottage would be so noisy.

Blair finished her wine, wishing she were drunk. She got up, poured herself another glass, sat back down and watched Amanda stare at her books. She looked around the living room and saw the bowl of water she had put out for Sweetpea next to the front door.

"Where does he live?" Blair asked finally.

Amanda looked up at her. She rubbed her eyes and blinked at her mother, confused.

"Mr. Hollywood," Blair explained.

"Potrero Hill," Amanda said.

"Nice house?"

"No big deal."

"Did you see the wife?"

"Yeah. She's a snoot."

"A snoot?"

"Uppity bitch."

"How could you tell?"

"The hair. Bleached blond and perfect. First thing in the morning. Sweetpea ran right to her. You'd think the dog would be smarter than that. Bitch left them. Someone should hold a grudge."

"I thought you didn't want Mr. Hollywood in our life."

"I don't."

"Did he . . . you know, say anything?"

"Like: 'Tell your mother to have a nice life'?"

"Or a nice death."

"God, Mom."

"No man wants to fall in love with a woman who's dying."

Amanda didn't answer. She seemed to be working again—even jotted something down in her notebook.

"He didn't say anything, huh?"

"No, Mom. He didn't say anything."

"I can't believe it."

Again Amanda buried her head in her notebook, her pen now flying across the page.

"I mean, what was that all about?" Blair asked, her voice rising. "Mr. Hollywood tornadoes into our lives, then blows on out, leaving us trampled."

"Leaving you trampled!" Amanda shouted. She stood up in the middle of her mess on the floor, kicking books in every direction. "I don't give a shit about Mr. Hollywood. You're dying and all we're supposed to worry about is Mr. Hollywood."

She stormed past Blair and into her room, slamming the door behind her.

• • •

Blair was making dinner in the cottage the next day—a night off from work—when the phone rang. She picked it up and heard Amanda's voice through a bad connection.

"Mom?"

"Where are you?"

"I'm going to be home late."

"Are you at the café?"

"No. I went to the beach with some friends."

"What friends? What happened to the job?"

"I quit. I can't hear you. I'm on someone's cell phone."

Blair could hear a dog barking in the background.

"What beach? What friends?"

"I have friends. You don't know everything," Amanda said, and Blair remembered the fight from last night, knew that she was not yet forgiven.

"When will you be home?"

"Don't know. Eat without me."

"I don't want to eat without you. How did you get to the beach?"

"One kid has a car. I gotta go, Mom. I'll be home in an hour or something."

"What something? Amanda!"

But she had hung up. Blair dropped the phone back onto the counter. This was what most teenage daughters did—but not hers, not Amanda, with no friends, no boyfriends, no world outside her mother, her schoolwork, her jobs, her music. Blair had never worried about her daughter because she herself had been so alone in the world, especially after the rape. And Amanda didn't complain about the social world of school. She seemed to want to spend her time at home, with Blair. When Amanda was with Blair, her daughter was happy, easy, fun—something Blair herself had never experienced as a high school kid.

She'll move on from me to others, Blair had always imagined. *When she's ready.* But now, Blair was leaving her before she was ready.

Maybe Amanda had a secret life of friends and walks with dogs on the beach after school. Maybe Blair was so suffocatingly close that her daughter needed to hide her own life from her. Maybe there were never jobs—the café didn't even exist—instead there were boys and drugs and all the paraphernalia of adolescent life. Maybe even the straight A's weren't true, and Blair didn't know a thing about her daughter.

One day Amanda had come home with a tattoo on her chest, ROVE. "What is it?" she had asked.

"A word," Amanda had told her. "Just a word."

Blair hadn't pushed—she waited for Amanda to tell her more. And so the word sat there, peeking above the top of her shirt, like a constant reminder: *You don't know everything.*

Blair ate dinner alone, forcing herself to finish the pasta with pesto because the doctor said she shouldn't lose more weight, should keep up her strength, her resistance. Resist cancer? Instead, her body seemed to have embraced it like a lover who was here to stay.

She read a book and watched it get dark. She drank a scotch, then another. When Amanda walked in, Blair looked up at her, relieved and angry, all the words she had prepared lost in her confusion.

"I'm going to my room," Amanda said.

Blair didn't respond. Amanda barely looked at her. She threw her jacket on the coatrack and crossed the room. Blair heard her in the kitchen, running water. Then she heard Amanda's bedroom door open and close.

Maybe this is her way of saying good-bye, Blair thought.

Chapter Eight

Where are you going?"

"For a walk."

"Where?"

"Just a walk, Luke. I need some air."

Luke turned away from Emily and headed toward his office. He sat at his desk and stared at the computer screen.

He heard Emily follow him into the room, could sense her standing behind him. She didn't say anything, and he waited.

"Luke," she finally said. "We can't live this way."

"What way?" he asked. He didn't turn around.

"You have to trust me. A walk is just a walk."

"How do I know?"

"Because I'm telling you."

"And before?"

"It's not before. I came back to start over. Fresh."

"I'm stuck on this, Emily," Luke said, and swung around in his chair to face her. "I keep running through last year in my mind. Did you sneak out in the middle of the night while I was sleeping? Did you come back from his bed and crawl into ours? And because I don't have any answers to those questions, I can't seem to work out how we live now. Are you really going for a walk? Did you really have a meeting with a client yesterday?"

"Stop," she said. She closed her eyes.

"And then there's this," Luke said, his voice quiet but insistent. "You look like the same person who walked out of my life without a word a few months ago. Except for the baby in your belly. Does that change everything?"

"Yes," Emily said, and she finally opened her eyes. She reached out and put her fingers on Luke's lips. "That changes everything."

"For you," Luke said.

Emily's hand dropped to her side.

"When you were gone," Luke said, his voice catching in his throat, "I wanted you back every moment."

"And now?"

"I don't know anymore."

Luke spun his chair back toward his computer. Emily was quiet.

"I'm going to write now," Luke said. "You go for your walk."

"Luke," she said.

"I need to work," he told her. "It's been a long time."

He heard her leave and opened the file for the bartender story.

He heard the front door open and close. *I could go to the window and watch her,* he thought. *I could see if anyone picks her up, if anyone meets her at the corner.*

But he sat there and began to work.

• • •

"If you hired me to walk the dog," Amanda said, running ahead of Luke on the beach, then turning and walking backward while she spoke, "then why are you here? You don't need me."

"Sweetpea loves the beach. You couldn't get to the beach on foot," Luke said, digging his hands into his pockets. Next time, he would bring gloves and a hat—a cold wind whipped at them from the ocean.

"You can drop me off here and pick me up in an hour," Amanda said. She picked up a stick, turned and hurled it toward the ocean. Sweetpea tore off and almost got it, but a wave scared her and sent her scampering back to Amanda's side.

"Happy dog," Luke said.

"You didn't answer me," Amanda said.

"Right."

They walked for a while, Amanda a few steps ahead of Luke, as if they might not be together, out for a stroll with the dog.

"How's your mom?" Luke asked.

"Fine," Amanda answered quickly.

"You're lucky," Luke said.

"That she's dying?"

Luke took a deep breath. Amanda didn't look at him. "No," he said. "That she's your mom. She's great."

"How would you know?"

Luke didn't answer. He watched Sweetpea run in circles around Amanda—when Amanda almost tripped over her, the girl laughed easily, leaned over to nuzzle the dog and skipped ahead.

"You remind me of your mother when she was in high school," Luke called ahead to her. It was her solitude that reminded him of Blair back then—the girl was always alone and never seemed to be bothered by that. All the other girls in school walked from class to class in bands of three or four and lunched at tables crowded with friends.

Amanda walked backward again. "My mother said you didn't really know her."

"She was a loner. It was hard to get to know her."

"Did you try?"

"No. I wish I had. I wasn't smart enough then."

"What do you mean?"

"She was different from the other girls. She didn't play their games. She didn't flirt or tease or hide. She was something else—something beyond the rest of us."

"She was lonely."

"Did she tell you that?"

"She hated high school. She hated you. Said you were a golden boy."

Luke walked quietly for a moment. Amanda found another stick, tossed it ahead for Sweetpea to retrieve.

"You have friends in high school?" Luke asked.

"No," Amanda said, not looking at him.

"Why not?"

"They're all awful."

"All of them?"

"I like to be alone."

"You're not lonely?"

"No."

"It's just you and your mom alone in the world?"

Amanda turned around and looked at Luke, hard. "You want me to walk your dog," she said, "next time, just drop us off. OK? I don't need this."

"I'm sorry," Luke said.

They walked in silence for a while. The tide was out, leaving the beach wide and freshly stocked with seaweed and driftwood for Sweetpea to explore. The cliffs stretched above them, cordoned off because of recent erosion. And the sea eased calmly onto the sand, then back again, the deep blue reflecting the last of the day's light. Luke took deep breaths of cold air, trying to clear his head. Amanda kept a few steps ahead of him.

"Did you tell your mother you're doing this?" Luke asked after a while.

"No," she told him.

"Why not?"

Amanda rolled her eyes at him. Luke smiled.

"She hates me," he guessed.

"Bright guy."

Luke tossed an abandoned tennis ball for Sweetpea.

"Did you tell your wife you're doing this?" Amanda asked.

Luke shrugged. "Guess I forgot to mention it."

Amanda looked pleased. Sweetpea delivered the tennis ball to her, and she picked it up, heaved it far ahead of them. Sweetpea bounded toward it. Amanda ran after her and Luke followed, close behind.

• • •

Emily got up from the table to clear dishes, leaving Luke alone with Dana. He looked at her. She was dressed elegantly for this dinner, as if they were dining at the Ritz rather than her own home. And her pregnant belly protruded proudly now, draped in a tight red silk skirt.

"You responsible for her return?" Luke asked.

Dana shook her head. "No one tells Emily what to do."

"That's not true, Dana. You've always guided her. She listens to you."

Dana shrugged. She offered him a quick smile. "And you think I would tell her to go back to you?" The smile was teasing, flirtatious.

"Yes," Luke said. "I think you would tell her that."

"You're right."

"Why?" he asked. "I can't even remember if we had a good marriage anymore."

He poured more wine in his glass. He filled Dana's glass with sparkling water.

"No one has a good marriage," Dana said. "It's a myth."

"You don't believe that." Luke leaned back, sipping his wine, eyeing his sister-in-law. Brady was in the other room, taking a business call on a Saturday night.

"Right now, I believe that. I'm pregnant and hot and my ankles are so swollen I can't walk."

"You look beautiful."

"That's all that matters, isn't it?"

"No," Luke said. "Maybe that's the problem with my marriage. We look sensational, don't we?"

"Do it differently now," Dana said. "Start over."

"Whose baby is it?"

"Oh, God, Luke." Dana stood up and headed toward the kitchen.

"Dana," Luke called out, stopping her.

"You can make yourself miserable," she said. "Or you can get back to your life with my sister."

"Do you know him?"

"I'm getting dessert." She walked through the door into the kitchen.

In her place Brady appeared, his face flushed from too much wine.

"Sorry, pal," he said, slipping into Dana's seat. "Had to take a business call. Got a real estate deal about to break. You know."

Luke didn't know. He didn't care but knew that Brady was about to tell him everything about this deal.

"Brady," Luke said, beating him to it. "You know this guy—Gray Healy?"

"Yeah," Brady said. "Squash buddy of mine. Whips my ass every time."

"You set him up with my wife?"

"What?"

Dana stood in the doorway, hands on hips.

"He doesn't know anything, Luke. Why tell the world?"

"I'm not talking about the world," Luke said. "I'm talking about me. The husband. I'd like to know a thing or two about my wife's lover. So, he plays killer squash. What else can you tell me, pal?"

Emily barged through the room, pushing past her sister in the doorway.

"Stop! Luke! Stop, goddamn it."

She moved around the table to Luke's side. She looked wild—her hair flew out behind her and tears streamed down her cheeks. Luke felt shame, felt it like a rock in his gut. He looked at her belly, round and full, taut against the fitted dress she wore. He leaned forward and pressed his face into her belly. She put her hands on his head, and he could hear her release her breath as if she had been holding it for too long. He reached his arms around her back, turned his head to the side and felt his cheek push into her belly.

"Emily," he whispered.

She held him. Behind her, he saw Dana gesture for Brady to get off his ass and get out of there. The two of them disappeared into the kitchen.

"Take me home," Emily whispered, her wet face on his neck.

They left without saying good-bye, without explaining or apologizing. Dana and Brady were hidden in the kitchen. They drove quietly through the streets of the city. At one point Luke reached out and took Emily's hand—she gripped and hung on.

At home they made love for the first time since she returned. Luke was gentle, slow, careful of her belly. He tried to move her onto her side so he wouldn't have to climb on top of her.

"No," she said. "I want to feel you. All of you." And she pulled him on top of her.

When he entered her, she began to guide him with her hands on his hips, urging him deeper, harder, faster.

"I don't want to hurt you," he whispered.

"You can't hurt me," she said, and he looked at her, surprised to see how dark she looked, how raw.

"What do you want?" he asked.

"I want to feel you," she said again. He had never heard her say this before. Was it something she said with Gray? Was he rougher than Luke? Was sex bigger, wilder with him?

Luke stopped moving for a moment, watching Emily.

"Don't stop," she gasped. "Keep going." She sounded panicked, her voice desperate.

"Emily," he said, and she looked at him. In a moment her eyes softened and she pressed him to her.

"Roll over," she whispered.

He did and she climbed on top, began to move over him, back and forth, her breasts rubbing against his chest. He watched her face—she had her eyes closed, a determined look on her face. Didn't they used to watch each other, eyes open, while making love?

He thought of Blair. No, it was Blair who surprised him by locking her gaze on him, so intense, so open, through all of their lovemaking.

If he was thinking of Blair, was she thinking of Gray?

He watched her come, watched her body arch and writhe, watched the smile spread across her face as she looked at him.

"Your turn," she said, kissing him on the chest.

• • •

This time Luke drove Amanda into the Santa Cruz Mountains, toward his cabin, to a trail he had taken once before in the middle of the redwoods.

"Can you stay out a couple of hours?" Luke asked.

"Sure," Amanda said.

"You want to call your mom?"

"No."

"She won't be waiting for you?"

"She works tonight. Besides, I'm a big girl."

They parked the car at the trailhead and watched Sweetpea bound ahead of them to the beginning of the trail.

"Sweetpea's been here before?" Amanda asked.

"I lived near here for a few months. After my wife left."

"Right. The hermit act."

Luke smiled.

Amanda ran after Sweetpea, and they disappeared into the woods. Luke grabbed a couple of water bottles and started after them.

The woods were thick and damp—Luke loved the rich smell and felt a pang of regret for leaving his cabin for life in the city. When he lived here, he walked every day, sometimes getting lost in these forests for hours. He knew he had been miserable then—drunk half the time, hungover the other half, mopey and mean. So why would he yearn for it again? He had Emily back; he was writing again. Still, he missed his woodworking, his walks. He missed something else—but he couldn't quite name it.

He caught up with Amanda, and they walked single file along the narrow trail.

They passed a grove of redwood trees and Luke called out, "Take a look at these."

Amanda stopped on the path and looked, leaning back, scanning up the long lengths of the trees to the sky.

"You see how these are grouped in a circle?" he asked.

She looked, nodding. The towering trees formed a circle, about five feet across, with nothing in the center. "Cool," Amanda said. "How'd that happen?"

"It's said that redwoods never die. If you cut one down, that trunk is gone forever and nothing grows where it stood. But out of the roots that have spread away from the base of the old tree, new trees begin to grow and become redwoods once again."

"It's like they're holding hands," Amanda said. "In a circle."

"Some people call them cathedrals," Luke explained. "From inside the circle of trees you can look up and see the heavens."

He was going to step between two of the trees and show her, but Amanda was already moving on, down the path. *I'm acting like a teacher,* he thought. *Very uncool.*

They walked in silence for a while, Luke close behind Amanda.

"How's school?" he asked.

"Just terrific," she said. "How's marriage?"

"Dandy," he told her.

She looked back at him. He grinned at her, and she rolled her eyes.

"You know what I hate?" she said. "Boys."

"All boys?"

"All boys. They're stupid."

"True," Luke said.

"You're one of them."

"When boys grow up, some of them get less stupid."

"Did you?"

"Probably not."

"You got that right," Amanda said.

Luke smiled again. He walked fast to keep up with her. She was fit, though he didn't think she played any sports or got very much exercise. She had her mother's body, small and lean. *What did her father look like? Did she wonder? When Emily's baby is born, will it look like me?* Luke wondered. *Or Gray Healy?*

Amanda's red hair was pulled into a ponytail, and it bobbed as she walked. Little-girl-like. But she was no little girl.

"Tell me about boys," Luke said.

"They hang around you and say dumb things, and they think that's supposed to make you like them."

"Have you had a boyfriend?"

"No. Yes."

They walked quietly for a while, and Luke waited for her to figure it out.

"Don't tell my mother."

"I don't see your mother."

"Yeah, right."

Again she was quiet. The woods closed in on them, making Luke feel safe, protected somehow. He liked talking like this, without facing each other. It felt something like therapy. You could say anything.

"Last year I went to a party," Amanda said. "I don't usually go to parties, but my lab partner in chemistry talked me into it. There was a guy there who I thought was cool. Not really good-looking. But there was something about him. You know."

Luke smiled. "I know."

"Anyway. We talked for a while, and he seemed different from other boys. He talked about real things—like we were figuring out why religion was so bogus, because it told people what to think instead of letting people find out on their own what they thought."

"Cool," Luke said. He wanted her to keep talking, and every time she paused, he thought he'd lost her again. But she was talking into the trees ahead of her, and his response or lack of response didn't seem to matter.

"We drank a beer, maybe two. Then we went up to the roof of the apartment, which was on Russian Hill—we had an amazing view of the lights of the city. I felt—I don't know—on top of the whole world. Like the stars were below me, and I was watching the universe."

She must have been remembering, because she didn't say anything again for a while, and Luke left her alone with her thoughts. They came to an opening in the forest and started across a meadow. The grasses were waist high—taller than Sweetpea, who was somewhere ahead of Amanda. Amanda walked with her arms open wide, skimming the tops of the grasses.

She didn't speak again till they reentered the dark womb of the forest, until the world closed in on them again.

"Tony told me to take off my clothes so he could look at me. I had never done that before. But I wanted to. It's crazy. Something about our conversation and the beer and being on top of the stars—it made me feel different, like I wasn't Amanda but some other girl, a wild girl. So I took off my clothes, piece by piece, while he watched me."

Luke was scared then, knew that this story would end badly, knew that she was telling him for some reason, and that he could fail her. She hadn't told her mother, didn't have a father. He knew this wasn't something she talked about with any of the kids at school, kids she had dismissed as being awful.

"He told me to lie down on an army blanket we found up there. Or maybe he had put the army blanket up there earlier, knowing that he'd do this."

Don't fuck her, Luke begged silently. *Don't fuck her. Don't humiliate her.* He had an odd thought as he waited for her to go on: *Emily will give birth to a girl, and some years from now, my daughter will be up on the roof with Tony.*

"I lay on the blanket, on my back, staring up at the stars. There were stars below me, stars above me. I felt dizzy, lost, like I was in some unreal world. I waited for him. He stood above me, looking at me, not saying anything. I said, 'Tony?' And he said, 'Shh.' I didn't really want to look at him, so I kept looking at the stars. I was scared. But kind of excited. I mean, I didn't really want to be a virgin anymore."

Luke slowed down as she slowed her pace. They were climbing the mountain now, and her breath was heavy. He took a drink of water but didn't offer her any. He didn't want to break the trance he felt—it was as if she had forgotten about him behind her and she was telling her story to no one.

"Finally he lay down next to me. He had taken off his clothes and his skin was like silk. I had never felt anything like it. He touched me all over, and he let me touch him, and then he taught me to make love."

Luke closed his eyes with relief—she deserved this. His own first time had been drunk and sloppy—this seemed almost magical. Good for her.

"Then he got up and left. And when I went downstairs, he was gone. He never talked to me again. At school he pretended he didn't know me—walked right by as if I were a stranger."

Luke felt it like a punch in the gut. He had an insane wish to wallop Tony. And he couldn't imagine what to say to the girl who walked in front of him, her pace even slower now, as if she had lost her energy in telling this story.

"I'm sorry," he finally said.

She swung around and faced him. "Why?"

"I'm sorry that happened to you."

She shrugged. "Lost my virginity. No big deal."

"It is a big deal, Amanda," Luke said. "And he's an asshole."

She turned again, kept walking.

"Do you want water?" Luke asked.

She shook her head. He followed her in silence.

"Take the left fork ahead," Luke told her. "That trail will swing around and bring us back to the truck."

They hiked for a long time without talking, now descending the mountain. When they reached the truck, Amanda climbed into the front seat, not looking at Luke.

Luke got into the driver's seat. Amanda turned her face away.

"Not all guys are like that," Luke said before he started the truck.

"I shouldn't have told you."

"I'm glad you told me."

"Then drop it."

Luke started driving. Amanda stared out her window, away from Luke's gaze. They drove through the mountains and back out to the freeway to head toward the city.

"Do you think I did that to your mother?" Luke finally asked.

Amanda didn't answer.

• • •

Luke entered the waiting room of the clinic, expecting to find Emily alone, waiting for her appointment. But there were dozens of women in the room, some of them hugely pregnant, all of them turning to look at him. He was the only guy in the room—where were the other husbands?

Finally he saw Emily, tucked into an armchair with a magazine on her lap, looking distinctly unhappy to see him.

He walked to her side, crouched by the chair.

"I wanted to surprise you," he said. "Meet your doctor. Listen to the heartbeat."

She didn't say anything for a moment.

"I'll be waiting forever," she finally offered.

"And I'll keep you company."

"You don't have to," Emily said.

"I know that."

"Go home and work. You'll have plenty of chances to see the doc measure my belly."

"I want to stay," Luke insisted.

"It's a bore."

"I want to meet your doctor."

"It might not even be Dr. Lewis. Sometimes it's someone else in the clinic."

"Give it up, Emily."

"I just hate taking your time."

He looked up, and all the other faces looked away. Was this such private territory that none of the husbands shared the experience? He had had an image in his mind, only seconds before he entered the clinic, of happy couples, hand in hand, being blessed by a beatific doctor who rubbed the wife's belly and pronounced the baby healthy. Instead, his wife seemed angry, and the other women glared at him, the intruder.

He stood, walked to the magazine rack, picked a copy of *Newsweek* and pulled a chair up next to Emily's.

"I thought you'd be pleased," he said quietly.

"I am," she told him.

He looked at her and saw the effort of a smile.

Luke reached for her hand. "I'm trying," he said. "To start over."

"I know."

"This is a way to do that."

"Jeez, girl," a woman in the chair next to Emily called out. "My man showed up here, I'd have a goddamn heart attack."

A few of the women snickered.

Emily leaned over and kissed Luke.

The woman whistled. "Honey, you can come to my appointment, too, if you want."

Luke smiled at her and shook his head. "One belly's enough for me," he said.

A voice boomed out: "Emily Peck."

Emily and Luke both jumped to their feet. Luke let Emily head to the door, and he followed her.

The nurse led them down a long hallway and into a small room.

"My husband wants to be here for the appointment," Emily said.

"Of course," the nurse said. "Why don't you take that chair." She gestured to the stool in the corner, and Luke perched there. "I'll take some information," she said, turning to Emily. "Why don't you sit right here."

Emily sat on the edge of the examining table. The nurse opened a file and looked at it. "Week fourteen. We'll wait till the next visit for your triple screen test. It's a preliminary test to determine the risks of Down's syndrome and spina bifida—Dr. Lewis will explain those in greater detail."

She pulled out the equipment to take Emily's blood pressure.

Luke began calculating. He was sitting behind Emily and couldn't see her expression, but he saw the slight hitch in her shoulders when the nurse began speaking. Week fourteen.

Emily walked out on Luke during the screening of *The Geography of Love.* November 27. Four months ago. She had told him she was sixteen weeks pregnant. That she must have gotten pregnant the last week before she left. Maybe that's why she behaved so irrationally. Hormones raging.

Week fourteen. He had already found his cabin in the woods. He had already given up looking for her, waiting for her.

She had called Gray Healy last April, during their ski trip. "I'm coming home." To Gray Healy, squash king. Father of Emily's child.

The nurse walked out, handing Emily a robe. She changed into it, her back to Luke, as if she were a modest, shy, virginal bride.

Awaiting her husband.

Who was silent, still calculating. Sixteen weeks since she had walked out of the screening. He had found the note on the refrigerator. Had she known she was going to leave when they drove to the screening or had she come home from the theater, posted the note under the penguin magnet and then dashed off to Gray Healy?

And a house in Noe Valley. Where Mr. Healy met her, spent days with her instead of going to work, calling home to tell his wife: "The meeting's running late, very late, don't wait up."

Emily sat on the examining table without turning around, without saying a word.

They waited for the doctor. Luke kept calculating.

How long until Emily would have told him: "The due date is wrong"? Or would she claim to be two weeks early, something so common no husband would start counting days?

Days when she made love with Gray Healy and stopped using her diaphragm.

The door opened, and a huge man stepped into the room, filling the space. *I thought doctors were thin, fit, healthy,* Luke thought, hating this man.

"Miss Peck."

"This is my husband, Luke Bellingham."

The man reached behind Emily with a bear paw, engulfing Luke's hand in it.

"Proud papa," the doc said.

Luke didn't answer.

"So how are we feeling?" the man asked, unbearably jolly, a Santa Claus of a doctor.

"We're confused," Luke said, and again he saw Emily's shoulders stiffen. She didn't turn around. "About the way you calculate weeks of pregnancy."

The doctor raised his thick eyebrows, glanced quickly at Emily, who faced forward, away from Luke.

"We just want to get clear on this," Luke said, his voice too loud in the crowded room. "Emily gets pregnant. Say November twenty-sixth. Or maybe November twenty-fifth, since I was up late working the night before the screening, the night before she left me."

"Stop," Emily said.

"Calculations. What are they? Numbers?" Luke asked. "Silly things. And yet, bear with me, Doctor. I need this."

"Yes," the good doctor said. He must have known now, what was coming. He sat heavily in a chair. He watched Emily, though she wasn't talking, and Luke couldn't seem to stop talking.

"We make love on November twenty-fifth. Hard to remember exactly, but there's a good chance we made love that night. We made love often in those days before Emily left me."

"Luke," she said.

"I'll get to the point," he told the doctor. "So, sex. She used a diaphragm but they're only—what?—ninety-nine percent effective? But those aren't the numbers I'm concerned with here, Doctor. It's how you calculate weeks. If the sperm does its deed, is she pregnant immediately? Day one and counting? Or do you give the sperm and egg a couple of weeks to hang out together, get used to each other, before you start counting days, weeks? Tell me, Doctor. How does that work?"

"We count from the day of her last menstrual cycle. Week one of forty weeks."

"So what you're saying is that would add a week or two."

The doctor eyed Emily, who looked straight ahead at the wall, at a poster on the wall. YOUR DEVELOPING BABY. Studying it for answers to his questions? Hoping he'd disappear from sight, and she could get on with the business of developing baby?

"And the good nurse said that my wife is fourteen weeks pregnant. Do you have a calendar, Doctor?"

"No, Mr. Bellingham."

"Because I'm having trouble with these numbers."

"Please leave, Luke," Emily said.

Luke stood up and felt light-headed, ready to faint. He closed his eyes for a moment, gaining his equilibrium.

"I'd like to speak with Emily alone," the doctor said.

"It might be a good idea," Luke told him. "Find out if a different proud papa might want to wait by her side in this fucking clinic."

"Luke," she said.

Luke squeezed past the doctor and pushed the door open, needing air, space to move, distance from his wife.

He moved down the hallway and out into the waiting room. All of the women looked at him—*They all know,* he thought absurdly. *The whole fucking world knows.* He kept going, through the waiting room and out of the clinic.

He found his truck in the parking lot, pulled out, started driving through the streets of the city, driving for hours, counting days.

• • •

Sweetpea leaped at him when he walked through the door.

"Damn," Luke muttered. "Amanda."

He was supposed to pick her up from school an hour ago, head to the beach with her and Sweetpea. Now Sweetpea was mad—he could only imagine how Amanda was feeling. Ditched, as she would have expected.

He couldn't call her, couldn't risk her mother answering the phone.

Though he'd love to talk to Blair right now, to sit with her in her impossibly small cottage and share a bottle of wine. Tell her: "I'm sorry. The days don't count out right. Take me back."

Back? He had never been there for the taking. He had just had a vision of something before it had disappeared.

The phone rang. He didn't want to answer, didn't want Emily to tell him some new version of mathematics that would make the weeks multiply, add, divide, subtract.

He ignored the phone, counting rings, and went to find a bottle of bourbon.

Sweetpea sulked. The phone stopped ringing, then rang again. He drank his first bourbon, standing in the kitchen, staring at the refrigerator. Imagining the note he would leave under the penguin magnet: *I can't raise someone else's baby. I can't love someone else's woman. I can't say good-bye.*

A taste of her own medicine. A note to rip your heart out.

He poured the second bourbon, and again the phone rang. This time he picked it up, feeling mellow, bourbon and unwritten notes easing the fury in his mind.

"Hello?"

"Luke, it's Amanda."

"God, I'm sorry."

"My mom's unconscious. I called nine-one-one. They're sending an ambulance. I'm scared—"

"I'll be right there."

"I hear the ambulance. Oh, my God. They're here."

"Go with her. I'll meet you there. UCSF?"

But she had hung up the phone.

He dashed out of the house and into the truck. He drove wildly through the streets of the city—now clearheaded, when he had just spent hours driving in a daze. He was angry that he hadn't answered the phone earlier, angry that he was with Emily at the clinic instead of with Amanda. Instead of with Blair.

He hadn't quite gotten the idea of Blair dying—it was something else that had made her exotic. She didn't wear her death in any way he could see, smell, feel. Even the time she had passed out at work and he had taken her to the hospital, he had felt somehow that he had taken care of the problem and she was getting better now. Male pride, male foolishness. She was dying. She never said it any other way.

He pulled into the hospital parking lot and rushed to admissions. They sent him to the ninth floor, and he found Amanda standing outside her door.

He put his arms around the girl, and she let him hold her.

She pulled away finally and wiped at her face with her sleeve.

"The doc's in there now," she explained. "She's conscious. She was out for a while, though. I was waiting for you. I should have gone home right away. I thought you'd show up. I didn't go home until late and she might have been unconscious all that time."

Luke pulled her to him again. "I'm sorry," he whispered, holding her, his head resting on hers.

The door opened and the doctor appeared. This one was thin and fit, clean-cut and doctorlike.

"You her husband?" he asked Luke.

"No," Luke said. "A friend."

"She OK?" Amanda asked.

"We'll have to take some tests," he said. "Her oncologist has been called. She's awake now. Resting."

"Can we go in?" Luke asked.

The doctor nodded and let them pass.

Amanda stepped in front of Luke, pushing through the door. Luke hesitated before entering the room.

Blair looked tiny under the sheets, girl-like and waifish, a woman who might really be dying. Her face was pale, and her eyes seemed sunken in their sockets. She had a bandage above her eye and her face looked bruised. Luke swallowed and could taste something metallic in his throat.

Blair looked at Luke, surprised, then immediately angry.

"I called him," Amanda said. "I was scared."

Blair nodded weakly. Her anger seemed to have passed in an instant.

Luke could hear something humming in the room. A pale green curtain closed off another patient—perhaps she was hooked up to something? The room smelled of ammonia and something else—Luke looked around. Flowers. The roommate had lined the window by the wall with vases of flowers.

Luke walked to the side of Blair's bed and gently put his hand on her wrist.

"How are you feeling?"

"Dandy," she said. "Wanna go dancing?"

"I'll give you a half hour to get ready."

"No problem."

Amanda looked alarmed. Luke smiled at her. "She's not going anywhere," he assured her.

"What did the doctor say?" she asked her mom.

Blair shrugged. "Why is it that everyone's an expert and no one knows a goddamn thing?"

"I'm sorry I didn't come home," Amanda said quietly.

"She's got a private life now," Blair told Luke.

"Mom."

Blair turned to Luke. "I think she has a boyfriend. With a car."

"Mom."

"It's a good thing, Amanda."

"If I had been home, I would have found you earlier."

"I was just napping. You make too much of a fuss."

"Next time you take a nap," Luke said, "lie down first. Easier on your head."

Blair put her hand to her bruised face and winced. "You're right," she said.

"Why'd you call him?" Blair asked Amanda.

"I told you. I was scared."

"But why him?"

"I don't know."

"I won't stay long," Luke said.

"Good," Blair told him.

"I walk his dog after school," Amanda said. "We both walk his dog."

Blair looked from Luke to Amanda and back again. Amanda was perched by the window, staring outside.

"He's the boyfriend?" Blair asked.

"No!" both Amanda and Luke said.

"I don't have a boyfriend."

"I hired her," Luke said.

"You hired her?"

"To walk Sweetpea."

"To walk Sweetpea?"

"Mom. Drop it. OK?"

"You're the boyfriend with the car."

"He's not my boyfriend," Amanda said, disgusted. "I'm the dog walker. Mom, this isn't so difficult."

"Well, I'm having trouble with this," Blair said. "This guy appears in my life, disappears in my life, reappears in my life, and my daughter's his dog walker?"

Luke smiled. "You're pretty fast," he said.

"And you couldn't tell me who you were sneaking off with after school."

"I wasn't sneaking off."

"But you couldn't tell me."

"You would have been mad."

"You're right."

"It doesn't make a lot of sense," Luke admitted.

"Try."

"I couldn't let go."

"Of my daughter."

"Of either of you."

"So you took walks on the beach with my daughter."

"Sometimes we went into the mountains," Amanda said. "It's beautiful there."

Blair closed her eyes. They were all quiet for a moment.

"How's your wife?" she finally said.

"I made a mistake," Luke told her.

• • •

Luke drove home to get Sweetpea and his laptop. He would leave Emily that note on the refrigerator, go back to his cabin in the woods. Maybe Blair would let him visit.

To his surprise, Emily was home, making dinner, waiting for him. He had imagined her in the house in Noe Valley, waiting for the proud papa.

She looked up when he walked into the kitchen. She stopped what she was doing—stirring something in a pot—and he saw her eyes catch his, look away; then she was stirring again, busy at the stove.

"I'm leaving," he said.

"Don't."

"I'm going back to the cabin."

"Please, Luke."

"Don't explain anything, Emily. It was so much easier when you just disappeared."

She picked up the glass of water on the table and sipped from it.

"Stay for dinner," she said. "Stay long enough for us to talk."

"No," he told her.

He turned from the room and headed up into his study. He packed his laptop into a briefcase.

He stopped in his bedroom, looked at the rumpled sheets, remembered making love with Emily the night before. He thought about Blair, a different Blair than the one he had made love to, now so tiny in her hospital bed. Suddenly Emily appeared at his side, standing in the doorway with him.

"I don't want Gray Healy here," Luke said. "We'll sell the house."

"Gray Healy will never come here," Emily told him.

"Will you stay here?"

"Yes. If I can."

"And the house in Noe Valley?"

"The lease ends this month. I'll move out."

"Where's Mr. Healy?"

"With his wife."

"Does he have other children?"

"No."

"Will he raise yours?"

She turned and walked away.

Luke entered the room, threw a sweater and an extra pair of jeans into the briefcase. He could leave all the rest—he had done it before. He didn't need much in the woods.

He headed down the stairs, toward the front door. Sweetpea waited for him there.

"Good-bye, Luke," Emily said. She was standing in the hallway, one hand on her belly.

He stopped and looked at her.

"Why couldn't you say good-bye the first time?" he asked.

"I'm not as brave as you are," she told him.

"I'm not brave," he replied. "I'm terrified."

"You could stay," she said.

He shook his head. He waited a moment longer, then turned and let Sweetpea lead the way out of the house.

• • •

The cabin was cold and dusty, and the garbage that Luke had forgotten to put out when he left weeks before smelled awful. But Sweetpea ran around the place like she had returned to her castle.

He cleaned the cabin, knowing that if he slept in the stink, he'd wake up feeling even more miserable than he did now. He set up his laptop, determined that this time he'd keep writing, without his muse.

When the cabin was clean, he walked out to his shop. He saw the table he had been working on and admired his work. He'd keep building furniture—there was something solid and real about it, as opposed to building stories based on flimsy words, characters he invented, plots he dreamed up. He wanted the result of his work to be something to sit on, something to eat on, something that lasted.

The night was cold, clear. Sweetpea scampered around his legs, excited to have the fresh smells to explore again. Luke looked at the sky, thick with stars, and breathed deeply. With his exhale he felt a strangled sigh escape from somewhere deep inside him.

Sweetpea began to whimper.

"I'm OK, girl. Just a little crazy after all these years."

He scooted down to pet Sweetpea, who fell to the ground and offered her belly.

"Come on, girl. Too cold out here."

He led the way inside, grabbing some logs for the fireplace. The cabin was warming up with the help of the space heater. Luke started a fire and chose a book to read, a Raymond Chandler mystery he had read before. He wanted no surprises.

He dropped into the old armchair and felt the fit like a pair of worn jeans. *I belong here,* Luke thought. *The hermit act.*

He thought of Amanda. He needed to tell them he was gone. He needed to say good-bye. He didn't look at the clock. He picked up the phone and dialed Blair's number.

Chapter Nine

You're home already," Luke said.

"I hate the hospital," Blair told him. She was lying in bed, wide-awake, and when the phone rang, she jumped on it. "I told them I'd come back tomorrow for tests. Amanda is not allowed to drag me to the hospital again."

"Amanda did the right thing," Luke said.

"By calling you?"

"That too."

"You want to save me."

"No, Blair. I know I can't do that."

"You do. You wrote a movie about the boy who should have saved me. And now you want that chance."

"No."

"I didn't need saving then, Luke. And I don't need saving now. That's your fantasy, not mine."

Luke didn't say anything for a moment. She could hear him breathing.

"Where are you?" Blair asked.

"Back in the mountains. At my cabin."

"You left your wife?"

"Yes."

"You doing OK?"

"OK would be a stretch."

"You want company?"

"Here?"

"I could take a drive. See the hermit in his lair."

"My god, Blair. I would love that."

"How long does it take to get to you?"

"An hour. Maybe less. Do you want to wait till morning?"

"No. I want to come now. I can't sleep. I'll leave Amanda a note."

"Wait. You passed out today. You just left the hospital. You can't drive out here now."

"Why the hell not?"

Luke didn't say anything.

Blair was already up, out of bed, moving around her room. She found a pair of sweatpants at the foot of her bed and pulled them on while anchoring the phone at her ear.

"Let me come get you in the morning," Luke said.

"I'm coming now. Just give me the address, some kind of directions. Your phone number, too. I drove to Woodside once and was lost for days."

She pulled on a denim shirt, slipped her feet into a pair of clogs. At her desk she grabbed a pen and paper.

"Go on," she said. "I'm ready."

"Blair—"

"Oh, don't get protective on me," she said. "I don't need that."

"What do you need?"

"I need to forget that I'm dying. You're good for that. If I remember correctly. And right now, all I can think about is that damn hospital and seeing my daughter's face when I came to and the fact that Dr. Hotshot Oncologist can't stop what's happening to me."

"OK," Luke said, and Blair took a deep breath.

"Directions," she reminded him.

He gave her the directions. She hung up, then scrawled a note to Amanda.

I'm going to visit Mr. Hollywood in the holly woods. I'll be back tomorrow. Call me there before you leave for school. His number is 650-555-9087. Stop worrying about me. Love you, Mom.

She put the note under Amanda's door, grabbed her backpack, headed out into the night. Casey's car waited for her in the driveway, the keys under the mat. He never used the thing—he certainly wouldn't miss it for a night.

She was glad to be driving, glad to have something to do, something to concentrate on. She had returned from the hospital with a worried and demanding daughter: "You can't leave; they didn't find out what's wrong with you." And when Blair said, "I know what's wrong with me. I'm dying. And I'd rather do it in my own living room, with a glass of wine and an old movie to watch," Amanda then sulked for the rest of the night. She went to her room early, not talking to her mother. But then again, she hadn't been talking to her for a couple of weeks. Since she had started sneaking off with Mr. Hollywood.

It was Blair's turn to sneak off with Mr. Hollywood. When he called, she had been thinking about him, about his sweet smile looking down at her in her hospital bed. He was sexy, and she wanted sex. Booze and sex. He was good for both. And she could get in her car, leave him in the morning, and not have to see him ever again.

She turned off the freeway and headed west into the mountains. The road was ridiculously curved, banking left, right. She could see the lights of Silicon Valley below, winking at her around every hairpin turn. She felt light-headed; but instead of the fear that gripped at her when she came to consciousness in the ambulance and while she was wheeled around at the hospital, she now felt free.

Free to have sex with Luke Bellingham. She would have fun tonight, leave him tomorrow.

• • •

She pulled into the long driveway and saw Sweetpea in her headlights. The dog danced from side to side, as if she knew the car, knew who was coming, knew that Blair liked her better than she liked Luke anyway.

She stopped the car at the end of the driveway, opened the door and let the dog nuzzle her for a few moments.

"OK. Take me to your master," she told Sweetpea.

"The master never gets such good treatment." Luke's voice came out of the darkness on the other side of the car.

"Where the hell am I?" Blair asked. "I've been driving for hours."

"We're close to Skyline," Luke said, and came to her side. "A quarter mile from the ridge. Head down on the other side and you get to the beach."

"Anyone else live out here?" she asked.

"Not many of us loonies," he told her. "Come on in. I've got a fire going."

He hadn't touched her. He was cautious—she could sense that right away. And something about him seemed different.

When she entered the cabin, she saw right away that this was Luke's true home. He belonged here. His cabin was cozy, warm—old furniture in dark wood and pale fabrics, fire lighting everything in a rosy glow. She had not seen his house in the city, but she couldn't imagine him anywhere but here. She saw the overstuffed chair, the stack of books on the floor, the line of candles on the fireplace mantel.

"Nice," she said.

He nodded, smiling.

"You look better, too," she said. He moved easier in this place.

"Drink?"

"Yes. Please."

"Scotch."

She nodded, wandering around the room, letting her hand slide over the small table where he had set up his laptop.

"Did you make this?"

"Yes. I'll show you my workshop in the morning. I had a ramshackle shed behind my house in the city that I set up as a kind of woodworking space. Escaped to it when I couldn't write. Out here, I've set up a real shop."

She checked out the mini-kitchen, saw the good cookware, the shelf of staples: brown sugar, pasta, rice, flour.

"You cook?"

"Not well. Maybe you'll make us dinner sometime."

"I'm off duty," she said.

"I didn't mean—"

"This isn't a regular thing," she said, turning toward the fireplace, scooting down and warming her hands in front of the fire.

"I know—"

"Just tonight."

"Here you go," he said, and she stood, taking the drink he offered. She looked at him, saw that half smile, the cocky boy/vulnerable man, breathed easier. Clinked his glass.

"Have a seat," he said, offering the armchair. He pulled the ottoman away and sat on that.

She settled in. "I'll never get out of this chair. This is a wonderful chair."

"I know. I've slept there a few too many nights."

"Why did you ever leave this place?" she asked.

"To find you," he said.

She rolled her eyes.

"I got back here tonight," he said, and he looked away from her, stared into the fire, "and I thought, good, I've left Emily. I'm glad to be here and not in the city, not in my house, not in my marriage. But instead of feeling happy, I felt incredibly lonely. I lived here for three months before and I never felt lonely."

"You'll get used to it again."

"No. I was lonely for you. I have been ever since I met you."

"That's crazy."

"I'm good at crazy," Luke said, smiling.

"Maybe you're just ready to start dating again."

"Dating? I don't think so, Blair."

"You forget. I'm not someone you should get used to having around."

"I can't forget that," he said.

Luke leaned forward and reached his hand out, stroking Blair's face. She closed her eyes. Somehow she felt his hand on her skin as if it touched her deep within her body.

"How 'bout we go for a one-night stand? That's kind of what I had in mind," she said softly.

He smiled.

"I'm serious," she said.

"I know you are," he said. "And you think I'm the one who's crazy."

"What's wrong with that concept? You need to forget your wife. I need to forget my illness. We're made for each other. We'll kiss good-bye in the morning."

"OK," Luke said, a huge smile spread across his face. "We'll do that."

He pulled her toward him and took her face in his hands.

"But I haven't kissed you hello yet," he said.

He kissed her, and kept kissing her. She opened her mouth and felt his tongue move through it as if he were exploring her. She felt undone. And then he pulled back and looked at her.

"Hello," she said. Her face—no, her whole body felt flushed.

"I love seeing you in my chair," Luke said, his voice soft, his face close to hers. "In my cabin. This makes me very happy."

"Good," she said. The kiss made her smile, and now she couldn't stop smiling.

"The last few weeks," Luke said, "I had it all back. Emily. My house. My work. And I never felt like I do right now."

Blair leaned forward and kissed him again. She put her hands around his back and pressed him to her.

"Don't forget," she whispered to him, her tongue at his ear. "I'm leaving in the morning."

"I dare you," he said, taking her hand and leading her to bed.

• • •

Blair and Luke made love, and Blair was surprised by how different it felt this time. Luke was fierce in his lovemaking, pulling her to him, and then seemingly through him, as if he couldn't get close enough to her body. He was inside of her, riding her, and then, before he came, he pulled out and buried his face between her legs, urging her on. When she came, he slipped back inside her again, and this time he came quickly, joining her. They held each other afterward, and he asked if she was watching the world spin inside her head, and she nodded, knowing exactly what he meant.

They then slept for a short time, Blair wrapped in Luke's arms, and when she stirred in the middle of the night, he awoke and began kissing her. They made love again, slower this time, and again slept, curled around each other.

When the phone rang in the morning, they were both sound asleep.

Blair thought about Amanda, forcing herself to emerge from deep dreams and Luke's tight embrace. She wiggled her way out and found the phone at the side of the bed.

"Hello?"

Luke opened his eyes, and she leaned over to kiss him.

"Uh—maybe I have the wrong number—"

It was a woman's voice—probably the wife. Well, that's one way to keep her away.

"You looking for Luke?"

"Yes. Tell him it's Dana."

"Dana?"

"Damn," Luke mumbled. He reached his hand out.

"He's right here." Blair handed Luke the phone, then curled around his back.

"It's early, Dana," Luke said into the phone.

Blair ran her fingers up and down Luke's long back. Then she pressed her mouth against the back of his neck. She felt different this morning than she had in a few long weeks—she felt healthy. *Sex cures melanoma,* she thought. *I'll tell the world, become the poster girl for the cure.*

"I know," Luke said into the phone after letting Dana speak for a while. "I know all that."

Blair ran her fingers up and down his back. "Don't go back," she whispered to herself.

After a pause he said, "That's my business. It's all my business, in fact. The woman in my bed. The wife I left. You've got nothing to say about any of it."

Blair ran a line of kisses down Luke's back.

"I have already decided the right thing to do," Luke said. He shifted around in bed to face Blair. He was smiling.

He let Dana speak while he stroked the side of Blair's body. She stirred under his touch, feeling her senses awaken, feeling her desire as if they had not yet made love even a first time.

"Funny," Luke said into the phone. "Three months here, and no one ever came to visit. No, Dana. Do not come out to the woods. We don't really have anything to talk about."

Luke climbed onto Blair and straddled her. He placed his hand on her stomach and she gasped, as if already she was feeling too much.

"I gotta go, Dana. Nice talking to you."

He listened for another moment, then hung up the phone, throwing it to the side of the bed and lowering himself on top of Blair.

The phone rang again.

"Ignore it," he said, his mouth in the curve of her neck.

"It might be Amanda," Blair said, her voice deep and breathy. "I told her to call in the morning."

"Do you have to get it?"

"Yes. Don't go away."

"I'm not going anywhere."

Blair squeezed out from under Luke and found the phone.

"Hello?"

"Mom?"

"Good morning, sweetheart."

"You sound cheery."

"Yeah. Well. You headed to school?"

"In a half hour. How you feeling?"

"Pretty terrific."

"Mom. I mean—"

"I know what you mean. I'm fine. I will not faint again."

"How do you know?"

"I just know. Go to school. Do not worry. I'll be home when you get back from school."

"You're coming back?"

"Of course I'm coming back."

Blair looked at Luke, who was shaking his head.

"Are you bringing Mr. Hollywood with you?" Amanda asked.

"Would you like me to?"

"I don't know. I don't care. It's none of my business."

"Well, I'll think about it."

"You do that."

"You sound mad. Are you mad that I left last night?"

"Pretty stupid, Mom. Driving after you were unconscious for an hour."

"I deserve to be stupid once in a while. Is that all you're mad about?"

"Listen, I've got to get to school."

"Good-bye, Amanda. Have a great day at school."

"Yeah. Right."

She hung up the phone.

Blair looked at Luke. "My daughter is not happy with me," she said.

"Maybe it's a little weird for her to think of her mother in bed with a guy."

"Maybe."

"Maybe her mother should get back in bed with the guy."

"Maybe."

Blair rolled over and on top of Luke. She leaned over and kissed him, a long, slow kiss.

"Now that's a good way to wake up in the morning," Luke said when she pulled away.

She lay down on top of him, letting her body settle onto his.

"I love the feel of your body," she said.

"Good," he told her. "Because I'm crazy about yours."

"Can we make love again?" Blair asked.

"You mean, before you kiss me good-bye and leave me forever?"

"Something like that."

This time their lovemaking was slow, careful, and in the light of early morning, they could look at each other, watch each other's expressions, hold each other's gaze.

"Luke Bellingham," Blair sighed when they were done, when they lay side by side in each other's arms.

"We should have started this in high school," Luke said. "We should have spent a lifetime already in each other's arms."

"No," Blair said. "We spent a lifetime getting ready for each other. Now we earned this."

Luke leaned up on one arm so he could look down at her.

"I don't want you to leave," he said.

"I have to," she told him. "I have a daughter and a job." She ran her finger along the side of his face. "But you could come with me."

She smiled, and he leaned over to kiss her again.

"Sweetpea too?"

"Of course."

"Back to the city?"

"Unless you want to kiss good-bye?"

"Not a chance."

Luke dove down, covering her with kisses.

"No more!" Blair urged, pushing him away. "I need food. Lots of food!"

"I'll make breakfast," Luke told her. "Then we'll take a walk with Sweetpea. Let me show you my mountain."

"I'd love that," Blair said. "I hate to take you away from your mountain."

"I want to be with you," Luke told her.

• • •

Luke made pancakes, which Blair admitted were the best she ever tasted, though she suggested that her judgment might be impaired. After breakfast they set out on a trail that passed behind the cabin. Sweetpea bounded ahead of them, deliriously happy to be back in the woods. The day was bright and cold—Blair borrowed one of Luke's sweaters, which hung down to her knees. She wore Amanda's purple hat, pulled down low on her head.

"This is beautiful," Blair told Luke only minutes after setting out. She took the lead, setting the pace as Luke followed. She felt tired, her legs achy. Too much sex? Or the damn disease, wearing her out. *I'll push through it,* she decided.

The forest was lush and thick, sweet-smelling from the pine trees, with a soft base along the trail. Sweetpea ran ahead and back again, as if urging her on.

"Sweetpea won't want to leave this place," she said.

"Sweetpea wants to be with you. Wherever you are."

"You're projecting."

"No. She had it all figured out way before I even had a clue."

"She's a smart dog," Blair said.

"Can you come back here and walk at my side?" Luke complained. "I need to touch you."

"If you touch me, I'll drag you back to bed," Blair tossed back at him. "Right now, I need to hike."

They hiked for a half hour, Blair willing herself forward with every step. At one point the trail ran along the ridge of the Santa Cruz Mountains, and they could see the Pacific curling toward the base of the mountains on one side, the suburban sprawl of Silicon Valley on the other side.

"This is heaven," Blair said, spreading her arms to the sky.

Luke came up behind her and put his arms around her, pressed his mouth onto her head. She turned around in his arms and kissed him.

"I may hate you soon," she said.

"Why?" He looked pained.

"Because I love this."

"Good," Luke said, looking confused.

"No," Blair said. "It's lousy. I don't feel well," she admitted. "I wish I could hike for hours with you." And she turned around, kept walking.

"Maybe it will go into remission," he called ahead. "Maybe we can find something—"

She stopped in her tracks and swung around. "*We* are not sick," she said, her voice dark and low. "*I* am sick. And I am not going to start fighting this, when there's no way to fight it. Remember that. I had just about figured out this dying thing and then I spend a couple of hours in bed with you and screw it all up."

Luke reached for her, but she pulled away.

"I changed my mind," she said. "I'm not bringing you back with me."

"Please, Blair—"

"Let's head back. I'm exhausted," she said, and suddenly she was walking past him, back in the direction they had come from.

"Let's talk about it, Blair. Please."

She shook her head and kept walking. She could hear him behind her and then he stopped. She walked for a moment, then turned back toward him.

"We don't have to talk about the rest of our lives," he said, and she saw the pain in his eyes. "We can talk about now. We can talk about tonight. We can turn this into a one-night stand. Night after night."

She smiled at him, swiping at the tears on her cheek.

He took a step toward her and she nodded. He fell into her arms and they held each other.

"OK," she said finally. "You can come back with me tonight. We'll have a go at it, then kiss and say good-bye in the morning."

• • •

Blair was getting dressed for work when she heard Amanda walking up the stairs of the cottage, heard the front door open. She had left Luke sitting in the dining room, working on his laptop. Her bedroom door was open—she could hear their conversation.

"So, you're here," Amanda stated, her voice sour.

"I'm here."

"Your wife give you a couple of days off for good behavior?"

Luke didn't answer right away. Blair could hear Amanda whispering to Sweetpea. She didn't want to walk out and interfere, make her daughter act like a civilized human being, make Luke find the right answers. Let them work it out between them. Or not. Blair pulled on her chef's jacket, worked the buttons slowly. Her hands felt thick and unsteady. She was bone tired now, even before a night at work.

"I left my wife," Luke finally said.

"You living here now?"

"No. I'm here for the night. Don't know about tomorrow."

Blair smiled. Smart man.

"Where's my mom?"

"Getting ready for work. I thought maybe you and I would make dinner here."

"And why would I want to do that?"

"Keep me company."

"I thought you just needed me for your dog."

"Right. Well, it was an idea."

"OK."

"Yeah?"

"I gotta eat, right?"

Blair figured it was safe to come out.

She walked into the dining room, saw Luke close the laptop quickly.

"You can work," she said.

"Amanda's home," he told her. "We're going to make dinner."

Blair kissed him and whispered, "You've always been able to charm the young girls."

"Except you."

"Took longer," Blair said. "I'm a challenge."

"You're telling me."

"Let me go say hello to my daughter."

"She's in her room."

Blair knocked on Amanda's door.

"I'm busy," Amanda called out.

"It's me!" Blair yelled. Music was blasting from within.

"Come in!"

Blair looked back at Luke, who raised his eyebrows. "I better keep working on the charm," he said.

Blair walked into Amanda's room, shut the door behind her. Amanda was sprawled on her bed.

"You don't look very busy."

"He bugs me."

"Why? Can we turn down the music?" Aerosmith wailed—Blair liked the fact that her own music had lasted into the next generation, made it seem like the whole rebellion hadn't disappeared with peasant blouses. Well, then again, peasant blouses were back, too.

Amanda reached out and turned down the volume on her CD player. Her room was painted dark blue—walls, ceiling, floor—with light blue paper lanterns hanging from the ceiling. Blair always felt peaceful in this room, as if she were tucked in some kind of cocoon. She sat on the edge of Amanda's bed and reached out, put her hand around her daughter's ankle.

"What's up?" she asked.

"I didn't trust him before. Now I really don't trust him." Amanda spoke with her face to the wall. She kicked Blair's hand away.

"I thought you guys had become friends."

"I was the dog walker."

"But you liked him."

"I didn't ask him to move in. You did."

"He didn't move in. He's just here. For a while. I don't know."

"Yeah, well, I live here, too. In case you didn't notice."

"I know that, sweetheart."

"Maybe I'll invite some guy to move in."

Blair flopped back on the bed. She gazed up at the ceiling. "I don't know what to tell you," Blair said.

They were quiet for a while.

"I wish you weren't sick," Amanda said finally.

Blair reached out her hand and found the top of Amanda's head. She stroked her daughter's hair—this time Amanda didn't push her away.

"You know, I don't think I've ever been in love," Blair said.

"Not with my father?"

"No. I was too young then. Not that you can't fall in love when you're young. You'll do that. But I was too unformed, too immature.

I loved him for a couple of weeks, enough to create you, but then he moved on or I moved on. . . . It doesn't even matter."

"Did he know about me?"

"No. I never saw him again. There were a lot of guys like that back then. We were sort of reckless in those days."

"How come you never fell in love?"

"I don't know. I got busy with my job and raising you. I stayed away from guys. I wanted a real life with you, and I thought they'd get in the way."

Amanda made a noise, and Blair rolled over to look at her. Her daughter was crying. Blair scooted up on the bed and put her arms around her.

"So why now?" Amanda asked quietly.

"Maybe it's not love," Blair said. "Maybe it's fear."

Amanda held her mother tightly.

"Or maybe I'm just looking for one last good time."

Blair smiled at her daughter and stroked her cheeks, wiping away the tears.

"Let me find out, OK?" she asked.

Amanda nodded. Blair leaned over and kissed her daughter's forehead.

"I still don't trust him," Amanda said.

"You will," Blair said.

The doorbell rang, and Sweetpea started barking.

"No one rings the doorbell," Amanda said, jumping off the bed, swiping at her eyes and looking in the mirror.

"I'll get it. You go wash your face," Blair said.

Blair left her daughter's room. Luke was already at the door, had opened it and was talking to a woman who stood in the doorway. Blair walked to his side.

The woman was glamorous, clearly someone from another part of town. She was perfectly coiffed and even more perfectly dressed in some kind of cream-colored pantsuit. Blair thought pantsuits were only worn by businesswomen. This was not a businesswoman. And she was pregnant.

"Blair, this is Dana, my sister-in-law," Luke said.

Blair stuck out her hand. Dana looked at her, confused. Finally she shook her hand once, dropping it quickly.

"Is this the dog walker?" Dana asked, peering at Blair. "I thought the dog walker was a kid."

"Dog walker's mom," Blair explained.

"Girlfriend?" Dana asked, turning to Luke.

"One-night stand," Blair boasted.

"You left my sister for her?"

"No. Your sister left me," Luke said. "Remember? During that time, somehow, I met Blair. Or remet Blair—we went to high school together."

"Want to come in?" Blair offered.

"No," Dana said. "I want to talk to Luke."

"There's nothing to talk about," Luke said, blocking the doorway.

"I need to tell you something about my sister," Dana said.

Blair turned to leave, but Luke reached out and grabbed her hand, pulling her back. "You don't have to disappear," he said.

Blair looked at him, surprised. "Really?"

"I'm not going anywhere," he told her.

Blair beamed at him. She had already been steeling herself for the exit: "Sorry, sweetheart, the wife wants me back. Gotta run. It's been grand." Blair took a deep breath and squeezed Luke's hand.

"Then invite the lady in," Blair said.

Luke gestured with a grand sweep of his arm.

Dana looked past them into the living room of the cottage, taking it all in.

"This is very hip, very bohemian," she said. "You never did like my life, did you?"

"I liked your life, Dana," Luke said wearily.

Blair took in a deep breath.

"My sister loves you," Dana said.

"Did she send you here to bring me back?" Luke asked.

"No," Dana said. "I'm here on my own."

"Why?"

"Because I think you're good for my sister."

"Good for her? What does that mean?"

"She was lost in your shadow, Luke. It wasn't your fault—it's hers. She never felt that she had much to offer except her beauty. But now, she'll have a baby. That will give her something real."

"Gray Healy's baby."

"Who the hell cares whose baby it is," Dana said.

"This is amazing!" Blair said. "You didn't tell me any of this!"

"She's very sweet, your little girlfriend," Dana told Luke.

"No one has ever called me sweet," Blair said. "Little, I admit, I've heard once or twice. But never sweet."

"Dana," Luke said, his voice calm. "Emily will be fine without me. I'm not going back."

"You owe her an explanation. She doesn't even know about the girlfriend."

"I don't owe her anything. How the hell did you find me?"

"The dog walker. Emily had the phone number. I did a little sleuthing."

On cue, the dog walker left her room and came to the door to join them.

"This is Amanda," Blair said, pulling her daughter close. "Amanda, this is the wife's sister. She wants Luke to go home now."

"Is he going?" Amanda asked, sounding hopeful.

"No," Luke said. "Good-bye, Dana."

Dana turned and walked down the stairs. They all watched her go. Finally Luke closed the door and leaned back against it.

Amanda pranced around the room. "I'm so hip; I'm *soooo* bohemian," she said in a deep voice, hand on hip, other hand fake-smoking a joint.

"You were listening in," Blair accused.

"Damn right," Amanda said, giggling.

"I'm sorry," Luke said, his voice serious.

"Why? I liked her!" Blair told him. "I was ready to invite her for dinner. She'll be my new best friend. She'll take me shopping and buy me pantsuits."

"You are *soooo* sweet," Luke said, and they all laughed.

Luke pulled Blair to him, wrapped his arms around her.

"Thank you," he said.

"For what?"

"For a lovely one-night stand."

Amanda stomped out of the room.

"Go to work," Luke said. "I'll deal with her."

"That's OK?"

"That's fine," Luke assured her.

"I don't want to go," Blair said when he released her. She stroked Luke's back, her hands pressing into his muscles.

"I'll wait up for you."

"Is your wife really pregnant with someone else's baby?" Blair asked, leaning back and looking up at Luke.

"I think so. I hope so. Then it makes leaving much easier."

"You really left."

"I really left."

"I'm glad."

"You'll keep me around for one more night?"

"One more night."

• • •

Blair kept smiling at work. She didn't tell Daniel about her latest seizure—she would have to quit working soon and she'd tell him everything then. For now, she wanted to feel good. What a concept.

"I figured it out," she told Daniel when he came in to bring her a glass of wine from an unfinished Bordeaux Grand Cru some diners had left.

"What's that?" He perched on the stool behind her. "Chop the onions finer. No one should see them."

Blair rolled her eyes and kept chopping.

"Why we never fell in love with anyone."

"Oh, that. I thought we were done with that. Please."

"Onions fine enough, my dear?"

"Perfect."

Blair tossed them into the oiled pan, added garlic and red pepper.

"Love is terrifying. The minute you have it, you're scared of losing it. And it's so big. It fills up all the space of your life. I mean, I'm not standing here making linguine with clam sauce. I'm thinking about him; I'm missing him; I'm getting ready for him; I'm planning when I can make linguine with clam sauce for him."

"You've lost it."

"I've lost it! You fall in love and you go crazy!"

"No, you fall in love and you get boring."

"But it's not boring. It's unbelievable. The whole world is charged. Like I've revved up all the ions around me, and they're all crashing into each other making little love explosions."

"I'm going up front. I can't take this."

"See. You're scared of it. You want a small world. A safe world. There's nothing safe with love."

"Stir, Blair. If you burn the garlic, I'm sending you home."

"But I wouldn't care! I'd be going home to him!"

"Please tell me you're kidding. This is all a bad joke."

Blair looked at Daniel and offered a half smile. "Sort of kidding," she said.

"Not good enough," he said, getting off the stool and heading back into the restaurant.

Philippe burst through the doors, carrying too many plates. He dropped them at Manuel's side, then slapped his butt to keep him from complaining. Philippe never organized his plates before depositing them for dishwashing—but all Manuel needed was a sexual tease to keep him happy.

"The boss says you are a mess, *ma chérie,*" Philippe said to Blair while swirling his finger in the sauce.

Blair slapped his wrist. "Get out of there."

"Are you sick again?"

"Sick in love," Blair said.

"The movie man?"

"Yes. He left his wife."

"For how long?"

"He's smitten. I've never seen anything like it. I never knew what smitten looked like before."

"It looks like hell in about a week. When the wife calls him home."

"Well, I'm not worried about a week from now."

"Bring him here," Philippe said, loading up the first-course dishes for his table. "I would like to serve dinner to the movie man and his smitten face."

"I'll do that," Blair said. "Get those plates out before they're cold."

Philippe pushed through the doors to the restaurant. Rianne emerged in his place.

"You're in love?" she asked, astonished.

"I'm not in love. Maybe I'm in love. I'm playing around with the idea. Nothing like a private conversation around here," Blair said. She was still smiling.

"The screenwriter?"

"Yes, the screenwriter. He's just a regular guy. No, he isn't," Blair said. "He's amazing. Regular guys aren't amazing."

"You're telling me," Rianne moaned. "Table five wants the steak cooked more."

"Tell table five the steak will be shoe leather if I cook it another second."

Rianne whirled around, carrying the plate, and returned to the dining room.

Blair had three more desserts to prepare; then she was done. She was wide-awake, her body physically exhausted, her mind whirling. When Daniel returned, asking, "Is it safe to come back here?" she kissed him and whispered, "Let me leave early. Otherwise I'll keep boring you with all this love talk."

"Go. Get out of here. It's downright frightening."

She kissed him again.

"Stop kissing me." Daniel swiped at his cheek.

"Go fall in love," Blair said, putting the desserts on their plates, grabbing her jacket and heading to the back door.

"Go hide until you're over this," Daniel called back at her.

"Can I take the flowers?" she asked, grabbing a bouquet on the counter.

"Go!"

"And a bottle of wine?" she called out, whisking a bottle of their house wine into her bag.

"Leave!"

She left the restaurant, smiling.

It was a warm night, unusual for San Francisco, and all of the inhabitants of the Haight seemed to congregate on the streets. There was a group of musicians on every corner, kids smoking pot, guys walking arm in arm, a whole city of people who had just fallen in love. Blair could tell—they kept smiling back at her.

When she arrived at her cottage, she could hear Amanda's African music coming from the open windows. A good sign—Amanda wasn't holed up in her room. Unless Luke had left. The sister-in-law had come back and taken him away, returned him to his rightful place in the world. Amanda would be in the living room, celebrating.

Blair ran up the steps, her heart pounding. She threw open the front door and saw Luke first, in the overstuffed chair, reading a book. Amanda sat in the middle of the floor, her homework spread around her.

They both looked up, surprised.

Luke got up from his chair, put his arms around her, whispered in her ear, "My God, I was just wishing you home. I never knew I had these powers."

"I couldn't work. I couldn't concentrate. I was acting like a goon in love," Blair whispered back.

"Are you guys going to make out right here in the living room?" Amanda called out.

Blair and Luke unwrapped their arms, let each other go.

"Maybe," Blair said.

"Spare me," Amanda said.

"How was your dinner?" Blair asked, handing Luke the flowers, offering one more kiss.

"Great," he said. "Amanda made me pasta with some perfect sauce and salad and garlic bread. I'm in food heaven."

Blair looked over at Amanda, who shrugged. "It's just the garlic-and-olive-oil sauce you always make."

"I'm impressed," Blair said.

"You thought I only knew how to cook an omelette."

"Well, maybe you should be cooking more around here."

"Maybe I will."

Blair leaned over and kissed her daughter. "I love you, sweetheart."

"I hate physics," Amanda moaned.

"I couldn't help her. I tried. She almost kicked me out of the house for trying," Luke said.

"I should have warned you," Blair said. "She asks for help. She doesn't really want help. She just wants to talk it out with someone."

"Where'd she learn that?" Luke asked.

"You don't know that about me," Blair countered.

"Just a sneaking suspicion," Luke told her.

"I'm going to open this bottle of wine and pour us two glasses. And then I'll join this scene of domestic bliss if you don't mind."

"I don't mind," Luke said, kissing her. "But why don't I do that."

He took the bottle and headed into the kitchen.

Blair fell into the armchair. She never wanted to feel her exhaustion, but sometimes it forced itself upon her.

"He's OK, isn't he?" Blair whispered to Amanda.

Amanda looked up from her physics book, shrugged, half-smiled. "We had fun, I guess."

"Thanks for making him dinner."

"I had to eat. What do you think I do every night while you're gone?"

"I know, Amanda. I'm just glad you're giving him a chance."

"I didn't say anything about that."

"Right."

"He's staying, isn't he?"

"For the night. That's all we've figured out so far."

"His wife is pregnant, Mom. This isn't a permanent gig."

"And I'm dying. Let's talk about permanence, here."

Amanda stood up, stormed from the room, and in a second Blair could hear her bedroom door slam.

"What happened?" Luke asked, appearing in the doorway, wineglasses in hand.

"I screwed up," Blair said.

Luke handed Blair a glass of wine, sat down on the floor in front of her.

"We did OK," Luke told her.

"I know," Blair said. "I could tell."

She leaned forward and kissed him. He put his hand on her cheek and kept it there.

"She's lovely," Luke said.

Blair smiled. "I know. Maybe you should fall in love with her. You'd have a helluva better chance at a future."

"I don't believe in the future," Luke said. "Take me to bed."

"I'll do that," Blair told him, and she stood, taking his hand and leading him into her bedroom.

• • •

In the morning Amanda was gone, off to school before either of them woke up. Blair read the note on the kitchen table: *I fed and walked Sweetpea. If Mr. Hollywood goes home, tell him to leave his dog here.*

Blair made coffee, took two cups back to bed. Luke was awake, waiting for her.

"My daughter wants your dog," she said.

"So I guess we stay," Luke told her.

"I woke up in the middle of the night terrified that you were gone," Blair said.

"I'm right here."

"For now."

"I'm not going anywhere."

"It doesn't make sense, Luke. You don't start a new life with a woman who's dying."

"It doesn't feel like you're dying."

"It will soon."

Blair thought about the pain in her head, the ache in her muscles. Each day there were new parts of her that hurt.

"Come back to bed."

"I want to talk about it."

"I can't talk about it," Luke said. "I think if we make love enough times, my brain cells will die and I'll never have to think about it."

Blair smiled, climbed into bed next to him.

"How did this happen?"

"I need you to live, Blair. I need you to spend a few more decades with me."

She lay down, her head on his shoulder.

"I can't do that," she whispered, pressing her face into the side of his neck, breathing him in, willing him to keep her alive.

Chapter Ten

Over the next couple of weeks, Luke could see that Blair's illness progressed, making her tired, occasionally weak. She sometimes moaned in her sleep and he would wrap his arms around her, wishing he had some power to take away her pain. If he asked her, she would say she was fine. She would tell him that it had been too long since they had made love. Which was daily, twice daily, never enough for either of them.

She wouldn't quit work, wouldn't slow down. She said she needed to cook, needed to see her friends at the restaurant or else she would disappear inside the Luke cocoon as she called it. "What's wrong with the Luke cocoon?" he'd ask.

He wanted nothing more than to be with her. He wanted long days in bed while Amanda was at school. He wanted walks on the beach with Amanda and Sweetpea after school. And he wanted quiet nights with Amanda in the cottage if Blair was working, quiet nights with both of them if she had a night off.

He finished the story about the man in the woods and the bartender's daughter. He was pleased, enjoying the process of fiction, the discovery of the story. He began a new story, this one about a high school boy, the golden boy, who fell for the odd girl, the loner. He would invent a shared childhood, let them marry, spend years together.

He wrote a few pages every day, letting the story find itself. He had never written this way before. All of his scripts had been crafted, scene by scene, before he wrote a word. He knew the stuff of Hollywood, the three-act structure, the necessary plot points to send the character on his filmic journey. Maybe he had become terrified of the unexplored territory. Maybe he hadn't written anything original since *Pescadero.*

So he took his time, wrote a few scenes and asked himself only: What happens next? Not: What happens at the end? Like his life. Writing as a one-night stand.

He loved the cottage, the coziness of the place. It was like his cabin in size, yet so unlike it in feel. The cottage was snug, full to the brim with women's things: gauzy scarves hanging over lamps and the backs of chairs, beaded necklaces draped and tossed everywhere, candles lit on every surface of every room as soon as night fell, incense filling the place with an earthy smell. Whenever he walked into the cottage, from an outing with Sweetpea or a trip to the supermarket, he immediately thought, *I'm home.* Home was Blair, Amanda, this place. He had never been home before.

He wrote in the morning while Blair slept. When she woke, he made coffee for both of them, then took her back to bed. They often strolled the neighborhood, hand in hand, like kids. Luke would buy them presents on these excursions: CDs, books, more candles, wine, cookware. "I have money," he told her. "I want to spend it on you."

She had a doctor's appointment—he asked if he could join her. "Yes," she said immediately. "I hate seeing the doctor. Come with me. I have a favorite bar we can go to afterward and get smashed together. I'll introduce you to my guardian angel."

"I thought I was your guardian angel."

"This one prepared me for you," she said, smiling.

"Then I'd love to meet him," Luke told her.

Luke remembered his last time with Emily, the doctor's appointment she didn't want him to come to, his intrusion into her secret life.

This clinic was shabbier, anything but elegant. They were in the middle of the Haight, and the patients looked ill, poor, lost. He wanted to take Blair somewhere else, somewhere they could save her. *No one could be saved here,* he thought.

But the doctor was smart, caring, attentive. He welcomed Luke, answered his questions directly, let him watch the examination and took the time to explain every step.

"I want to do more," Luke told him, his voice catching in his throat.

"You're doing a lot," the doc said. "I'm glad she's got someone."

"Are there trial drugs, some kind of treatment—"

"Stop," Blair said. "You promised."

Luke had promised to respect her decision not to fight the inevitable. But in the doctor's office, with Blair's white skin exposed on the examining table, it was impossible not to dream of miracle cures.

"She's making the right decision," the doctor said. "We can talk about how to make the end easier, not harder."

"Isn't there something? Some new treatment—"

"Stop," Blair repeated, sitting up on the table, looking more scared than angry.

"I think Blair's right on this," the doctor said. "It benefits us—the medical profession—to have her try one thing after another. But I know what's out there. We would only be prolonging her life by a short time. And the quality of that life would diminish substantially. The drugs would kill her instead of the disease."

Blair sank back onto the table, and Luke nodded his head, silent.

"I've talked to Blair about ways to alleviate pain, the stages she'll go through, the way we can make it possible for her to stay home and out of the hospital."

"Good," Luke managed.

"Has the level of pain changed?" the doctor asked Blair.

"Some. The pills work fine so far. I don't need anything else yet. Maybe something for my boyfriend, who's going to be in great pain if he keeps this up."

Luke looked at her and smiled. "I'll shut up," he said. "You never called me your boyfriend before."

The doctor smiled. "Lucky guy," he said. "I thought she was a pain in the ass when I first met her, but she grows on you."

"She's been growing on me since high school."

"He's lying," Blair said. "He never talked to me in high school."

"Guys don't need to talk," the doctor said. "They lust just fine without words."

The doctor patted Blair's shoulder. "You can get dressed now. I'll see you in another month. Unless something comes up sooner. It might now. The pain and fatigue indicate that the disease has advanced farther. You can expect some changes."

"What kind of changes?" Luke asked.

"More severe pain. Perhaps more seizures. Stay close to home or take this guy out with you when you do leave the house. You might think about quitting work. Save your energy. If you exhaust yourself, you'll fire up the disease."

Luke shook the doctor's hand and watched him leave.

"I can't stand this," Luke said when he closed the door behind him.

"You have to stand this," Blair said, sitting up.

"I know. Give me an hour. And a trip to that bar you were talking about."

"Great," Blair said, smiling.

"Good doctor," Luke said.

"Yeah, I hated the bastard at first. Easier than hating what he told me. But he's OK."

"I love you," Luke said. "Girlfriend."

"Don't get possessive," she teased.

"Not a chance. Get dressed. Let's get smashed."

• • •

"You hang out here?" Luke asked when they entered the bar. It was the kind of place that you passed without noticing, no sign, no light, a dark door open just a crack. But Blair pushed open the door, flooding the place with light. The few patrons, old men and a couple of middle-aged women, squinted at them, clearly annoyed at the intrusion of daylight.

"I came here once. After an appointment. I say we make it a tradition."

"I don't like building traditions around doctor appointments," Luke said.

"We don't have much choice," Blair said, heading right for the bar.

"Let's take a table," Luke suggested.

"Nope. The bar. It's part of the tradition."

Luke reluctantly sat at the bar, joining the grimmest set of characters he had ever seen in the city. No one was talking—they all seemed intent on hearing every word of Luke and Blair's conversation.

"Hi, angel," Blair said, and Luke looked up at the bartender.

He was young, too young for this place. Not bad-looking. Very pierced. Did Blair go for younger guys?

"Hey, you," the bartender said. "Looking better."

"That's easy," Blair said. "I was looped by the time I got to you last time. This is Luke."

"Her boyfriend."

Blair smiled and elbowed him in the ribs.

"Did she ever call you her boyfriend?"

"Nah. Just her angel," the guy said.

"He wouldn't sleep with me," Blair explained.

"You didn't try very hard," the bartender said, smiling. "What can I get you?"

"Scotch for me. Bourbon for the boyfriend," Blair said.

"Doubles," Luke said.

"I knew that," the bartender said, and turned to make the drinks.

"You jealous?" Blair asked.

"I don't know," Luke said. "The idea that you had a life without me drives me just a little crazy. It's a guy thing. I'll get over it."

"Don't get over it," Blair said.

"Easy for you to say."

The bartender slid their drinks across the bar to them.

"How's your daughter?" he asked Blair.

"How well do you guys know each other?" Luke asked.

"You find out a lot when someone crash-lands on your bar stool," the bartender said.

"She's OK," Blair said. "When she's a little older, I'll tell her to stop by and fall in love with you."

"How long do I have to wait?" he asked.

"How old are you?" Blair asked.

"Twenty-three."

"She's sixteen. You've got two years."

"She look like you?"

"Better. And she's nicer."

"Maybe she doesn't need her mom to set her up," Luke suggested.

"Took me more than forty years to find a good man. No reason she should flounder around for so long," Blair told him.

"Maybe she'll be better at it than you are," Luke said.

"Maybe she'll spend the rest of her life looking for a man just like you," Blair said. "Won't she be disappointed."

Luke leaned over and kissed her. The bartender disappeared.

"This is a very cool place," Luke said. "But why is he your angel?"

"One more drink and I'll show you," Blair told him.

They ordered another round of doubles when they finished the first. They drank, talked about whom they remembered in high school and made up stories for what might have happened to each.

When the bartender returned with sandwiches and chips—unordered—Blair beamed.

"My angel," she said.

"I figured I had to feed you or save you again. Feeding you is easier," the bartender said.

"I still want to be saved," Blair said.

The bartender put his elbows on the bar and leaned toward them. "What can I do for you?" he asked, smiling.

"I changed my mind," Blair said. "I don't want to die."

The bartender nodded, thinking. "I can see that," he said.

"You gonna grant me a wish here, or what?" Blair asked.

"I don't want you to die, either," the bartender said quietly.

"Bad for business," Blair muttered, drinking the last of her scotch.

"How soon?" he asked.

Blair shrugged.

Luke saw that she was crying. He put his arm around her.

"I'm turning into a sloppy drunk," Blair whimpered.

"Two more," Luke told the bartender. "She promised me we'd get smashed. I'm not even close."

The bartender turned away reluctantly and went to make their drinks. Luke pulled Blair close to him and held her.

"I hate you," she whispered.

"I know," he told her.

"I want you out of my life," she whispered.

"I know," he said.

"Don't let go," she told him, and he held her tightly.

• • •

They walked home slowly, with great difficulty. The day had almost disappeared, though dusk, with its soft light, covered everything in Day-Glo pink. They held each other, weaving slightly, making their way through the early-evening crowds on the sidewalks.

They didn't speak—they hadn't had much to say to each other after their third round of doubles. They had kissed sloppily, and the bartender had finally bestowed his blessing: Come back again, many times, many doctor's appointments, a lifetime of bar visits after death sentences.

Blair had kissed the bartender good-bye, promising him her daughter.

They walked home to the daughter, hoping the sandwiches and the walk and kisses along the way would sober them up, make them presentable. It didn't work.

And when they opened the door to the cottage, having pushed each other up the long row of steps, they discovered someone waiting for them in their living room. Emily. Abandoned wife and pregnant woman.

They both stood up straight.

Emily sat in the armchair, watching them.

Amanda raced into the room from her bedroom and skidded to a stop in front of them. "She came a while ago. I let her in. I hope that's OK. I couldn't let her wait outside."

"It's OK," Luke said. "Hello, Emily."

Emily stood up slowly, one hand on her belly.

"This is Blair," he said.

Emily nodded.

"I'm outta here," Amanda said. "Too much homework." She fled the room.

"I'd offer you a seat, but you already took mine," Blair said, and started to giggle.

"I don't think Emily needs to stay," Luke said. "If she wants to talk to me, she and I can go for a walk and talk."

"You're drunk," Emily said.

"That's true," Luke said.

"In the middle of the day," Emily stated. She looked confused.

"It's now the end of the day," Blair said.

"I mean . . . I shouldn't be here. I'm sorry." Emily looked away from them.

"Would you like to leave?" Luke offered.

"No. I don't feel well," Emily said, and her hand reached out for the chair, but she misjudged the distance and leaned on thin air, so that her body, swollen and round, started to topple. Both Luke and Blair raced to grab her and bumped into each other, so that they all struggled to stay on their feet, to stand up, straighten up, separate themselves from the mess of each other.

"I'll leave," Emily said. "I shouldn't have come."

"Let me get you a glass of water first," Blair said.

Emily stood with her hand now firmly planted on the back of the armchair. "Water. That would be nice."

"You OK?" Luke said. Suddenly he wondered if Emily was drunk.

"I'm just fine," she said, her old voice returning. "I'm having a fine time visiting my husband and his girlfriend."

"I'll be right back," Blair said, heading toward the kitchen.

Luke sat down on the couch, and Emily slid back into the armchair.

Neither of them spoke for a moment, and Blair didn't return with the water. Luke sat up straight, as if that would make him less drunk.

"This is what you wanted," Emily finally said.

Luke looked at her, baffled. She opened her arms and showed him the cottage.

"I didn't know what I wanted till I found it. I wanted you for a long time. Remember that."

"I remember," Emily said. "I'm having a hard time forgetting that."

"You forgot it for three long months."

"I never forgot it, Luke."

"Gray Healy was there to comfort you."

"Is this about anger?" she asked, pointing to where Blair had disappeared. "To do to me what I did to you?"

Luke shook his head slowly. "No. Blair was an accident. A wonderful accident."

"Goddamn you."

Emily put her head back on the chair. She closed her eyes.

"I don't want to have this conversation here," Luke said. "It's not fair to them."

"I don't give a damn about them," Emily said wearily.

"I know that, Emily. But I do. Let's go for a walk."

Luke stood and offered her his hand. She stared at it for a moment, as if it were something unrecognizable. Then she took it and stood. He turned and walked toward the door, then held it open and let her pass in front of him. He waited a moment, hoping that Blair would return, but when she didn't, he followed Emily out of the house, closing the door behind him.

They walked quietly for a while. He turned away from the direction he had just come with Blair. Minutes ago, he and his girlfriend were walking, kissing, bumping shoulders, giggling. Now he and his wife walked solemnly, side by side, not touching.

"I want a divorce," he said finally.

"No," she said.

"Please, Emily. I don't want to hurt you. This has been painful enough."

He stopped walking and waited. Emily turned back to him.

"You know what I figured out?" he asked. "You were right to leave our marriage. You were incredibly brave. I would never have been bold enough to do what you did."

"Stop, Luke—"

"No, listen. We both need something that we can't get from each other."

"I need you," Emily said.

"No," Luke told her gently. "You'll be better without me, I'm sure of that."

She was quiet, and he could tell she was crying. They walked again, slowly, and he felt his mind becoming sober, clear, and his body seemed weightless, his limbs fluid and smooth.

"I'm sorry about the baby," Emily said. "Isn't it possible to forgive me?"

Again he shook his head. "I don't need to forgive you, Emily," he said.

She looked at him, confused.

"What I think or don't think doesn't matter," Luke said.

"I want our lives back," she said.

Luke didn't say anything for a while. They walked along deserted streets, away from the noise of the Haight. He felt lost—they had turned so many corners that he no longer knew which direction he was headed.

"I'll call a lawyer and we'll move forward," he finally said. "You won't have to worry about money."

"That's not what I want," Emily said.

"It's what I want," he told her. "You don't have a choice anymore."

A man was walking toward them, a huge hulk of a man dressed in motorcycle leathers, and Emily pulled close to Luke, wrapping her arm around his. He felt the heat of her body, the weight of her rounded stomach pressing against him, and he held her for a moment, until the man passed. Then he let her go and felt, with an ache, the hard stomach, the soft arm, the smell of her, pull so far away that he thought he might topple over, as if he had lost his own balance without her.

He stopped and straightened up. She looked at him.

"Which way back?" he asked.

"Are you OK?" she said, concerned.

"I want to get back to the cottage."

"It's straight ahead. Another couple of blocks."

"Where's your car?"

"On Haight."

He started walking again, and she hurried to keep up with him.

Then she grabbed his arm and stopped him, pulling him back around to her.

"Luke," she pleaded. "I want to talk—"

"I'm done talking, Emily."

"Will you have a family with her?" she asked.

Luke shook his head. "I wish I could," he told her.

Emily looked at him for a moment. "I really lost you," she said, her face darkening. Then she turned and walked away. He waited until she was out of sight before he made his way back to the cottage.

• • •

Blair was sitting on the porch, her legs dangling over the edge. From a distance, as Luke approached, she looked like a little girl, her legs kicking back and forth. Then she took a swig of beer, her head tilted back so it caught the light of the moon, and she looked like Blair again. Luke wolf-whistled at her.

"You coming back to me?" she called out.

"I never left you!" Luke shouted back. He neared the cottage and looked up at her. She tossed down a bottle of beer, which he caught and opened. "Why sober up?" he asked.

"She's beautiful," Blair said.

"You're beautiful," he told her.

"No. I'm interesting. She's beautiful."

"You're interestingly beautiful. And I love you."

"She still loves you. She wants you back."

"She'll get over it."

"Come sit next to me."

Luke climbed the stairs and squeezed in next to Blair on the ledge. He leaned over and kissed her, slowly, tasting the beer in her mouth.

"If you pack up your things and leave, I'll understand."

"What would you understand?" Luke asked.

"Real life. Wives, babies, the future. That sort of thing."

"I'm not leaving."

"You think you're in love."

"I think I'm in love."

"I've never been in love before."

"Really?"

Blair shook her head.

"Neither have I," Luke said.

"What was that between you and the tall, gorgeous blond woman?"

"Something else. Something completely different."

"Not love."

"Maybe it was love," Luke said. "But it was nothing like this."

"I'm drunk," Blair said.

"Me too," Luke told her. "Can we sleep out here?"

"I don't think so. But it's nice to sit here."

"What's Amanda doing?"

"Homework," she said. She breathed deeply. "I'm going to miss all this."

Luke slipped his arm around her. They stared out into the dark street, legs dangling, sipping their beer.

• • •

In the morning Luke headed for the kitchen to find Advil and water. Blair was still sleeping. He wore his boxer shorts, no shirt. As he opened the cabinet door, he felt someone standing behind him, and he turned around.

"Good morning," he said to Amanda, who was standing there, dressed for school, backpack on her back.

"You should get dressed before you walk around here," she said.

"I thought it was the middle of the night," Luke said. "I've got a headache."

"I read your story," she said.

"What story?"

"On the computer. The one about you and the girl."

Luke turned back to the cabinet, took out the bottle of Advil. He poured three into his hand, then filled a glass with tap water. He took the pills, then drank the glass of water. And his slow, groggy mind tried to process this information: She read the story he had written about a man who has sex with a young girl. When he put the glass in the sink, he turned back to Amanda.

"You shouldn't be reading something on my computer," he said calmly.

"Well, I did," she said.

"The story wasn't about me and a girl. It was fiction. Made up."

"Did you have an affair with a sixteen-year-old girl?"

"No. And it's none of your business."

"Which answer."

"Both."

"I bet you did."

"Amanda—I'm upset you read my work without asking."

"Yeah, well, I'm upset you write about having sex with young girls."

"That wasn't for you to read."

"Too private? No one should know what you do?"

"It wasn't about me. I told you that."

And then Blair was standing in the doorway, watching them.

"What's going on?" she asked. "I have a roaring hangover."

"I'll get you some Advil," Luke said. "Let's go back to bed."

He knew Blair must have heard some of the conversation because she wasn't moving.

"What are you two fighting about?"

"We're not fighting," Luke said.

"I read his story."

"Without my permission."

"Did he ever tell you about some bartender's daughter out in the woods? Some sixteen-year-old babe he had sex with."

"Amanda!" Blair said.

"Maybe he didn't mention it."

"Go to school, Amanda," Luke said. "I'll talk to your mother about this when you leave."

"Don't tell me where to go. It's my house. You're not my father."

"If I were, and you read something private, I'd punish you. Right now, I don't quite know what to do," Luke said. He held on to the kitchen sink—his head was pounding.

"Yeah, I know what you'd like to do—"

"That's enough," Luke called out.

"Clue me in," Blair said, leaning back on the wall.

"I wrote a story," Luke said. "Fiction. Made up. Invented. About a man who falls for a sixteen-year-old. Amanda read it."

Blair nodded. She looked at Luke for a moment, then at Amanda, who then pushed past her and out of the room. Luke and Blair waited a few seconds, then heard the slam of the front door.

Still, they waited, watching each other.

"Fuck," Luke said. He leaned back against the sink.

"What was it?" Blair asked.

"A story. A story that she shouldn't have read."

"Did it happen?"

"No!" Luke poured himself another glass of water, then held the cold glass against his cheek. "I have never had an affair with a young girl. Believe me, Blair."

"Where'd the story come from? Desire? Lust?"

"I don't know. I'm living with a sixteen-year-old who happens to be beautiful. The thought crosses my mind that a man could fall for her. I fell for a woman ten years younger than I am. She was a kid, unformed. I must have wanted that. So in my story, I throw a man into a relationship with a girl. It's a way of playing it out in my mind. Not doing it. Not even wanting to do it. But it's something to explore."

He finished talking, and she didn't say anything. She wasn't looking at him—instead, she watched her hand run across the countertop. He felt nauseated—by the hangover, by the image of Amanda up in the middle of the night, reading his story.

"Christ, Luke," Blair said. She sat down on the floor.

Luke walked over, slid down the wall and sat next to her.

"I'm sorry," he said. "I never thought about her reading it."

"She doesn't trust you anyway," Blair said softly.

"I know that."

"How much did we drink yesterday?" Blair asked, her hand on her head.

"Too much," Luke said. He put his arm around her and drew her close.

"You have to believe me, Blair. I would never—"

"I know," she said.

"Take the Advil," he offered. "It's either that or a Bloody Mary."

She reached for the bottle, took a couple and swallowed them with Luke's glass of water.

"I'm scared I've lost her," Luke said quietly. "We had become friends. Or so I thought."

"I'll talk to her."

"No. It's between her and me," Luke said. "I've got to work it out with her. I can't stay with you and have her against me."

Blair nodded.

"I'll talk to her tonight," Luke said. "I've got to make her understand."

"I'm going to quit work today," Blair said.

"Good," he told her. He watched her, pulling her close to him.

"It's the last thing I want to do," she told him.

"I know."

"Maybe it will give us more time. If I'm not so tired."

Luke nodded. Blair put her head on his shoulder.

"Can I come eat in your restaurant?"

She looked up at him, smiling. "If you promise to fend off Philippe and Rianne. They'll both try to seduce you."

"I only go for sixteen-year-old girls," Luke said.

Blair punched him in the arm.

"Bring her for dinner," she suggested.

"Good idea," he said. "If she'll let me."

• • •

Luke waited for Amanda on the street in front of her high school. Throngs of kids left the building, lighting up cigarettes the moment they were out the door, throwing arms around each other, waking up from a day spent listening to teachers talk at them. No Amanda. Luke stayed in his truck, Sweetpea at his side, and waited.

When the kids were all gone, Amanda came out alone. She walked slowly down the long stairway from the school, seeming to get heavier and slower with each step. *She doesn't want to leave,* Luke thought. *She doesn't want to go home.*

She looked up finally, at the bottom step, and saw the truck. She turned away, took a step, then stopped again. She waited a moment.

Luke stepped out of the truck.

"Amanda," he said. "Come for a walk on the beach. We need to talk."

"I don't want to talk," she said, not looking at him.

"Then come walk Sweetpea. Please."

Reluctantly Amanda turned back toward the truck and opened the passenger door. Sweetpea jumped out, hopped up in front of her, pranced around. Amanda leaned over and nuzzled the dog, then climbed into the truck. Sweetpea settled in at Amanda's feet.

Luke got in, started the truck, drove toward the beach. He let Amanda fiddle with the radio. *I have to win her,* he thought. *All over again.* He felt exhausted, not quite over his hangover, confused about who should be courting whom. She shouldn't have been reading files on his computer.

They drove in silence, and when they parked at Fort Funston, Amanda jumped out of the truck and led Sweetpea down the long stairway to the beach before Luke could begin to catch up.

He let them go. He stayed behind, watching her transform from depressed teenage girl to delighted kid romping with her dog at the beach. *She needs this,* he thought. And then he surprised himself with the next thought: *She needs me.*

"Amanda!" he called out. "Wait up."

Miraculously, she did. He jogged ahead, joining Sweetpea in some kind of hopping race to Amanda's side.

"Glad you came with me," he said, slowing to a walk with her at his side.

"Did you ever think about me that way?" she asked, not looking at him.

He thought for a moment, trying to track the conversation they hadn't been having. He ran through the morning's episode in his head. He wished his mind were clearer, sharper—but instead, he felt mired in the hangover fog, worse even than this morning.

"No," he said finally. "That story was not about you."

"I know that," she said.

"I don't know any bartender's daughters in the woods," he said.

"Too bad," she told him.

"No, it's not too bad. I created a short story. That's all."

"Funny choice of subject matter," she said.

"Writers write about all kinds of material. We challenge ourselves in our writing. I wrote the story as a challenge."

"Why?"

Luke didn't answer right away. He picked up a stick and threw it far ahead of them on the beach. Sweetpea raced after it, but then ran around with it, finally dropping it far away from him. She never quite got the concept of playing fetch.

"Did you know that *Pescadero* was your mother's story? At least the premise was. I didn't know her story, but I was upset by it. The story stayed in my mind and wouldn't let go. So I invented my own version of it. In the end *Pescadero* had nothing to do with what really happened."

"Maybe you should leave us alone," Amanda said.

"I can't leave you alone," Luke told her. "I'm in love with your mother."

"I don't see what that has to do with me," she said sullenly.

"I want to be with her. All the time," Luke explained. "And up until this morning I wanted you around, too. Now I'm angry that you sneaked around on my computer, and I'm embarrassed that you might think that story is true."

"It's not a bad story," she said.

He looked at her. She watched her feet as she walked.

"Do you believe me?" he asked.

"I don't know. I guess."

"Good," he said.

"You can go out with my mother without me hanging around," Amanda said.

"I don't want to," he told her. "You're the center of your mother's life. I want to join her, not drag her away from you."

"Yeah, well." She didn't say anything else. They walked for a long time, along the edge of the surf. Sweetpea ran ahead of them, then back, checking up on them, then taking off again.

They turned around after a half hour and started back. The day was cold and windy—they wrapped their sweatshirts and fleece jackets tight around themselves. There weren't very many people on the beach, and the noise of the wind made Luke feel comfortable in their silence.

"Your mom's going to quit work tonight," Luke said as they neared the stairway back to the parking lot.

"Why?"

"The doctor thinks it's a good idea. She needs to save her energy."

Amanda didn't say anything for a while.

"I can help out. Financially. Your mom can take it easy for once."

"What else did the doctor say?"

"That she's looking good. For now. But things will change."

"She loves her job," Amanda said.

"I know that. This will be hard for her."

"Shit," Amanda muttered, kicking at the sand as she walked.

"Let's have dinner at the restaurant tonight," Luke suggested.

Amanda looked at him warily. Then she shook her head and looked away.

"I've got too much homework," she said.

"Last chance," Luke told her.

"Fuck you," she said, and she started running, Sweetpea on her heels, and kept the pace all the way up the stairway.

Luke trudged up the stairs slowly, the wind whipping his face as if it were slapping him, the noise in his ears like an echo of *fuck you, fuck you.*

When he reached the truck, he expected Amanda not to speak to him, perhaps ever again. He kept blowing it, saying exactly the wrong thing, finding it impossible to imagine what she felt, what she thought. But he sat down, put the key in the ignition, felt her hand on his arm.

"I'd like that," she said. "Dinner at Mom's restaurant."

He looked at her, but she got busy with the radio. He nodded and drove them back to the cottage.

• • •

Luke kissed Blair good-bye as she headed to work in her chef's clothes. He held her for a moment, close to him.

"You can still cook for me. Every night. I'll be the most appreciative audience in the world," he said.

"It's not the same."

"I know."

"I've loved cooking. Even on the longest, lousiest night. Put me in that kitchen and I'm a happy woman."

A couple of hours earlier, she had called Daniel to tell him it was her last night, had made him promise there would be no fanfare for her departure. She had cried—or rather, tried not to—for a few moments. Then she asked him to hold a table for Luke and Amanda.

"I wish I had years of this," Luke said. "Kissing you good-bye. Watching you dash off in your sexy chef's outfit. Waiting for you to come home."

Blair held him close, then pulled away, opened the door and headed out.

"See you later, Amanda!" she called out.

Some muffled noise came from Amanda's room.

"We'll see you at seven," Luke said. "I want the most decadent chocolate dessert on the menu."

"It's yours," Blair said, and headed out into the night.

Luke poured himself a glass of wine and sat in the living room. He read while he waited for Amanda to do her homework—in her room this time, rather than on the living-room floor—and get dressed for dinner.

When she emerged, he was surprised. She had transformed herself from punk teenager to knockout woman. She wore a long black skirt and a red tank top. She draped a silk shawl over her shoulders—something her mother might have worn in high school. Instead of her army boots, she wore high-heeled sandals, strappy things that wrapped around her ankles. And she had rimmed her eyes in dark liner and had given her full lips a coat of red lipstick.

"Wow," Luke said. "You look terrific."

"Yeah. Well." She kept her face half-turned away from him, but Luke could see her shy smile.

"Your mother will be very happy."

Amanda looked at Luke quickly, then looked away.

"You ready?" Luke asked.

"I guess." She sounded timid, unsure—Luke had never seen this side of Amanda. She looked older, seemed younger. He imagined her on a date and knew that it would take a boy a long time to get to know her.

"Let's go."

They walked to the restaurant, slowly because Amanda was unsteady on her heels. She seemed cold, and Luke offered his jacket, but she said no, then went back to not talking.

At the restaurant Daniel greeted them, kissing Amanda, complimenting her so much that she blushed, then led them to a table in the corner.

Daniel didn't talk to Luke. Luke wondered if he was the enemy for taking Blair away from the restaurant or for taking her away from him. A gay man can fall in love with a straight woman—Luke was sure of that. He may never want to sleep with her, but then, no one else should, either.

Rianne rushed to their table, kissed Amanda, kissed Luke. "We met once before. The night you dumped her," Rianne explained breathlessly.

"Sorry about that," Luke said.

"Don't ever do it again," she said.

"I promise." She looked at him mischievously—testing him out?—then gave him another kiss. "You're as handsome as she says," she whispered, and moved on to another table.

"What did she say?" Amanda asked.

"She said your mom's cooking up a storm," Luke told her.

"She did not."

"What's good here?"

Philippe appeared, presenting a bottle of champagne. "Daniel's gift," he said, "and the lovely girl can even sneak a glass."

Amanda's eyes lit up.

"Bon soir, monsieur," Philippe said, offering Luke his hand for a shake.

Luke felt the waiter's appraisal—was it for Blair's sake or his own? *Or both,* Luke decided.

"Nice to meet you," Luke said.

"If there's any champagne left over, bring it back to the kitchen after dinner," Philippe whispered.

"If we need to, I'll buy an extra," Luke told him.

"I have school tomorrow," Amanda said.

"You, *chérie,* have to learn to be a teenager. Drinking champagne is a very good thing. I bet I hear you giggling tonight." He turned to Luke. "Amanda is not a giggler. A young girl should know how to giggle."

The waiter exited with a wink at Amanda.

"I don't think you should take lessons from Philippe on being a young girl," Luke said.

"He's *sooo* cute," Amanda said, leaning close to Luke across the table.

"And off-limits," Luke said. "For several reasons."

"You're not my father."

Luke felt himself sink a little lower in his chair. "I know that, Amanda."

Amanda picked up the glass of champagne and took a sip. She wrinkled her nose, then took another sip.

"Should I giggle?" she asked, and then—amazingly—she giggled.

Luke smiled and clinked glasses with her. "I'll call Philippe over next time."

"Don't you dare," Amanda said, and giggled again.

Luke took a deep breath.

And then he felt Blair's hand on his cheek, and he turned around.

"Welcome," she said, smiling at him. She wore her chef's jacket—no hat—she had told him she found the hat thing silly. She leaned over and kissed him.

"If you hadn't come out to say hello," Luke said to her, "I would have come into the kitchen and risked the wrath of Daniel."

"Did you meet everyone?"

"Rianne was flirting," Amanda said.

"No she wasn't. She was being Rianne. You look lovely, my daughter," Blair said, leaning over to kiss Amanda.

"Daniel gave us champagne," Amanda said, lifting her glass.

"Don't let her drink more than one," Blair said, smiling at Luke. "Hey. I'm glad you're here."

"Me too."

"I gotta get back there. Daniel agreed to cover for me in the kitchen—he gave me three minutes. He's so upset that I'm quitting, he doesn't quite know what to do tonight."

"Go," Luke said. "Come visit at the end of our dinner. Please."

"I will." She headed back to the kitchen.

Amanda sipped more champagne. "It's OK," she said. "First taste was gross. But now, I kind of like it."

"Uh-oh," Luke said, smiling.

"The kids at school get drunk. I've had two beers in my life."

"Well, now you've tried champagne. I bet they're not drinking champagne."

Amanda smiled. She looked beautiful, and Luke wished she hadn't read the story, wished they were anywhere else rather than sitting at a table for two in a romantic restaurant.

"Remember the story I told you about the boy who took me up to the roof?"

"Yes, of course I remember that story," Luke said.

"He's been hanging around me lately. Talking to me."

"I hope you're not talking back to him," Luke said.

"He's OK."

"He's not OK. He left you alone on that roof. Amanda. You deserve a helluva lot better."

"Well, he invited me to a party on Saturday."

"No."

"You can't tell me no."

"I know that. I'm talking to you as a friend, not as a father. The guy's a shit."

"Well. We'll see."

"Amanda."

"I know how to take care of myself."

"I know you do."

Rianne arrived, ready to take their orders.

"We haven't looked at the menu," Luke said.

"I know the menu by heart," Amanda said.

"Go ahead," Luke offered. "I'll find something quickly."

They ordered, and when Rianne left, they sat quietly, sipping champagne. Philippe appeared, refilling both glasses. Luke saw Amanda glance at him, daring him to object, and he said nothing.

"My mother's going to be a mess when she stops working," Amanda said. "You think she's going to be happy because she's spending every moment of the day with you, but she's not."

Luke nodded. "I know it will be hard for her."

"You think you can step in and take care of everything," Amanda said.

"No, Amanda. I'm not trying to do that."

Amanda finished the glass of champagne, putting it down too hard on the table.

Rianne arrived with the first course—salad for Luke, soup for Amanda. They ate quietly for a while.

"This is delicious," Luke said.

"Taste the soup. It's one of Mom's specialties."

Luke reached across the table and tasted.

"It's great," he said.

"I helped her make it up. Years ago. We were fooling around in the kitchen, and suddenly we had invented Blair's Bean Soup."

"You're lucky," Luke said. "Growing up the way you did."

"What do you mean?"

"With a mother like Blair. So close."

"Yeah, well. I used to think my life sucked. Everyone else I knew had fathers. Then all the parents got divorced, and all the kids have to deal with moms in one house, dads in another."

"Did you wish your mother would get married?"

"Like, did I wish she'd fall in love and marry the guy and live happily ever after? Fairy-tale stuff. Doesn't exist."

"Yes, it does."

"You grow up around here and it's hard to believe in fairy tales. Everyone's divorced. Or still married and miserable after all these years. It's all the kids talk about. No one wants to be like their parents. At least my mom had some fun along the way."

"I wish I had fallen in love with your mother a long time ago."

"You were busy being married."

"Right. Bad timing."

"Well, didn't you love your wife?"

"Yes. At one time."

"So love disappears. In thin air. Poof. It's a dream."

"No," Luke insisted. "Not if it's the real thing. If I could, I'd marry your mother and love her for as long as I live. I'm sure of that. You find love, real love, and you put it at the very center of your life. The way your mother put you at the center of her life. That kind of love lasts."

Amanda finished her soup and reached for her champagne glass. It was empty. She looked at Luke but didn't say anything. He watched her. Then she picked up the bottle and poured herself another glass.

"You're going to have a hard time waking up in the morning," Luke said.

"Well, that's my problem, isn't it?"

"Amanda, I wish you weren't so angry with me. We were doing pretty well there for a while."

"You're in the way. My mother is dying, and you're all over the place."

"I can help you both."

"I don't want your help. I want to be alone with my mom."

This time Luke was quiet, and he finished his salad, drank his champagne, told Rianne when she came to clear the plates to give his compliments to the chef.

They never got to the second course. Amanda reached for her glass, which tipped over and spilled all over Luke. She stood up and raced to the bathroom, awkwardly with her high heels, and stayed there for a while. Finally Rianne went after her, brought her out, her face white, her hair wet from the water Rianne had splashed on her.

"She was sick," Rianne told Luke. "You better get her home."

So he walked her home, and though he wanted to put his arm around her and help her, he didn't touch her. She wobbled her way back to the cottage.

Once inside, Luke gave her some Advil and a glass of water, told her to go to bed. She looked at him—he recognized the old you're-not-my-father look, but she didn't say anything. She started toward her room and then said, "Can I lie in my mom's bed and watch TV a little while? My head's kind of spinning."

"Of course," Luke said. He noticed that she had asked permission.

Amanda disappeared into Blair's room. He heard the TV. She hadn't shut the door.

He changed his champagne-drenched clothes, found his book and went into the living room to wait for Blair. He knew she'd be disappointed—he was, too—but he'd take Blair and Amanda out to dinner someplace nice—the three of them—to make it up to both of them.

An hour later, the phone rang. Amanda didn't pick up in the bedroom—he figured she was long passed out. He reached for the phone near him and said, "Hello."

"Luke." It was Emily's voice. "I need help. I'm bleeding. I've got some kind of pain, in my belly. I can hardly breathe. I'm so scared. I don't want to lose the baby."

He didn't say anything for a moment.

"Please, Luke. Come get me. I don't want to go to the hospital alone."

"I'll be right there," he said.

At the door, Sweetpea nudged his leg. "Come on, girl. Let's go for a ride."

Chapter Eleven

Blair walked home in the cool night, tipsy from the champagne the staff had shared at the end of the evening. Leon, the pastry chef she had never met, had shown up to say good-bye. He was bad-boy handsome and wickedly charming, and happily she kissed him good-bye so she could head home to Luke. "Some man's got your heart," he had teased. "Yes," she had told him. "He's got my heart."

She was feeling too many things—pain at saying good-bye to her dear circle of friends at the restaurant, fear about what was going on with Amanda, and an erotic charge about slipping into bed with Luke. She was also feeling bone-numbing exhaustion.

She walked slowly, breathing in the cool air, trying to clear her head, calm her heart. She wanted to get home—Luke would be there—and she wanted to walk for hours in the quiet night. Once she got home and undressed, she would no longer be a chef. For now, in her chef's jacket and pants, well stained by hours of hard work at the stove, she was still a chef. Anyone passing by would see that. They could not see—not yet, not tonight—that she had quit work and was getting ready to die.

She reached the cottage and walked quietly up the steps to the front door. The house was dark—perhaps Luke would be sleeping, though he would awaken when she slipped in beside him.

She opened the door and heard something—a noise that made her heart stop for a moment. It was a kind of wail, almost inhuman, a long stretch of a cry, and though it sounded muffled, it was shrill enough to chill Blair's overheated body.

She listened for a second more, than ran toward her bedroom. The door was open, the room dark. But in the corner of the room, on the floor, she saw Amanda huddled in a ball—the wail was coming from her.

"My God," she called, and ran to her daughter's side. "Are you OK?"

Amanda first pulled back from Blair, her body stiffening. She had her head buried on her knees, and when she looked up, her expression was one of terror. An animal trapped.

"Amanda," Blair said, pulling her daughter to her. "What happened?"

Finally Amanda let go of herself and fell onto her mother. She still kept her body rolled into a ball, but now the wail got louder, and she clutched at her mother's legs.

"Talk to me!" Blair shouted. "Tell me what happened."

Amanda shook her head, cried louder.

"Where's Luke?" Blair demanded, and the wail intensified.

Finally Blair grabbed Amanda's shoulders and sat her up, holding her up in front of her. "What's going on?" she asked, her voice strong and calm. "Tell me what happened."

Amanda blinked as if Blair had turned a spotlight on her. Her eyes couldn't seem to adjust to her mother's stare. Her face was streaked with tears. She wore a T-shirt and boxers, and she pressed her arms tightly around her body.

"Amanda," Blair said again.

The girl nodded. She blinked again. She swiped at her face with the back of her arm, wiping off the new run of tears. Then she wrapped her arms around herself as if she were freezing. She nodded again.

"He—he—he tried . . . Luke"—and then she shook her head again, lowered it, and her body began to tremble.

Blair reached for Amanda's chin and pulled it up, kept the girl looking at her.

"He tried what?"

"To have sex with me." This time she kept looking at her mother, her eyes wide and terrified.

"Amanda," Blair said.

Amanda nodded, then fell forward into her mother's arms.

Blair held her awhile, trying to take it in. Amanda sobbed in her arms.

"Where is he?" she finally asked.

She felt Amanda shrug in her arms.

"Did he—did you . . . ?"

"No," Amanda said, her voice buried in Blair's shoulder. Then she picked her head up, and the story exploded in a rush. "No. I was sleeping. I thought it was a dream. A hand on my body. Someone leaning on me. It was dark. I couldn't see anything. He was naked. He just climbed in bed, and I felt his thing on me, and then I knew I wasn't dreaming. He put his hands all over me, up my shirt and down my shorts, and he kept pressing on me. . . ."

Finally she stopped, and the wail began again, lower, more mournful.

Blair held her and rocked her in her arms. She fought off the images that sprang to mind immediately—the men at the beach who tore at her flesh as if she were nothing. One man first pushed his fingers inside her, and then finally his penis thrust into her, through her, it seemed. She remembered the pain and the terror.

"Tell me all of it, Amanda," Blair said.

Amanda got quieter, her cry subsiding. She pulled back, spoke in a quiet voice, her eyes lowered to the floor.

"I woke up. I mean, in the middle of it. I knew it wasn't a dream. But I was so scared. I didn't know what to do. I mean, I should have screamed or something, but I didn't want to. I don't know, I was embarrassed or something. It doesn't make sense, I know, but I was scared. I pushed him off me, but he just kept moving his hands everywhere. And then he pulled my shorts off, and when he climbed on top of me, I could feel it—it was hard and pushing against me—and finally I screamed and he stopped for a second and then he ran out of the room, just like that. Just took off. I heard the front door slam. Like he thought I wanted it, and when I screamed, he just flipped out or something. Oh, my God."

She crumbled again, and Blair pulled her close, held her tightly.

"Shh," Blair said.

"I was so scared," Amanda said, and finally she cried quietly, her head on her mother's lap.

"You're OK," Blair said, stroking her head. "Shh."

Blair imagined Luke, not her rapists, not any rapist, but Luke, the man she loved. Maybe he had been drinking, maybe he had always wanted Amanda, but Blair hadn't seen it. Maybe she was blind in love.

Her daughter would be all right, she told herself. He had scared her, done something awful, but she had stopped it in time. Then Blair thought back to sixteen, her own sixteen, and knew that this night mattered. This experience, even if he hadn't finished what he had set out to do, had the power to pierce her soul.

"When did it happen?" she asked quietly.

She felt her daughter shrug.

"An hour ago?"

"Maybe," Amanda said.

"He won't come back," Blair said, and she felt the weight of it all. "He can't come back."

Amanda didn't say anything.

And then Blair thought of the fight that morning, thought about Amanda's anger about Luke being there now, all the time.

"You aren't making this up," Blair said as gently as she could.

Amanda pushed herself away from Blair, scrambled to stand, turn away from her, run to her room.

Blair waited for the slam of the door, then hung her head, sighed deeply. She pushed herself up and moved after her daughter. *Oh, my God,* she thought. *Both possibilities are awful.* That Luke could do this. Or that Amanda could create such a lie.

She knocked at Amanda's door. After a moment she called out, "I'm sorry, Amanda. You wouldn't lie. I'm sorry I said that."

The room was quiet. Blair put her head on the door, exhausted now.

"Can I come in? Please."

She didn't hear the answer. There was a noise at the front door, and then Sweetpea was barking. Blair moved toward the door.

Just as she got there, the door opened, and Luke stood there, his key in hand.

"Goddamn you," Blair said.

"What?"

"I should call the cops. I won't if you get out of our lives. Leave now and don't ever reappear."

"Blair—"

Luke started to move toward her, and she reached for the phone by her side. "I'll call the police. Right now. Leave. Before I rip you to shreds."

"What happened—"

Blair stared at him. She waited a moment. She looked at the closed door behind her. "Amanda . . ." She started and then stopped, watching him.

"What happened to Amanda?" he asked.

"You know what happened."

"If I knew what happened, I wouldn't be asking."

"Goddamn you," she said, shaking her head. "Get out of here. Now."

"Blair. What happened to Amanda?" He stood solidly in the doorway, not moving.

"You tried to rape her," Blair said, her voice low and mean.

"What? Someone tried to rape her?" He started to move into the house, and Blair held out the phone, but he kept moving, past her, and toward Amanda's door.

"Stop it! Get out of here!" she shouted.

Luke stopped in front of the closed door. "Amanda! Amanda!"

"Get out of here," Blair said, and she grabbed his shirt, started pulling him away from the door.

"I didn't try to rape her!" Luke shouted, angry now. "Goddamn it, Blair. Tell me what happened!"

Blair pulled at him and then let go of his shirt, falling back against the wall.

"How could you?" she asked.

He leaned toward her. "I didn't. I don't know what you're talking about. Emily called. She was miscarrying. She needed someone to take her to the hospital."

"Liar," Blair said.

"Blair, listen. Maybe your daughter is lying."

"Get out of my house," Blair said.

"Call the hospital if you don't believe me."

"Amanda wouldn't lie about something like this," Blair insisted.

Luke turned from her and started toward the door. He took a few steps and stopped. "Blair, don't let her do this to us."

"Leave," Blair said.

He walked out the door.

Blair sank to the floor.

"Amanda," she said loudly enough for her daughter to hear through the closed door. "Please come out and talk to me. I have to know if you're all right."

Amanda didn't answer.

• • •

In the morning Amanda wouldn't go to school. She wouldn't get out of bed, though she let her mother bring her a bowl of oatmeal, let her sit at the side of her bed and stroke her hair.

Amanda didn't speak much, and her face still looked swollen from crying. Blair finally leaned over, kissed her and said, "Take a day off. It won't hurt you. I'll go rent some movies for us."

But Amanda stayed in her room, curled in her bed, and didn't come out to watch a movie, or to eat any meals, or take a shower and get dressed.

Blair was sick—from exhaustion and worry and a dull pain that pulsed behind her eyes. She remembered her own slow recovery from the rape—she stayed in her house for weeks, watching TV, sleeping, silent, and when the summer ended, it was the headmaster of the school who came and talked her into returning to classes. She remembered the day she got up to go to school that first time. She had examined her body and found that all the bruises and cuts had healed over the couple of months since her attack. She looked at herself in the mirror and thought, *They're all inside. All the bruises are hiding now.*

Blair let Amanda sleep. She took a Vicodin and tried to float through the day, tried not to think about Luke, where he was, what he was thinking, what he had done. Or not done.

But Amanda wouldn't lie, and she wouldn't keep lying. He must have been drunk. Blair must have been wrong about him. He was just a guy, like any guy, lusting after a sixteen-year-old girl.

But then she would think about the Luke who came with her to doctor's appointments and sat by her bed and held her all night. He wasn't the same man who slipped into bed with her daughter, who pushed himself at her, terrifying her.

She hated the noise in her head, and the Vicodin did nothing to quiet it.

The phone rang, but she didn't answer it.

She took Sweetpea for a walk—Luke had left Sweetpea, and she wasn't going to give her back. She walked slowly—every muscle in her body ached. Sweetpea urged her forward gently, as if the sweet dog knew Blair was sick. They made it to the video store, where she rented movies—mysteries, detective stories, thrillers—anything to keep her mind busy. She sat alone in her bedroom, eating popcorn, watching film after film, waiting for Amanda to emerge from her room.

The next morning, Amanda still didn't get out of bed, still refused to go to school.

"You have to get over this," Blair said. "You can't hide in your room, sweetheart." Eerily, her mother's voice echoed in her head. She remembered telling her mother, "I'll never get over this." Had she? Can you get over rape? Or does it become a permanent wound, hidden deep inside your body?

"I'm not leaving," Amanda said, curled around a pillow, hiding her face in her hair. Blair held her shoulder, felt like shaking it.

"At least get out of bed," Blair urged her. "Take a shower. Get dressed."

"No," Amanda said.

"What can I do for you?" Blair asked, exasperated.

Amanda didn't answer.

"Come walk Sweetpea with me," Blair suggested. "We'll go to the beach."

"No," Amanda said.

"Tomorrow you'll go back to school," Blair told her.

She left her in bed, and Blair walked with Sweetpea back to the video store, rented more movies, bought more popcorn. She took a Vicodin and bought a bottle of wine. She didn't answer the phone.

When Amanda refused to go to school the next day, Blair told her they needed to do something. "I'll take you to a doctor," she said. "A therapist."

"No," Amanda said. "I just want to sleep."

"You can't. You have to get back to your life. I know it was awful, Amanda, but you've got to be strong enough to recover from this."

Amanda didn't answer.

"What if we went away for a few days?" she suggested.

Amanda looked up at her from the bed.

"I'll get Luke's cabin. You have spring break next week. I'm done with work. We'll go live in the woods for a while."

"No," Amanda said. "Not Luke—"

"We won't see Luke," Blair said. "I'll tell him I'll kill him if he shows up. He owes us this."

Amanda didn't argue. Blair left her room and headed toward the phone. She found his number in the woods and dialed.

"Hello?"

"It's me."

"Blair." She could hear the sadness in his voice. She could hear him breathe deeply, and she felt for a moment that he was next to her. She could almost smell him.

"I don't want to talk to you. I want your cabin. Amanda's a mess. She won't go to school. Just give us your cabin for a week or two. Maybe that will help. I don't know what else to do."

"Will you listen to me?"

"No. I don't want to listen to you. You'll tell me my daughter is lying, and I don't believe that. It's easier to believe that you're a monster, and I'm a fool for not seeing that."

"I would never touch Amanda," Luke said.

"I'm just calling to ask for the cabin. Can we have it?"

"Yes. Of course."

"You can't stay here. I don't want you here ever again."

"Blair—"

"Just leave, and put the key under the mat. Don't show up or I'll kill you. We'll stay for a while—I don't know—until she's better."

"I can't bear this, Blair."

"We'll be there tomorrow. And you better be nowhere near the place."

She hung up the phone.

She sat there, her body shaking. She felt her heart pounding in her chest. Her body felt weak, as if she could crumble on the spot. She didn't want to stand up, didn't want to reach for her glass of wine on the bookshelf, didn't want to tell Amanda that they were leaving tomorrow.

She would borrow the car from Casey. They would leave tomorrow.

• • •

Amanda seemed to sit up straighter as they drove into the Santa Cruz Mountains. She kept her head to the side, staring out the window, or avoiding her mother's glances.

Blair felt sick, worse than she had yet, and knew that some progression of the illness had started, knew in her bones that she would not feel right again.

"I love it here," Amanda said quietly when they turned off onto one of the small roads heading up the mountain. The woods closed in on them, creating a canopy of leaves over their heads. "It feels safe," she said.

Blair smiled. She followed the curve of the road, hugging the side of the mountain, hiding her nervousness about Luke. That he would be there. Or that even the feel of him in the place would disturb Amanda. She thought about the feel of Luke in that cabin and realized she was worried for herself, worried that she'd be hit by the loss of him finally. And she wasn't ready for that.

She remembered the turnoff, the long driveway, the warm glow of the cabin as the sun hit it in the early morning. He was gone—no truck in sight. Sweetpea was whining in the backseat, an echo to the sound in Blair's own heart.

She stopped the car, and Sweetpea pushed herself up toward the front seat, urging them out of the car.

"She's happy to be home," Amanda said.

Blair nodded, looking at the cabin, not quite ready for it.

"It's cute," Amanda said. "Now we'll be hermits."

"For a week," Blair said. "That's all."

Amanda opened the door, and Sweetpea climbed over her, racing up the path to the cabin, back to Amanda, back up the path again. Blair sat watching them. *Does Sweetpea miss Luke?* Blair wondered. *Does she feel his absence like an ache in the heart?*

She saw Amanda stop at the door, turn back and wait for her. She had to propel herself forward. *What kind of ridiculous idea is this,* she thought. *Heal my daughter. Ruin myself.*

She pushed the door open and forced herself out of the car. The cool air slapped at her, alerted her. *Wake up. Find the energy. He's not here. He's gone.*

She walked to the front door, lifted the mat, found the key. Sweetpea pranced around them impatiently.

Blair opened the door and let the light sweep through the one-room cabin.

"Wow," Amanda said. "It's so cool."

It was clean, neat, ordered. Not like Blair had seen it last time. That helped. But it was inviting, with its warm woods, upholstered armchair, small dining table with its two chairs. As if he had eaten there for months, waiting for her to fill the second chair.

She wouldn't look toward the bed. She wouldn't imagine Luke in the armchair, at the stove, sitting with her at the table, eating pancakes. She breathed deeply and imagined that the smell was the cabin smell, not the man smell.

"I want to go for a walk," Amanda said. "It's all so beautiful."

"Go ahead," Blair said, relieved that Amanda was being Amanda again. "Take Sweetpea."

"Don't you want to come?" Amanda asked.

Blair couldn't look at her, couldn't let herself feel her daughter's need. Maybe it was better for her to walk on her own anyway.

"You go ahead. I'll unpack, get us moved in."

"Where do I go?"

"Follow the path behind the cabin. It leads up the hill for a while. You'll come to a meadow that's filled with wildflowers."

"Cool," Amanda said. She headed out the door, Sweetpea on her heels. When she left, Blair moved to the back window and watched her daughter come around to the back of the house and head up the trail. Amanda looked better than she had for days, her step lighter, easier. *She'll get better,* Blair thought. She turned away from the window.

She looked at the bed, neatly made, pillows stacked high. She moved toward it hesitantly. She lay down and placed her hands on her heart and began to cry.

Chapter Twelve

Luke drove down the mountain, taking the long route to 280 so that he wouldn't pass Blair's car as she headed to his cabin. He had cleaned all morning, thrown a few things in the back of his truck, set out for the city with one mission: to find out what had happened to Amanda.

He didn't think she would lie—he wanted to give her more credit than that. She was drunk—was she drunk enough to imagine something and decide it was real?

He would start with the theory, though, that something had happened, that someone else had come into the cottage and tried to rape her. He had to discount all scenarios before he faced the real possibility of a hatred so profound that she had invented the story to destroy him.

He drove into the city along 280, wishing he were heading toward Blair, instead of away from her. He didn't know where he would go, what he would do. He imagined that Emily was back at the house on Potrero Hill. She had miscarried that night—all the time he was in the hospital with her, taking care of her, someone was undoing the life he had created with Blair. He wanted to hate Emily for pulling him away that night, and he wanted to blame her for everything that followed. But he couldn't. Instead, he felt a terrible pity and sadness.

When the doctor had told them it was a miscarriage, Emily had cried for a long time.

"I wanted the baby," she told him sadly.

"I know," he said. She lay in the emergency room, her hair damp against her face, her skin pale against the white sheets. He sat at her side and thought about the months ahead with Blair. He had vowed to keep her out of the hospital.

"You can come back," Emily had said, her voice almost a whisper. He was sitting on the edge of the bed, his hand on her arm. "We can try to start a family."

"No," Luke had told her gently.

When the doctors advised that she spend the night in the hospital so they could continue to monitor her, Luke had said good-bye. He had leaned over and kissed her cheek, felt her arm wrap around his neck and press him to her.

And then he had driven back to Blair's cottage. As he drove through the streets of the Haight, he had remembered a moment from high school. His creative-writing teacher had called on Blair Clemens, the girl who had been raped on the beach only months before. "Miss Clemens," the man had said, his voice a rumble through the classroom. "What's the worst thing that could happen to the character in your story?" And Blair's voice was clearer than he had ever heard it. "She could be raped."

When Luke got to Blair's cottage that night, she had called him a rapist.

Luke took 101 into the city and headed to the Haight again. He drove to Blair's cottage, found a parking space in front and sat in his truck, staring down the long driveway that ran behind the purple

Victorian. He looked over at the porch of the big house, remembering Casey, the landlord. Maybe he had heard something. If he wasn't too stoned to notice. Luke would start with him.

He got out of the truck. The house looked deserted, but then it always did. There were no curtains on any of the windows, and the windows stared blankly at him, as if the house had been emptied. Ghosts might roam the hallways there, but there was no sound of humans, no light, no visible movement within.

Luke walked up to the door and paused for a moment. He hated the guy, irrationally perhaps. Because he had tried to keep Luke away from Blair? Because he claimed a familiarity with Blair that he didn't deserve, just for being her landlord? Maybe he would be jealous of any man who had known Blair for all those years when she was absent from his own life. Yes, it wasn't rational. The guy was just a rich hippie, with a great tenant.

He rang the doorbell. The sound echoed within the house. He waited a moment, then rang again. He turned and looked back at the street just as Casey ambled down the sidewalk.

Casey walked with a long, lanky stride, his arms wrapped around a grocery bag. He looked over at Luke and nodded, the barest recognition, then started up the path.

"I'm Luke. I don't think we officially met."

"Yeah. I'm Casey. Hey, where'd Blair go? She borrowed my car and disappeared." He stood a few steps away from Luke, at the bottom of the stairs, eyeing him, holding his bag in front of him. He squinted at Luke, though there was no sun in his eyes.

"She and Amanda went to my place in the Santa Cruz Mountains for a week."

"How come?"

"Vacation."

Casey looked away then and rearranged the bag in his other arm. "You want a beer?" he offered.

Luke shook his head. He hadn't even eaten breakfast.

"Are they OK? Blair and Amanda?"

"Yeah," Luke said. "They're OK."

Casey fidgeted with the bag, then put it down. He reached inside, pulled out a Budweiser can, flipped back the top and drank. When he was done, he sat down on the steps, his back to Luke.

"Whadda you want?" he asked, his voice low.

Luke took a step down and sat next to Casey.

"Were you home last Tuesday night?"

"What are you, a fucking cop?"

Luke reached over, into the bag, and pulled out a beer. "No, man. I'm not a cop. I'm trying to help them out."

He opened the beer and took a long drink. He felt exhausted already and hadn't found out a damn thing.

"What's wrong with them?" Casey asked.

"You hear any noises or anything? Tuesday night. Sometime after ten?"

"What kind of noises?"

"Screams. Amanda might have screamed."

Casey looked at Luke for a quick second, then looked away.

"She didn't scream," he said. "She never screamed."

Casey put his beer down by his feet. He hung his head low, between his knees. Luke could see his back rising and falling with his deep breaths. He waited for him. Finally Casey sat up and stared ahead of him, out toward the street.

"I got high. A woman was supposed to come over—Fran, someone I get together with once in a while—but she didn't show. I thought we were going to make love, and then I felt sort of awful about spending the whole night by myself, no woman. I get high and want sex the way some people want food. And Blair's cool—I mean, she was until she got sick. Then she didn't want to screw around anymore. And you were hanging around all the time. I was sitting outside smoking when you left. I figured you had a fight and she kicked you out. She'd be lying there, wanting sex, just like me."

He stopped, and Luke closed his eyes, imagining the rest of the story without hearing it. But Casey's voice went on, smooth and quiet like it could slip right past him, never bother a soul. Already Luke wasn't breathing right, couldn't seem to find enough air in his chest.

"I got a key. Hell, it's my place. I go in, see Blair's door open. It's dark, but I figure she's lying in bed, and, damn, she'll be happy when I slip in there with her. I go into her room, and she's sleeping. No noise, just the soft sound of her breathing. So I take my clothes off and slide under the covers. I'm as high as a fucking kite. There's nothing like waking a woman like that. It's a rush, man. So I'm ready for her, just like that, and she's moving in her sleep like she wants me, and then I start to climb onto her and she's pushing me away, pushing herself to the other side of the bed, and, goddamn it, it's Amanda. How the fuck am I supposed to know it's the kid? In her mother's bed. I mean, they're the same size and the lights are out and fuck it all if it wasn't the kid."

He picked up the beer and was about to take a swig when Luke slammed it away from him. The can flew past him, beer spraying.

"What the hell," Casey mumbled.

Luke stood, pulling Casey up by his shirt.

"Goddamn you," Luke said, his anger surging through him so that his whole body trembled. "She's a kid. A sixteen-year-old girl."

Luke punched him, a solid punch that connected with his jaw. Casey was loose, a bag of bones, waiting to be hit. He flew back and dropped to the ground. He lay there, not moving, his body breathing hard, his face lowered to the dirt.

Luke watched him a moment, feeling the punch reverberate in his own body. "You're a monster," he spat.

"Tell her I'm sorry," Casey muttered, his voice barely audible.

Luke walked away. He got in the truck and drove back to the mountains.

• • •

Luke drove up the long driveway to his cabin, saw Blair's car, heard Sweetpea's barking. He hadn't let go of his rage at Casey. Now, for a moment, he could begin to feel something else—relief. Perhaps hope.

He parked behind the car and walked up to the front door. It swung open before he reached it.

"Get the hell out of here," Blair said.

She stepped out and pulled the door closed behind her. Blocking him from her daughter.

"I know who did it," he said.

She stood, staring at him.

"Listen to me, Blair."

She shook her head but didn't say a word, didn't move away from him.

"It was Casey," Luke said. "He saw me leave, let himself in, thought he'd have sex with you. Amanda was in your bed."

Blair stared at him, her expression confused. She looked angry enough to slug him—and then, a second later, she looked scared, ready to flee. Her skin was white, her eyes swollen as if she had been crying.

"Casey?" she asked, taking it in.

Luke nodded. "I would never—"

Blair sank to the ground, sitting there.

"Casey," she said weakly.

"I think I broke his jaw," Luke said.

She looked up at him. Her eyes were still dark, angry.

"How could you have imagined . . . ," Luke started to say.

"I don't know," Blair said. "It was crazy. She was so sure."

Blair patted the ground next to her, and Luke moved toward her, sat down next to her, took her in his arms. She began to cry, and he pressed her to him. Her body shook with her tears. *She's gotten so thin,* Luke thought, feeling her ribs as he held her.

"I'm sorry I thought it was you," she said into his neck, hanging on to him.

"Shh," Luke said. "You had to believe her."

"But I couldn't," Blair said, looking up at him. "I couldn't make sense of it."

"And I couldn't believe she would lie," Luke said. "She wouldn't do that."

"Stay here," Blair said. "I'll go tell her."

She got up, wiped her eyes on her sleeve and walked back into the house.

Luke sat for a long time, Sweetpea at his feet, looking out at the forest in front of him. Sweetpea seemed happy to be home. *Maybe I'm home, too,* Luke thought.

When the door opened, it was Amanda who came out and sat beside him. He looked at her, imagined Casey pushing himself on her, felt rage like a stone in his gut.

"I thought it was you," she said quietly.

"I would never do something like that," Luke said.

She looked away from him, stared out toward the trees.

"It was awful," she said.

"I believe you," Luke said.

"I was so confused. I thought maybe you liked me—"

"I love you, Amanda," Luke said. "Like a daughter. Don't you know that?"

She looked at him quickly, then lowered her head. *My daughter*, he thought.

Amanda glanced at him, then shrugged. "I guess. I mean, I felt that. But you're still a guy. And you wrote that story. I don't know."

"You know what I kept thinking these past few days?" Luke said. He felt Amanda's eyes on him, but he looked straight ahead. "I couldn't stand losing Blair. It would kill me. But there was something else. Something new. I couldn't stand the idea of losing you in my life."

Amanda put her hand on his elbow and kept it there. They were quiet a moment.

"You beat him up?" she finally asked.

Luke smiled. "One solid punch. He deserves more."

"Good," Amanda said, nodding.

Luke put his hand over hers.

"I don't want to go back there," she said.

"You can stay here," Luke told her.

"I have school," she said.

"We'll figure that out."

The door opened, and Blair stood there, looking down at them. "I made soup," she said. "Should we invite the hermit for lunch?"

Amanda nodded.

• • •

They sat at the table, with a third chair added, which Luke brought in from the workshop. They were cautious with each other. Amanda talked about her hike with Sweetpea earlier in the day. Blair told them about a time when she was young and spent a summer in a cabin in the Sierras with her parents. Luke watched them talking, listened and smiled. He had never imagined both of them here, in his private one-room cabin. He felt incredibly lucky.

After lunch Amanda sat outside in the sun with a book to read. Luke stood at the doorway while Blair brought her a glass of lemonade. In just a few days Blair's body seemed changed, too thin, too frail. She moved as if each step hurt. Watching her, Luke's heart ached.

Amanda took the drink and placed it on the arm of the chair. Blair bent over and kissed Amanda's head, then rested her cheek there, as if she couldn't pull herself away.

She must have felt Luke's attention—she looked up and smiled. "Want to go for a walk?" she asked.

"Can you?"

"A slow walk," Blair said.

They headed to the trail, Sweetpea at their side. Luke took Blair's hand and she let him hold it tightly in his.

"Can you give Amanda and me one night alone?" Blair asked him.

"Of course," Luke said. Too quickly. He felt the pain of his disappointment. "I'll miss you," he added.

"I know," she told him. "But I need a night alone with Amanda. To see how she is. About your being with us."

"She's OK with me," Luke said. "I can see that."

"I know you're right. Maybe it's for me," Blair said.

Luke looked at her, but she was watching the ground in front of her as she walked.

"Why?" Luke asked.

"Just one night," Blair said. "Come back tomorrow."

"Don't change your mind tomorrow," Luke said, taking her hand again. "I've missed too much time with you already."

"I'm getting sick now," Blair said. "It's happening so quickly."

"I'll take care of you," Luke told her.

She looked at him and smiled. "You will," she said. "I know that." She looked away, followed the ground in front of her with her eyes. "But I'm scared. Really scared. And loving you gives me more to lose."

• • •

Luke drove back into the city again. This time Blair said he could stay at her cottage for the night. He would gather some of their things to bring back to the mountains. "Beat the crap out of Casey if you run into him," Blair had suggested. But Casey was nowhere in sight. Luke parked at Blair's cottage, but couldn't go inside.

He walked through the Haight, stopping to buy things for the cabin. Flowers for Blair. *What flowers does she love?* he thought. Would he have enough time to find out, to develop the habits of couples? He chose blue irises.

He bought food for the cabin, CDs for Amanda, a warmer blanket for their bed. He walked through the streets of the city, his arms weighed down by so many packages. He saw a young couple standing in a doorway, making out. He wanted to be sixteen, in high school, with Blair Clemens in his arms. He wanted years that he wouldn't have.

When he reached Blair's cottage, he felt the pain of her absence. He went right to the phone and dialed his number at the cabin. On the first ring Blair picked up.

"Hello?"

"I woke you."

"No. Yes. You can wake me every day for the rest of my life and I won't care."

"I can't spend the night away from you," Luke said. "I've missed too much time already."

"Then come home," she told him.

Chapter Thirteen

Amanda and Blair headed out on the Ridge Trail, Sweetpea in the lead. The trail wiggled across the top of the Santa Cruz Mountains, sometimes descending into the thick forest on the Pacific side, sometimes roaming through meadows on the valley side. Along the peak they could see the Pacific licking the edge of Half Moon Bay, and to the east they could see the sprawl of Silicon Valley and the wide expanse of San Francisco Bay. The day was surprisingly warm, though fog was threatening to move in from the ocean.

Amanda had taken a leave for her last half semester of school, doing all the work on her own at the cabin, heading into the city for major tests. She had told the school her mother was dying, that she wanted these last couple of months with her, and they had agreed. She was disciplined enough, and smart enough, to pull it off. She moved into the workshop, setting up a cot, hanging sheets from the windows so she'd have some privacy. Sweetpea slept in there with her. During the days she studied, read in the sun, hiked with Luke. Blair could manage a short, slow walk every few days, though on her return she'd sleep for hours.

This time Blair and Amanda had headed off together while Luke fixed a broken sink in the cabin. Amanda had told Blair that she had something to show her.

"Mom?" Amanda called out when they neared a turn on the path. Ahead was a cluster of redwoods.

Blair was struggling to keep pace with her daughter—she didn't seem to have enough air in her chest.

"Up ahead," Amanda said. "I want to show you my favorite spot. My hiding place."

Blair nodded and headed off the path behind her daughter. Amanda squeezed through two of the trees and reached back to take her mother's hand and guide her through. Inside, they were encircled by the redwoods, tucked inside a space just large enough for one person to sprawl on the soft ground. Light filtered through the trees, shimmering down on them.

"But now that I know this place," Blair said, "you won't be able to hide here anymore." She felt the need to whisper. The sounds of the outside world seemed muffled now, and the enclosed space was filled with a kind of hush.

"I'm not hiding from you," Amanda said.

Blair flinched. Luke. But Amanda and Luke had been doing well. For the first days at the cabin, they had been cautious, circling around each other, talking to Blair but not to each other. Luke would give it time, let Amanda come to him. And she did—each day Blair noticed that Amanda trusted him more. She asked for his help in hanging curtains in the workshop. She helped him set up a picnic table in the backyard. She showed him her essay on American film directors. And he had liked the essay, told her she was smarter about film than most of the directors he knew.

"Who are you hiding from?" Blair finally asked.

"The world," Amanda said. "When I finish studying every day, I feel crazy. I can't figure out what I want. Why I'm reading all these books, learning all this stuff. My mind gets too crowded. So I come here. My escape from the world. Then I sit here a few minutes and I figure out: This is the world. I see the trunks of the trees and the insects and the leaves, and if I lie down, I see the sky and the clouds through the branches above me, and I've forgotten about all the stuff of books. I can just rest."

Blair smiled.

"You think I'm crazy," Amanda said.

"I think you're incredibly smart," Blair said. "That's what living in the cabin with you and Luke makes me feel. Like nothing else matters—the past or the future. I can just rest."

"This is called a cathedral," Amanda said. She leaned back and looked up.

"I can see why," Blair told her. The branches of the redwoods stretched like vaulted arches toward the sky.

"I love how cozy it feels," Amanda said. "The trees wrap me up inside them."

"It's a very cool hiding place," Blair told her.

Amanda squeezed back through two of the trees, and Blair followed her.

"Should we head back?" Amanda asked.

"I think we better," Blair said. "I'm beat."

They started back along the trail, Sweetpea racing ahead, then circling back. Amanda started to pull too far ahead.

"Slow down," Blair finally called out, and Amanda turned back, peered at her, worried.

"You OK?"

"Yes. Tired. That's all."

Amanda waited for Blair to catch up.

"Should we rest?" Amanda asked.

"I don't know," Blair told her. She felt a knot of pain behind her eyes, and the feeling was oddly familiar—had she felt that before she fainted the other times? Maybe she shouldn't be so far from the cabin.

"Is Luke coming back soon?" she asked. She couldn't remember where he had gone: To the store? Back to San Francisco? Why was it so cold in the beginning of May?

"Mom, sit down," Amanda urged. "You look awful."

Blair sat in the middle of the path. Sweetpea bounded back across the field to her side.

"Where's Luke?" Blair asked. She could see glittering points of light at the edge of her vision, as if an electrical storm were brewing on the horizon.

"He went to the hardware store," Amanda said. "Rest a bit and we'll head home."

Blair remembered. Something about the plumbing—a leak under the kitchen sink. But when she tried to picture it, she could only remember the kitchen sink in her cottage, not this one in Luke's cabin. The thought of Luke's cabin calmed her somehow. They had been living there for a few weeks, and she had thought of these weeks as Amanda's healing, while she knew she herself was failing fast. Luke. She needed Luke.

Her body was trembling.

"Mom? Mom? What should I do?"

"Wait. It'll pass."

Amanda took off her fleece jacket and wrapped it around Blair's shoulders. Blair breathed easier in the warmth and thought: *My daughter will take care of me. She can do that. My wonderful girl.*

She kept her eyes closed and still the light seemed to dart around the inside of her eyes, sending little jolts of pain.

She felt Amanda's hand on her back, rubbing it, creating a warm bath down her spine. *I used to rub her back to put her to sleep, my baby.*

"Should I run back to the cabin?" Amanda asked. "I'll see if Luke's back yet?"

Blair shook her head. *Don't leave me.*

"Can you walk?"

Again Blair shook her head. "I can't open my eyes," she said finally.

She felt Amanda's hand on her back, moving in slow, warm circles. She heard Sweetpea's labored breath in her ear. *Poor sweet dog,* she thought. *Scared. They're both scared. I'm not scared. I just want to lie down.*

But someone was lifting her, easily it seemed, until she was standing again.

"Lean on me," Amanda said. "We'll take it slow. We can't sit here."

She felt Amanda's arm wrap around her back and tuck under her arm. When Amanda moved, somehow Blair moved with her, her feet shuffling along the path. *My daughter's so big,* Blair thought, *and I've become so small.*

They walked like that for a long time. Blair kept her eyes closed and still her eyes hurt from the light. There was a noise in her head, a kind of humming, like a lawn mower somewhere in the distance.

She could hear her daughter's voice as they walked. Amanda was telling her something about the mountains, how beautiful it was here and that they would stay here and take care of her. Luke. Amanda kept saying his name. Luke would be home when they got back. They were making their way home.

Amanda, her baby, carried her home. *I've done well,* Blair told her guardian angel, the bartender from the Haight. She imagined his face, smiling at her, the glint of a lip ring shining in her eye. "I told you," he said. "You've done enough. She can take care of you now. Just keep watching."

I'm watching, she told him silently now. *I'm not going to miss a minute of her sweet life.*

• • •

Blair pulled herself out of a nightmare. Sweetpea was whimpering—was that the dream or was the dog really crying?—and someone was hurting the poor dog, except Blair felt the pain. When she woke, she still felt the pain. She opened her eyes and saw Sweetpea, watching her, whimpering.

"You were crying in your sleep," Luke explained. He was sitting on the bed, his hand stroking her hair. "Sweetpea got upset."

"It was in my dream," Blair said. Her mouth was terribly dry, and Luke lifted a glass of water with a straw to her lips. She smiled, thanking him. She hadn't even asked for it.

She had not imagined the disease would spread so quickly, would take over her body and transform her so completely into a dying person. Since her seizure on the Ridge Trail, she had been bedridden, and the shape of their days had changed. On most days Luke wrote, sitting at the little table in the cabin, typing away at his laptop. He said it was going well. He wouldn't talk about it, wouldn't share any of it with her. But he thanked her every day for being his muse.

Amanda studied in the morning, then hiked with Luke every afternoon, Sweetpea at their side. Blair slept. She seemed to sleep for hours at a stretch, even in the middle of the day. At night Amanda read stories from her contemporary short story class to her mother and Luke. Afterward, she and Luke would argue about the stories or the characters, and Blair would doze off, would end up dreaming new endings for the stories. Happy endings. No one died.

"Did I sleep long?" she asked Luke, and let her head fall back against the pillow.

"No. Only a few minutes."

She shook her head. "I wake up to be with you."

"Do you want your morphine?"

"No. Not yet. Where's Amanda?"

"Outside studying. I have to take her into the city for her math exam soon."

"I'll sleep when you leave."

She closed her eyes and felt Luke's hand on her forehead, then his lips on her dry mouth.

"Climb in bed with me," she whispered.

He did.

"Not with your clothes on, dummy."

"I have to leave soon. I'll hold you all night."

"Hold me now."

She felt him pull her into his arms, felt herself give something up, as if he could carry her pain away. She was sleeping again, easily now, floating in his arms.

She was in her bedroom, her childhood room, lying on her bed. Her mother walked in. Blair felt a rush of happiness at seeing her mother after so long.

"I'm here to take care of you," her mother said.

"You can't take care of me," Blair told her. "You died a long time ago."

"You need me," her mother said.

Blair felt terrified for a moment and wrestled to lift herself from the dream. In her half consciousness she heard a door open and close. Amanda.

"Mom," Blair said, her mother still lurking in the back of her dream, in the shadows of her girlhood room.

"I'm here," her mother said impatiently. "I don't have all day."

Blair peered at her mother and could see that she was wearing her apron, ready to get to work in the kitchen. *I forgot about that apron,* Blair thought, both in the dream and out of the dream. A white apron with red strawberries.

"I've got Luke now, Mom."

"Luke?" her mother asked suspiciously.

"He takes care of me."

"No one could ever take care of you."

"You did, Mom. Remember that summer—"

"Don't talk about that," her mother said.

And in her dream she knew she had been raped, weeks before, her body still raging with the physical pain, her mind still numb. Her mother kept bringing her things: letters from teachers, magazines, new records. Nothing interested her. She wanted to sleep.

"Come on, Blair. Get out of bed," her mother urged.

"I'm dying, Mom. Let me rest."

Luke moved in her arms, waking her. She didn't open her eyes. She felt him ease away from her, and she felt herself sinking, someplace darker. *Stay with me,* she wanted to say. But she heard Amanda talking and remembered the exam.

Finally she opened her eyes. Amanda had her back to her and was lifting her backpack.

"Good luck, sweetheart," she said.

Amanda turned and looked at her. She leaned over and kissed her mother's cheek.

"Easy A," Amanda said. "I'll prove to them that I don't need school at all."

"You're going back to school in September, my dear," Blair said. "Don't get any dropping-out-of-school ideas."

Amanda turned away. Blair knew Amanda wouldn't talk about September. Her mother wouldn't live that long.

Now Blair often dreamed the moments she didn't want to miss: In one dream Amanda had a baby in her arms, a redheaded girl, and she showed the sweet thing to her mother, her face beaming with pride. Blair was sure the dream was true, some kind of lucky glimpse into the future. In another dream Amanda was painting a huge canvas, filling it with bold splashes of color, and the effect was so thrilling that Blair wanted to charge inside the painting. In the morning she asked Amanda, "Did you ever think of becoming a painter?"

"You're weird, Mom," Amanda had said.

"What do you want to be?" Blair had asked impatiently, wanting to see it all ahead of her.

"Your daughter," Amanda had insisted.

My daughter, Blair thought. *You will always be my daughter.*

In one dream Luke was kissing another woman. When Blair woke up, she had told him, "You'll love someone else."

"Not like this," he had said, kissing her better than he had kissed the dream lover.

"I gotta go, Mom," Amanda called, blowing her a kiss from the doorway, bringing Blair back to the present. It was so hard these days to stay awake, to stay in the present.

Luke leaned over Blair from behind, placing a fresh glass of water on her bedside table.

"I want you to take that morphine now," he told her. "Don't let the pain get ahead of you."

She pressed the button on the pump at her side to release the morphine into her system. She leaned back heavily on the pillow.

"How long will you be?" she asked.

"A few hours," he told her. "Should I call someone to be with you?"

Blair shook her head. "Who? The bartender at the Lookout Bar? I don't think so."

"I won't leave you after this. It's her last exam."

"English?"

"That was yesterday."

"I forgot."

"Can you sleep again?"

"No," Blair said. "Not without you. I'll watch a movie."

Luke had bought a TV and VCR and a collection of old movies. Blair was now too tired to read, too weak to do anything else. Movies filled the hours. Luke moved to the set.

"Which one?" he asked.

"I know," she told him. "Put in *Pescadero.* I want to watch your movie again."

"My favorite fan," Luke said, smiling.

"Your leading lady," Blair said, correcting him.

He set up the movie, kissed her good-bye.

She pushed herself up in bed, wiggled her fingers good-bye to Amanda.

She pulled a pillow behind her back and leaned against the cool wall. She didn't want to sleep, was scared of the demons, of fighting them off and finding herself alone in the cabin.

She pressed the play button, started the film. She had seen it dozens of times now.

She began to doze again, sitting upright in bed, the movie playing. When the rapists appeared in the dunes, they told her not to run. She wasn't scared, found herself watching them with an ease she had never imagined before.

"He's running away," one of the men said, and she turned, watched her boyfriend scamper up the side of the hill.

"He's scared," she told the men. "I'm not scared."

"We might kill you," one man said.

"I know," she said.

This time, when they came toward her, she didn't fight. She didn't scream. She sank deeper into the dream and thought, *I'll die. I can let myself die.*

And then she was awake, her body drenched in sweat. She reached for a towel she kept at the side of the bed and dried herself off.

I can die, she thought. *I can do this without a fight.*

She stayed awake for the rest of the movie. She got herself out of bed, made it to the bathroom, then back to bed again, exhausted by the effort.

She slept until Sweetpea's barking woke her. They were home again.

Luke appeared at her side, then sat next to her in the bed, leaning forward to kiss her and stroke her. She loved how he touched her, always, and kept touching her, as if he spoke to her through his fingers. She wanted his hand on her body all the time now.

"I love your movie," she said.

He lifted the glass of water for her and she sipped.

"Did you make it all the way through?"

"I fell asleep at one point. In my dream I was ready to die."

Luke nodded. "I can tell," he said. "I wish I could say the same for myself."

"You were a fool to fall in love with me," Blair told him.

"No," Luke said. "It's the smartest thing I've ever done."

They held each other for a while.

"You're so good to me," Blair said.

"I adore you." Luke pulled back a bit and looked at Blair. "I thought I loved Emily. I didn't know anything about love before I met you."

"You did love her," Blair said. "But it was just one of the things you did in your life. Right now, all you do is love."

He smiled. "My full-time job," he said.

"I may give you a raise," Blair said, grinning.

He leaned over and kissed her gently. "You're beautiful," he said, stroking her face.

Sweet lies, she thought. She was emaciated and gray now. She knew that she looked awful, but he never mentioned it.

"When I watch *Pescadero,*" Blair said, "I imagine I look like the actress, that she's really me."

"I'm sorry that I used your life, or some idea of your life, to make my film," Luke said.

"No," she told him. "Don't apologize."

"And in the real version of your life, I can't save you," he said sadly.

"You saved me," Blair said, and she saw that he knew what she meant.

He leaned over and kissed her again.

"Guess what we got in the mail today," he said.

"Tell me."

"An invitation to our high school reunion."

"You're kidding. Should we go?" she teased.

"Absolutely," Luke said, his voice breaking. "I want to dance the night away with you."

"I get to go to the prom with Luke Bellingham," Blair mused.

"On the back of the invitation, there's a list of lost alumni. My list of Lost Souls," Luke told her, smiling. "You're still on it."

"Keep it that way," Blair said. "I'll be your secret."

"We'll have our own private class reunion," Luke whispered, pulling her close to him.

"Where's Amanda?" Blair asked after a while.

"In the workshop. She'll come in to help me make dinner soon."

"How was her exam?"

"Easy," Luke told her. "And she's done with school. Until September."

"Senior. She'll be a senior." Blair's voice cracked.

Luke didn't hide his tears, and Blair smiled at him.

"What will—"

"We talked about it in the car on the way home," Luke said. He held his hand on the side of Blair's face.

"Tell me," Blair said softly.

"I'd like to take care of her. For as long as she needs me."

He put his head down on her chest, and they were quiet for a while.

"What did she say?" Blair finally asked.

"She said she'd like that," Luke told her.

"I'd like that, too," Blair told him.

Luke lay next to her, holding her in his arms for a long time. She imagined a scene as if it were happening: Luke driving Amanda to college in his truck, all her gear piled in back. Amanda's prattling on with nervous energy about everything about to happen. Luke's face full of his beautiful smile. He would love her through all of it. Lucky Amanda.

Blair slept for a while, and when she woke up, it was dark. He was still there, next to her.

"Are you sleeping?" she whispered.

"No," he said. "I'm holding on to you for dear life."

She rolled over in his arms and kissed him.

"You and Amanda need dinner," she told him. "And I want to sit right here and order you both around in the kitchen."

Luke lifted himself up and away from her. She felt herself catch her breath, as if she weren't quite ready to breathe on her own. He looked at her.

"Dinner," she said, urging him on.

Luke left to find Amanda in the workshop, and Blair pushed herself up in bed, clicked on her morphine pump, sipped at her water. When Amanda and Luke got back, they started work on a complicated paella dish. Luke had bought the ingredients in the city while Amanda had taken her test.

Blair watched them prepare dinner. They moved around each other in the kitchen as if they had been cooking meals together all their lives.

"Anytime you want to throw out a command or two," Luke called back to her from the stove, "your sous-chefs are ready."

"You'll do just fine," Blair told them.

Luke chopped and Amanda stirred. Their busy arms seemed everywhere, reaching, moving around her. Sweetpea rested her head in Blair's lap. Blair closed her eyes and let the morphine take hold. There was the empty space in the center of a circle of trees. The redwoods. Amanda's cathedral. Blair lay in the middle, taking small breaths, listening: Luke humming a forgotten tune, the rustle of leaves, the clatter of pots and pans, an owl settling in the canopy above, a murmur from Sweetpea and Amanda's voice, stronger now. Then in the circle of their arms, in the glow of the last filtered light of day, Blair slept.